Readers love
RUSSELL J. SANDERS

All You Need Is Love

"*All You Need Is Love* is a beautifully written deeply touching story about coming of age in a very difficult time, and I highly recommend it!"
—Gay Book Reviews

"This story is well written and engaging. I think that Russell did an excellent job capturing the essence of 1969 in a precise, accurate manner."
—Rainbow Book Reviews

Colors

"Amazing story. Beautifully written. Simply incredible."
—Prism Book Alliance

The Book of Ethan

"I really enjoyed the diversity in this book… I will probably be on the look out for more from this author."
—Scattered Thoughts and Rogue Words

By RUSSELL J. SANDERS

Published by HARMONY INK PRESS
www.harmonyinkpress.com

RUSSELL J. SANDERS

YOU CAN'T TELL BY LOOKING

Harmony Ink

Published by

HARMONY INK PRESS

5032 Capital Circle SW, Suite 2, PMB# 279, Tallahassee, FL 32305-7886 USA
publisher@harmonyinkpress.com • harmonyinkpress.com

You Can't Tell by Looking
© 2018 Russell J. Sanders.

Cover Art
© 2018 Aaron Anderson.
aaronbydesign55@gmail.com
Cover content is for illustrative purposes only and any person depicted on the cover is a model.

Trade Paperback ISBN: 978-1-64080-389-3
Digital ISBN: 978-1-64080-388-6
Library of Congress Control Number: 2018900250
Trade Paperback published October 2018
v. 1.0

Printed in the United States of America

This paper meets the requirements of
ANSI/NISO Z39.48-1992 (Permanence of Paper).

For all LGBT Muslims who are struggling to find their way in the world and facing condemnation from their families and peers.

ACKNOWLEDGMENTS

I'VE WRITTEN many novels, both published and unpublished, where I've gotten invaluable help from mentors and other writers. They've all been named specifically in previous acknowledgments, so I won't repeat them here. Instead, some comments about Dreamspinner Press. I had a lovely experience with my first publisher, but when I discovered Dreamspinner Press, I found a home. I've learned and grown from the editing process, and I've now worked with some incredible Dreamspinner editors, most specifically the wonderful, patient, and supremely capable Dawn Johnson. My last several books have had thought-provoking, evocative covers by Aaron Anderson. And I always feel appreciated by office staff, editorial staff, publicity staff, and everyone else. I almost never contact anybody at Dreamspinner who doesn't return my email within hours, if not minutes. And I believe Elizabeth North is the best publisher on the planet. I bless the day I discovered Dreamspinner Press/Harmony Ink Press. Their support, their encouragement, and their responsiveness make the sometimes-thankless task of writing novels worthwhile.

AUTHOR'S NOTE

YOU CAN'T Tell by Looking began as a personal quest to explore aspects, both light and dark, of a religion that is ancient and peace-loving. Islam is one of the largest religions in the world, second only to Christianity, and yet, because of a small group who have distorted and politicized this faith—and they are a small group, compared to the millions of other Muslims in the world—Islam is vilified by many. I set out to paint a different picture. One that not only shows followers of Islam are as "normal," decent, and law-abiding as the rest of the world's citizens, but that among those followers, like all religions, there are LBGT people who are as devout as their fellow Muslims. If one person, gay teen, straight teen, parent, Christian, Jew, or other, reads my book and has a change of mind and heart, then my quest is fulfilled.

SEPTEMBER

CHAPTER 1

Gabriel

"THAT IS the most gorgeous creature I've ever laid eyes on!"

Did I say that out loud? Or did I just think it? Whatever. I'm standing here, at the end of the first day at my new school, gazing across the commons at a guy who is mesmerizing. His slender stature—straight and tall like a soldier and muscled like one as well—says he has the confidence of a lion. His jaw is square, his closely cropped black curls shine, and even this far from him, I see eyes as black as midnight that sparkle as he laughs with his friends. I can't look away from him.

"So how was your first day?" I hear my cousin's voice, and I want to respond, but I am entranced by this magnificent specimen across the way.

"Gabe?" Shaun is almost shouting in my ear, but I continue to ignore him. "Earth to Gabriel, Earth to Gabriel." Shaun's call pounds into me, but it doesn't break my concentration.

Not taking my eyes off the god I've just discovered, I say, "What, Shaun?" trying to keep the annoyance out of my voice.

"What's up, Gabe? I'm trying to get an update on your first day here, and you're blowing me off."

Shaun is right, and to be fair, I shouldn't be doing this. But my eyes don't want to leave this vision. They're glued to the guy.

"Oh, I see, you've discovered our resident towelhead." His use of that disgusting slur rips me away from the object of my attention for a moment.

"Shaun, you know as well as I do name-calling is lower than low. I'm surprised at you." My cousin and I have never been close, but we've been raised in the same family with the same values—or at least I thought so. I'm reasonably certain my aunt, my dad's sister, would not like hearing her son say what he did.

"Look, Gabe, I'm only calling it like it is. That guy you have the hots for is a Muslim. Is that the term you'd rather I use? Either way, he's just one jihad away from blowing this school sky-high."

"Are you kidding me? You really believe that about all Muslims? That they are all waiting for the chance to strap on a bomb and take out the world?"

"Gabriel, my man, this ain't the little town you spent your life in until now. We don't leave our front doors unlocked. We don't ask just anyone into our lives. We're cautious. And when someone like him, the one you're drooling over right now"—he points to the object of my fascination—"is around, you need to be on your guard. No telling what's going on in his mind."

I truly want to go off on Shaun right now. He's being blatantly bigoted, and it pisses me off, but Shaun has been so good to me this past summer. When my dad announced we were moving here and I wouldn't be graduating from my school back home, leaving the friends I've always known, Shaun took it upon himself to make the transition easier for me. He spent the entire summer texting me and skyping with me, trying to get me ready for the day I'd just spent. I stayed with Gram and Pop while Mom and Dad moved here at the beginning of summer. I'd spent the last three summers teaching little kids how to swim at the Y, and I wasn't about to give that up. So my parents told me I could live with my grandparents while they got the new house set up and Dad started his new job. He was an insurance salesman in our hometown, but now he's working at his company's headquarters here in the city. A big promotion for him. So I didn't raise much of a ruckus when I was told I'd be moving. And Shaun's wrong about our "little town." It has a hundred and fifty thousand residents, give or take a few, so it's not a tiny place; granted, it's not as big as this ginormous city.

Anyway, given my status as the new kid and my cousin's eagerness to make me feel welcome, I had no right to deal with his attitude at the moment. That might come later, if he kept it up.

"Okay, okay," I say. "But who is that guy?" I had to know more.

"Off-limits to you, gay boy." I have to give Shaun this: he isn't bothered by the fact that I'm gay. I guess that's a big-city thing.

"Sure, Shaun, sure. But just tell me a little about him."

"Okay, but only so you'll point your dick toward some other guy."

That was pretty crude, I think, but again, I've only been in this town for two days, so I need to get the lay of the land before I start popping off.

"That *guy*"—Shaun's contempt is palpable—"is the senior class president."

Well, that blows my mind. Does Shaun hate him because he's Muslim or because he's popular? Even though my school back home was much smaller, I know how teenagers think.

Shaun continues, "I don't know how he got elected, but I guess he has everyone else but me fooled. They'll live to regret it. You know, that camel jockey"—I wince at the term—"disappears every day at lunchtime. Some say he works in the library, but no one I've talked to has ever seen him checking out books or anything. If you ask me, he meets with his buddies to plot."

I try not to sneer at Shaun.

"Anyway, his name is Kerem Uzun, his dad's a heart doctor, his mother's a lady-parts doctor, and he's the only one of *them* in this school."

I make a mental pledge to teach Shaun a thing or two about tolerance or die trying. "Well, I'd jump him if he was willing."

"I'd jump him too," Shaun says, "if it wouldn't get me arrested." He quickly changes the subject. "Did you find all your classes without a problem?"

He knows I did because he'd shown up at my locker or accosted me in the halls a zillion times during the day. But I smile and say, "Yeah."

"And your teachers? Okay? I've never had Bergen, but I hear he's a real hardass."

"He was okay. Seemed to have pretty high standards. Time will tell."

Shaun suddenly yells at someone passing by. "Kramer, come here!"

A good-looking guy stops, glances over at Shaun, and then changes his trajectory and heads for us.

"Kramer, this is my cousin Gabe; Gabe, Lou Kramer."

As my father taught me, I reach out my hand for this guy to shake. He takes it and smiles as he gives me a hearty shake and greets, "Welcome, welcome. You'll like Compton High. Junior? Senior? When'd you get to town?"

He's friendly, I'll give him that. "Senior. And I just got to town yesterday. I was tying up loose ends back in my hometown. My folks moved at the beginning of the summer. Thank God I had grandparents I could stay the summer with."

"Glad you've joined us. You play sports? Band? Drama? Debate? Art?"

This guy is bordering on being nosey, but I chalk it up to his just trying to make me feel welcome.

"Gabe's a swimmer," Shaun answers for me.

"Great swim team here," Lou Kramer says. "I've got a couple of friends on the team, and they love, love, love the coach. They say that all the time, just that way. You know girls. I'll introduce you to 'em. You might hit it off with one of 'em. Some great guys on the team too."

Shaun doesn't point out that I would be more interested in the guys than the girls, and I figure it's too soon for me to make that known to this virtual stranger.

"Well, it was good meeting you, Gabe," Lou says. "I gotta run. My boss'll kill me if I'm late to work." And he rushes off.

"I'm pretty sure he bats for your team." Shaun winks. "That's why I hooked you two up. Who knows, if all goes well, you two might *hook up*." He piles on every bit of sleazy sexual innuendo he can muster. "Come on. I'll Uber you home."

I glance over and see Kerem start to walk away from his friends. "No, Shaun. I'll walk home. Beautiful day. I need the fresh air after being cooped up all day long. I'll see you tomorrow."

"Whatever. If your ass is draggin' by the time you get home, don't blame me."

I watch until Shaun is safely gone, and then I scan the landscape for Kerem. A canvas cylinder of some sort and a backpack now both slung on his shoulder, he's on the sidewalk and strolling away. He doesn't seem to be walking with much purpose, so I can easily catch up to him. But what will I say when I do? *Hi, I'm the new guy. I want to have sex with you.*

Good luck with that, Gabe.

I swear I'm not a sex-crazed stalker, but I find myself following him. As he meanders, I stay far enough away that he's oblivious to my attentions. I talk big, but at this point, I'm not really looking for someone to date, much less bed. There's something about him that draws me. I just want to get to know him. To gaze in his eyes. To stand close enough to feel his breath. To sidle up close to that perfect body.

We've been walking for a good ten minutes or so when I see we're at a park. There are no signs, so maybe it's not an official park, but it's a heavily wooded area. I know from studying Google Earth that we're about a half mile from the school, and these woods have a stream running just behind them, on the east side. Why has Kerem stopped?

He turns and walks with purpose toward the trees. I stand a moment, my eyes tracking him like an undercover detective stalking his prey. He disappears into the woods. God help me, I can't let him out of my sight, and if I don't follow him, I will lose him.

With the stealth of a leopard, I approach the trees, and when I get close, I spy him, in a small clearing just out of sight from the sidewalk. I slip, like a Native American brave tracking his dinner, past the first trees and hide myself, but I take a position that gives me a clear view of Kerem.

He takes a small packet of something from his pack. I can't read what it is, but he pulls a white square from it and begins wiping his face, his arms, his hands—so apparently it is a Handi Wipe. We aren't generating much sweat out here on this relatively cool day. Maybe he feels dirty for some reason.

Next, he pulls the drawstring on the canvas cylinder and takes out something that is rolled up. Facing the stream, he unrolls his cargo. It is a small rug, which he places on the ground. He steps from his loafers and stands on the carpet.

He raises his hands in the air and speaks, quietly. I've never heard the language he is using. It sounds vaguely Middle Eastern, like something I've heard on the nightly news. Yes, it is something I've heard. "*Allahu Akbar.*"

He folds his hands on his chest and speaks a short speech, still in the foreign language.

Then he bows three times, each time speaking a short phrase, again the same language—or at least I assume it is the same.

Again, he says, "Allahu Akbar," and then he falls on his knees, puts his hands flat in front of him, and leans over, placing his forehead between his hands. Again, he repeats something three times.

I watch in wonder. Was Shaun speaking truth? What is this ritual? Surely it's not some private terrorist thing.

I stand, quiet and still, peering at him, feeling a mixture of wonder and embarrassment and a tinge of fear that I hate myself for. I'm witnessing something that looks to be very private. I'm intruding. I shouldn't be here. But I can't pull myself away.

He stands and again performs the entire ritual. Then he sits on his heels and recites more strange words. Finally I hear him breathe, a long, cleansing breath, and then he turns his head to one side and speaks, then turns his head to the other and speaks again.

My stomach growls, and it is a growl to wake the dead. If a walker were nearby, he would instantly head my way to feed on me, and I'd be forced to shoot him in the head. I'm a huge *Walking Dead* fan. I pray the gurgle was just loud to me and Kerem didn't hear it.

But he jumps up. "Who's there?" There is fear in his voice. Do I keep quiet and hope he ignores what he's heard? What if he finds me here? What will I say? I want to run, but I think, *Well, bozo, you wanted to meet him. Now's your chance.*

Like a dork, I say, "I come in peace," hoping to make light of my eavesdropping. But it comes out like a line from some old movie where the settlers are huddled around the campfire and Chief Running Deer shows up.

"Why are you following me?" Kerem's voice this time is fear mixed with anger—not a good thing for me—but it does show that he has a backbone. I like that. Even though I could get my block knocked off at any minute.

I hold up my hands in surrender and take two steps out of my hiding place. "I'm sorry, guy." I think quickly and lie—not a good first move, but it might be self-preservation time. "I saw you up ahead going the direction of my house—I just moved into a house on Eden Way—and I thought maybe this was a shortcut." *Lame, lame, lame.* Not even a total imbecile would believe me.

He looks at me, sizing me up. "Eden Way? Where on Eden Way?"

"It's two-three-two-three."

"I'm at two-three-two-four—right across the street. There's only a man and a woman living at two-three. They moved in at the beginning of June. I've never seen *you* before." He is still cautiously assessing me. And rightfully so. I could be a rapist.

"They're my parents. I've been at my grandparents' house all summer. I only got here yesterday."

"Well, this isn't a shortcut. And I don't appreciate your interrupting my prayers. I was just finishing, thank Allah."

"Prayers? That's what you were doing?"

"What did you think? That I was planning a jihad?" The fear is gone; the anger remains. "You know, we're not all terrorists. And a jihad is not always a bombing. That's what you people think, but jihad, for your information, means a search. Most of the time, it's a search for meaning and purpose in life." He pauses a millisecond, like he's trying to figure me out. "But why am I telling all this to a rapist?"

"No—no, no, no. You have me all wrong. All right, I admit I didn't think this was a shortcut home." He takes a step away. "But I didn't follow you to harm you. I heard a little about you today in school, and I wanted to know more. Granted, stalking you is not the best way to foster understanding, but as clumsy as I said it before, I do come in peace. Let's start this over. Whaddaya say?" I step toward him, and I smile with my hand outstretched. "Hi, I'm Gabriel, and I want to know more about you." With that somewhat inarticulate greeting, I guess I get through to him. I'm told I have an engaging smile. By Gram and my mom, but still….

"We don't shake hands," he says, "but we fist-bump." He holds his fist up, and I bump it. "My name's Kerem."

"Good to know you, Ker." His face squinches up. I guess I shouldn't have shortened his name like that. But it's what I do. I determine to pile on the charm and make it all right. "Gabe. And I am sorry. About before. And shortening your name like that."

"The name thing's okay. I've just never had anyone do that before." He smiles. "But I kinda like it."

I breathe a tiny sigh. Of relief? Of happiness? Of what?

"The stalking thing? We can't be too careful. Lots of haters out there. Some of them at Compton."

"But I hear you're class president, so there can't be too many of them."

"Only takes one, Gabe; only takes one." As he talks, he takes up his prayer rug, rolls it, and puts it back in its canvas bag.

He turns toward the sidewalk and motions for me to join him.

"So tell me about these prayers. What language was that?"

"Arabic. My dad's Turkish, and I don't speak Arabic fluently, but the Holy Quran was given to Muhammad in Arabic, so Muslims always pray in that language because our prayers are verses from the book. At the end, we can speak in our native language to ask Allah for favors or blessings or whatever we need to say to Him."

"But you didn't say anything after you did that thing where you turned your head to the sides. What's up with that?"

He laughs. "Tell you the truth, when I heard you—that's some stomach you got there; it would attract a hungry walker in a millisecond—I was praying silently, 'Please don't let him hurt me, please don't let him hurt me.' I'm not exactly trained in tae kwon do." He laughs again, and it's a joyful, at-ease expression that tells me we are going to be friends, Ker and I.

"You like *The Walking Dead*? Best damn show ever."

"Wouldn't miss it. I watch the streaming episodes over and over," Kerem says.

"You're kidding. That's about the only show I have on my Netflix watch list."

"Be still my heart. A *Dead* fanatic like me." He puts his hand on his heart. "But I didn't answer your question. The head-turning thing?" He looks at me with a smile. "We're talking to angels who sit on our shoulders. I know, I know… it sounds weird, but it's just part of our religion, and if you know anything about any religion, there are a lot of unexplainable things going on in all of 'em. Besides, when we pray in groups, like in our mosques—that's what we call our churches—we are actually speaking to the people on either side of us, wishing them peace, for the Arabic words translate to 'may the peace, mercy, and blessings of Allah be upon you.'"

"Just like in our church. At the end of the service, we do what we call 'giving the peace.' We turn to the people near us and wish them well."

"Exactly."

"Only we worship God. You worship Allah."

"Allah is Arabic for God. We worship the same God you do. You know Abraham? In your Bible?"

Despite the fact Mom and Dad have always taken me to church, I'm not much of a Bible scholar, but I do know that story. "The guy who God told to sacrifice his son, and he almost did it."

"Yeah, that's him. Forgive my guessing that you're a Christian. I suppose you could be an atheist, Buddhist, or whatever, but we don't have a lot of those, if any, in our school. What denomination?"

"Methodist, born and raised. But my parents aren't the kind to be at the church every time the doors are open."

"Mine aren't either. Some Muslims are at mosque half their waking hours, or at least it seems, because they are so devout."

"Sounds like my grandparents. I think their devotion pushed Dad away from the church until he met Mom. Now they go regularly, but they're not church-*crazy*."

Kerem smiles at that. "Sounds a lot like my family. Oh, we do go to mosque regularly, but our traditions are pretty modern—American, you might say. There are a zillion different ways to be Muslim. Each country, sometimes each community, and yes, each family, has their own traditions. I suppose my family has adapted—a little bit old-world, a lot new.

"But we were talking about Abraham. Muslims are descended from Abraham, just as Jews and Christians can trace the beginnings of their beliefs to him as well. Lot of similarities. I'll tell you sometime if you're interested."

"Ker," I say again, and he smiles at me. "We're on." I would listen to him read the dictionary to me if it meant I could hear his voice and be in his presence. "But maybe right now, you can get me up to speed about Compton. Seems like a good school. Of course, I've only been there one day. My cousin Shaun—Shaun Gray, you may know him—" A slight quiver in Ker's body stops me.

"Oh, I know him." I can't read much into his tone, but from what Shaun was spouting earlier, I wonder if Kerem has either heard something about Shaun and his attitude or actually encountered Shaun at some point. I do know that I want to distance myself from that sort of thing.

"Look, Ker, Shaun can be a hardass. I don't know him real well. He's helped me a lot, easing me into this move, but before that, I'd only seen him a couple of times a year as we grew up. Just know that whatever you think of Shaun, I'm not him, I'm not like him, and apparently I wasn't raised like he was. 'Nough said?"

"Okay. Good to hear. Because if you're going to be living right across the street from me, we'll be seeing a lot of each other. Who knows? We might feed our addiction with a *Walking Dead* date in our future."

CHAPTER 2

Kerem

"WHAT'S WITH the scarf? Having a bad-hair day?"

My sister is looking very traditionally Muslim as she waltzes into the breakfast room this morning. Something's up.

My cousin Timur, who lives with us, says, "It's called a hijab, Kerem."

"I know, *kuzin*." I roll my eyes at Timur. "I'm just funnin' with my sister. Is that okay with you?"

He doesn't respond. Sometimes it's hard to communicate with Timur. He's a year older than me, and he's lived with us for nine years. You'd think we'd be like brothers by now, and in some ways we are, but in other ways, I've always felt we just don't connect. Still, I tell myself to tone it down. Mama would not like it if Tim and I got into it this sunny morning.

"You look lovely, dear," Mama says.

"Aysel, my love," Dad says, "you would be beautiful no matter how you dressed."

"Oh, *Baba*, you are decidedly prejudiced. I could be ugly as the *cadi* in the forest, a giant wart on my nose, and you would say I'm beautiful." There's a lilt in her voice. My sister is, indeed, beautiful. A little ditzy sometimes, but beautiful nonetheless.

"You favor your mother, *benim küçük kızım*." Dad grew up in Turkish Kurdistan, and he peppers his speech with his native language. He's prone to call my sister "my little daughter" and me "my little son." But strangely he doesn't have any affectionate term for Timur. Baba is kind to Timur—after all, he took him to raise as his own—but maybe it's because Timur is a bit standoffish that Baba treats him differently than he treats us.

"When I saw your mother for the first time," Baba continues, "she was dressed head to toe in a burqa, complete with niqab across her face. The only part of her body uncovered was her eyes. I looked into those eyes, and I thought, 'this is the most beautiful creature on earth.'"

"Aram, it's a sin to tell a lie. It's in the Quran—'woe to every sinful liar.' What you tell our children…. I've never dressed like that in my life, and you know it." Mama's words are stern, but there is love in them.

Baba just laughs. "I'm only joking, my dearest. Allah enjoys humor." Then he turns his head to Aysel. "But your *anne*—my heart, my Maria—is beautiful, and so are you."

Aysel turns red as a beet.

"Now, tell us why you are suddenly the obedient Muslim woman. I would bet a man is involved. Am I right?" Baba probes, mischief in his eyes.

Aysel turns even redder. "Well…."

"Darling," Mama says as she places toast in front of us, "no man has the right to tell you how to dress."

Timur looks at Mama. I can't read what's in his eyes.

"I know, Mama," Aysel answers. "I am *choosing* to wear the hijab. It is a symbol of my faith. It shows a reverence to Allah."

I can see in her eyes, in her hesitation, in her body as she reaches for toast, she is withholding. "Spill it, sister."

"Okay, okay. What I said is true. My decision to wear the hijab is mine alone, and it is for those reasons. But I *have* met someone."

Baba looks at me, nodding with an I-knew-it smirk on his face.

Mama sits down with her cup of coffee. She's eager to hear the tale of her daughter's first boyfriend, I can see. "Well, don't just sit there, love, after dropping such a bombshell. Tell us."

"His name is Hasan. He was the graduate assistant who taught my summer class." Aysel is about to be a sophomore in college. "He has seen me many times with uncovered head, so I'm not doing this entirely for him." Ah-hah! The *entirely* gives her away. She obviously is trying to please her new boyfriend with the hijab. "We crossed paths when I went in to register for the fall semester, and he invited me to coffee today. Hasan comes from a very orthodox family. I could tell that from little things he said during class, even though it wasn't a religion class at all. Anyway, I like him, and I want to please him, and I've felt for a long time that I would like to be stricter than our family is when it comes to traditions." That last sentence started slow and picked up speed. Now Aysel looks down at her toast, tearing it into small pieces, waiting for a response.

"My love, if you get to know this Hasan and he makes you happy, your father and I will be very pleased. I've told you often enough I didn't grow up with orthodox traditions."

Aysel and I interrupt her in unison. "Born into a fourth-generation immigrant family, went to mosque sporadically, parents weren't that strict."

"Stop it, you two. Am I that predictable?" She smiles.

Aysel and I laugh.

"Enough, little ones! Your mother was talking." She feigns anger. "Where was I? Oh, yes. Because of me, I suppose, your father has discarded much of his childhood ways, but that doesn't mean we don't support your decision to wear the hijab proudly. Just make sure you are doing it for all the right reasons."

"Benim küçük kızım," Baba adds, "we want you to be happy, and if Hasan makes you happy as you get to know him, we support you. Two things: finish your degree and make us some grandchildren. That's all we ask any of you three." He often includes Timur when he speaks of grandchildren, although technically Timur's children would be nephews or nieces to Baba. I usually cringe a little when Baba gives the grandchildren speech, for I fear his only source will be Aysel.

Aysel brightens, the burden lifted. "Well, I must go. I have class at nine; then I'm meeting Hasan at ten thirty." She is her bubbly self again as she jumps up from the table and retreats.

"And what's new with my son?" Baba asks. "We have a few minutes before we all leave for our day, so I think a family discussion is in order." Strange how he says it that way, like it's some sort of business roundtable or an inquisition. But that's just Baba's way.

"I met the new neighbor," I tell him.

"Which one, the man or the woman?" Mama asks.

"Neither. They have a son. My age. Started at Compton yesterday. We met after school." I omit how he almost interrupted my afternoon prayers. "Last night, we skyped."

"It is good that you are welcoming him to the neighborhood. You are performing a blessing, praise Allah." Baba says this as he gets up to pour himself more coffee.

"Tell us more, dear," Mama says. "What is he like? Do you have things in common? Is he Muslim?"

I laugh at that. "No, Mama, I'm still the only one at Compton. Diversity is still alive and well there, thanks to me."

"It's a good school, it's nearby, and your father and I believe public school is best for you. So many Muslims hide their children away in private schools. Your sister and Timur, and now you, are spreading the word that we are as normal as anyone else. That's a good thing."

I smile at her. She didn't grow up orthodox, and she and Baba have modified Islam a bit to fit their busy schedules and American suburban life, but they still brought us up to be good Muslims, and they want us to be role models, dispelling the notion that all Muslims are terrorists.

"I know, I know. And like most schools, Compton has its bullies, its haters, but I guess our family has taught the community something."

"They elected you president of your class, didn't they? Huge step toward understanding." Baba's so proud of my elected office. And I am too, since it's such a popularity contest. I guess people like me.

"You were going to tell us about this new neighbor," Timur says. He usually changes the subject when my parents talk about my popularity.

"Oh, yeah. His name is Gabriel—"

"Like the angel who brought the divine revelation to Muhammad, PBUH," Mama says.

That means "peace be upon him," and we Muslims always add that when speaking the name of the prophet—or at least *think* it. Or when we speak of any of the prophets—Moses, Abraham, Jesus, or the rest. They are all revered in Islam.

"Yes, Mama, like the angel. Gabe is a swimmer, and he plans to be on the team this year. He won medals on the team at his last school. His parents are Methodists, and they go to church mostly, he said, regularly. He wants to know more about Islam, and I told him I'd tell him anything he wanted to know. What else? He's about my height, sorta sandy hair, sea-blue eyes, and freckles across his nose." I stop, wondering why I added that description of him.

"Well, he sounds like a very nice young man, dear. And quite handsome." She doesn't make much of my detailed description, and I'm glad.

"Timur, how's the new job?" Baba turns his inquisition to my cousin.

"Okay. Boss seems to like me. Or at least he likes what I can do on the computer."

"Well, it's a great honor to be hired in as the computer consultant for that firm. Most men your age would need a degree for such a position, but you've proven yourself with skills. I'm proud of you."

"Thank you, *Amca* Aram." I see a trace of pleasure on Timur's face. He is pleased with Baba's praise. That makes me feel good for him.

"And now," Baba says, as he pushes his chair from the table, "we have to get to our offices. Another day of healing, if it pleases Allah, is beginning for us. You boys make your lunches and get out of here. Never, ever be late, be it for prayers, school, or your jobs." Baba means what he says, but he, like the rest of us in this busy world, is sometimes unavoidably late for prayers.

As he and Mama leave, I begin to make chicken sandwiches. I turn to Timur. "You want me to make you a sandwich for lunch, Tim?"

He takes a last gulp of coffee and rises. "No, I'll get something out. I'm going to go brush my teeth, and then I'll drive you to school if you want."

"Sure." I enjoy walking home so I can pray by the stream, but Tim takes me to school most every morning. I finish the sandwiches and bag them as I wait for him to finish with his teeth. He's very particular about his hygiene. He brushes after every meal, while I brush before morning prayers and sometimes forget to do so later in the day.

THE MORNING at school goes well. We have morning activity period, a time for finishing homework or club meetings or parent conferences. This morning, my cabinet and I meet to discuss our fall fund-raiser. This year we've decided to raise money for flooding and tornado victims. So many people across the nation have been devastated by weather this past summer that we feel we need to help them, if only in a small way. We're hoping to divide what we raise between two organizations: one for flood relief, the other for tornado-ravaged folks. We discuss how, even though we will be raising funds all year long for these causes, the wheels of FEMA and other government agencies move so slowly that money given in nine months will be as welcome as donations given now. I'm particularly happy about my fellow class officers' enthusiasm, because charity is one of the most important things in Islam. In fact, one of the things Islam is based on is zakat, the giving of money to the poor. Like tithing in Christian religions. Helping others is so important, and we can help anyone of any faith, anyone who is in need.

Lunchtime comes around, and I head to the library. Gabe gets there before me. Our paths crossed before school. Well, actually I was looking for him, and I was so glad when I saw him. I quickly told him I'd be in the library during lunch period and he should meet me there, but I didn't fill him in on why. I was glad he didn't ask because explaining's easier in person.

The librarian calls out, "How's it going, Kerem? Having a good morning so far?"

"Really good, Ms. Fox, really good."

"Who's your friend?"

I introduce Gabriel as the new student at Compton.

"Good to meet you, Gabriel. You've made a good friend already." She looks at me. "Room's all ready."

"Come with me," I tell Gabe. And the two of us enter the small workroom of the library. Long ago, when I came to Compton, I asked the principal if there would be a private place for me to do my noontime prayers. He talked to Ms. Fox, and she agreed her workroom would be a good spot for me. She even pushes her worktable out of the way each day before I arrive. Afterward, I put it back for her. She is such a good person, and I appreciate having her in my life.

"So this is where you spend your lunchtime?" Gabe asks.

"This is it. I wash, I pray, I eat. No terror plotting, as a certain fringe element around here seems to think." I see something in Gabe's eyes that tells me he's heard from this fringe, and I suspect what he heard came from his cousin Shaun. "You said you wanted to know more about me and about Islam. This is me, five times a day. First I wash—"

"The Handi Wipe yesterday?"

I nod. "Yeah, sometimes we have to make do. Luckily Ms. Fox has paper towels and a sink here." I go over to cleanse before prayer as Gabe watches.

Clean and ready to present myself to Allah, I unroll my prayer rug and place it on the floor, facing east toward Mecca.

"We use a rug to pray because a clean place is required, and the rug insures that. Luckily for me, Ms. Fox lets me keep this one here. I do have the one in my locker that I carry home each day so I have it when I pray in the woods. You see how I placed the rug carefully? We must always face toward Mecca, the holy city, when we pray. Oh—we also always remove our shoes to keep the place clean." I remove my shoes as Gabe gazes, hanging on my every word. I find myself fascinated by the blue of his eyes. Earlier I'd called it sea-blue, but now it is more sky-blue.

"And now I begin, always with the declaration of faith 'Allahu Akbar,' said three times. As I said yesterday, the entire prayer is in Arabic, quoting from the Quran. If I'm interrupted, I have to start all over, so please sit there"—I point to a chair—"and I'll be finished quickly."

I go through my prayers, ending in English with "Allah, thank you for bringing my new friend to me. May he reap Your blessings always." I sit a moment, letting the quiet reverence seep in, then rise, and roll up my rug. And while I do so, I look at Gabe.

"Thanks for the shout-out," he says.

"You're welcome." I put the rug back on the counter where I keep it.

"You can always put in a good word for me to God. Compared to our way of praying, your way seems somehow holier. Like God will listen more—" He pauses like he's searching for a word. "—intently. Pretty impressive, your prayers," Gabe says as he helps me move Ms. Fox's table back to the center of the room.

"Each section has a name and a purpose."

"Five times a day? Really?"

"Most definitely: morning, midday, early afternoon, sunset, and evening. It's very centering, if you know what I mean."

"Like yoga. My mom does yoga."

"I suppose our prayers are sort of like that."

"But doesn't life sometimes get in the way?"

I can't believe someone my age, a guy no less, and a Protestant Christian at that, is so interested in me and my way of life. I've known Gabe for less than twenty-four hours, and I already feel close to him.

"You know, life gets in the way of anything. You have a test to study for and you really want to watch *Walking Dead*. You have a class officers' meeting and you run into a wall and the nurse takes you to the emergency room."

Gabe laughs.

"Don't laugh. It happened to me. You want to get to the mall as soon as the stores open so you can pick up the latest Nikes, and you have to take out the garbage, the bag breaks, and you spend the next twenty minutes sweeping up coffee grounds and desiccated banana peels. Yeah, that happened to me too. My point is that we make time for prayer, and if something comes up to keep us from it, we accept it as Allah's will. Sometimes, you make it up later in the day, or sometimes you just go on with life, knowing you've tried your best."

"That's all fine and good, but I've seen things on TV in Iran and those places, where a horn sounds and people drop everything to go pray."

"Believe me, they don't all drop everything, but most do. That's because Islam is part of the governments there, and they are very strict.

In some ways, they've perverted our religion for their own purposes, to keep people in line. People who do dare skip prayers live in constant fear of being found out. But here, this is the US of A. Separation of church and state, you know. Everybody adapts. Your Methodists do it, and so do us Muslims. My baba sometimes has emergencies that keep him from midday prayers. Or his morning appointments run overtime. He tries to work in the prayers, but he admits that sometimes it's just not possible. Doing prayers is worship, a chance to get close to God five times a day. But missing prayers does not make us bad people. We cope."

Gabe's hanging on my every word. I feel like a celebrated imam, a great Muslim scholar, and it feels sinful to be enjoying his attentions.

"But enough about praying. Let's feast!" I open the sack of food I prepared this morning and pull out my two chicken sandwiches. "Hope you like chicken. Nothing but water to drink in here, but that's okay, isn't it?"

Gabe gets up and grabs two cups from the nearby counter and fills them with water from the sink, and then he sits back down.

"Your sandwiches are probably a lot better than cafeteria fare, if yesterday is any indication. And I love chicken. My favorite. My mom likes ham, but I always make her buy chicken too."

"We don't eat ham," I say. "No pork. Like the Jews. And yes, some Muslims, just like their Jewish brethren, eat a lot of bacon. But my family has never had pork and never will. It's strange. There are Muslim traditions about food. You only eat halal meats. Those are meats from animals that must be prayed over before being killed or else they're considered haram, unclean, forbidden. Pork, prayed over or not, is considered haram. Anyway, my family doesn't eat strictly halal, but we don't eat pork. I think it's one of those Dad things. He grew up not eating pork, being taught it wasn't allowed in Islam. Dad's changed an awful lot over the years. He, thanks to Mama's influence, believes we have to adapt to the world we live in. Some traditions stay, others go. We strictly observe prayers but don't eat halal. But he still won't touch pork and forbids it in our home."

"What if a really strict Muslim accidentally had some? I don't know, like he ate a bit of deviled egg that had bacon bits in it?"

"No prob. We're covered. Accidents are okay. It's the on purpose that's a sin. For my family. And a lot of other Muslims. But don't get me wrong, all religions change and adapt. Muslims who eat pork are not going to hell. You mentioned your mom. Tell me about her. And your dad."

"Well, my mom is one of the greatest cooks on the planet. Learned that from her mom. Grandma could whip up a fantastic meal in fifteen minutes flat. You can come over for dinner sometime. I'll make sure Mom doesn't make her beloved ham. She sews for people too. That's something else her mother got her into. I'm not talking about just putting on a button or mending a rip in the seat of your pants. Mom can look at anything someone is wearing, and before you know it, she has whipped it up in your size. And smart. If I have a math problem I need help with, I always go to Mom. My dad is useless with math."

"She sounds amazing. What's her name?"

"Mary."

I laugh, and he stares at me like I've offended his life's blood. I'm horrified. I quickly say, "No, I'm laughing because my mother's name is Maria. Mary, mother of Jesus, is a big deal in the Quran, and a lot of Muslim women are named Maria, Miriam, Maryam. My mom's parents chose Maria for her name because their ancestors were from Catalonia, a region in Eastern Spain. Spanish Muslims. Who'd a thunk it, huh? But my Mom's maiden name was Vila. Mary/Maria. Looks like your mom's parents and my mom's parents think alike." Now he laughs with me. "What about your dad?"

"My baba?" he says, and I smile. "I figured it out. You call your dad that. Is that a Muslim thing too?"

"No, that's a Turkish thing."

"Well, my baba, is—was—an insurance agent. He was the cream of the crop in my hometown, not just in his company, but from what I've heard, every company in town. That's why he was transferred here and given a big promotion. I'm not sure what his new job entails, but I do know he has a fancy job title and is making a lot more money. I'm very proud of him. As proud as you are of your doctor parents, I'm sure."

I stare at him, taken aback, wondering how he knows my parents are doctors. I don't remember it coming up. Not in our walk home yesterday or our Skype session last night.

"How'd you know my parents are doctors?"

"Shaun told me." I try not to look disgusted at the mention of his cousin's name. "Your dad's a cardiologist and your mom's a gynecologist. Am I right?"

"Yep. Baba came over from Turkey to attend university here, and they met. Mama's American born and raised, and Baba's naturalized. To hear him tell it, it was love at first sight." I think of his morning story involving the burqa and the niqab, and I smile. I love Baba so much. And Mama too.

"So did your mom grow up Muslim?"

"Yeah. Not super strict, but they kept the traditions some. Her ancestors fled Catalonia because they were Muslim. They came over here, and within a generation, the Vilas were apple pie American. Her parents weren't too happy she fell in love with a foreigner, a Kurd no less, but they met my father, and they fell in love with him as fast as Mama did."

"What's a Kurd? Haven't I heard that before?"

"Probably. Lots of Kurds in Iraq. Kurds are an ethnic group from the mountains of the Middle East, Iran, Iraq, Syria, and Turkey. The parts of those countries the Kurds are from are collectively called Kurdistan." I'm surprised at my scholarly explanation. I remember it, rotely, from a report I had to give in fifth grade entitled "My Genealogy."

"And I guess from your grandparents' initial reaction that Kurds are bad?"

"Not really. The stereotype is that Kurds are violent people. They fought for recognition during World War I and some're still fighting today for their rights. And since we're mountain people, city folks look down on us, I guess. Despite the fact that Baba came from all this, he doesn't talk much about it. And what I've just told you might be my projection, rather than absolute truth. I'm American. I don't really care a whole lot about my ancestry." I pause. "What's yours?"

"I don't know much. Mom and Dad haven't told me a lot. What little I know about our heritage came from my grandparents, the ones I lived with this summer—Dad's parents. They knew my mom's folks well, so when I asked, they filled me in somewhat. Mom's folks lived in our little town forever. I do mean forever. Her great-greats were among the first settlers there. Dad's family came, originally, from England. They were Methodist since before arriving in this country, so that just got handed down from generation to generation. Like you said about yourself, we're just Murricans." He says that like a hillbilly with a twinkle in his eye and a funny little smile, and I melt.

But I can't let him see that I like him. I've just made a friend, and he can't know I'm gay. That might ruin everything.

CHAPTER 3

Timur

I REMEMBER everything. Most people think a kid of ten would block it all out, banish it. But I didn't. It's still as clear as when it happened.

I remember that man bringing her back. His shouting in Turkish. I never learned but bits and pieces of my parents' language, but I remember how angry the man was.

He thrust her into the room as he ranted. My father tried to push him away while grabbing her and pulling her from him. Baba answered the man's anger with anger of his own.

Finally the man went away, leaving her on the couch beside me. Baba raved at her, gesturing wildly, his face filled with fire. I'm not sure she knew what he was saying. I understood nothing except the one English word he used, *honor*. I'd heard the word before, but I wasn't sure what it meant. Or why he kept saying it over and over.

At last, he calmed. She sat. Weeping. Quietly. His unintelligible words had broken her. Baba left the room. After a time, he came back, holding his *hançer*, the dagger he'd shown me proudly so many times.

I sat, wondering. One moment I was content, watching the TV that still blared the cartoons I loved so; next I was thrust into the turmoil of all this.

Baba walked with purpose, came behind the couch, and stood right behind her. In a flash, the hand holding the dagger sliced it across her throat and blood spurted everywhere. I don't know if the sound I heard coming from her was a tiny scream or the sound of a final gasp of breath.

"I do this for our family's honor," he said, no emotion in his voice.

As she bled out, he came round and said, "Come." I got up and followed him.

Baba took me out of the apartment, into his work truck, and we drove. Ten minutes later he pulled up in front of my uncle's house.

Opening the truck door, he once again said, "Come."

We walked up the sidewalk. He knocked. I heard the faint sound of crickets in the night, waiting for Amca to come.

The door opened, and there stood Amca Aram, Aunt Maria behind him. They must have been shocked by the blood on Baba.

"Sivan, what has happened?" Amca said, alarm heightening his voice.

"I've killed my Delal. For the family's honor." Baba spoke slowly and deliberately. Then he pushed me toward Amca. "You must raise Timur now. I must go to the police and turn myself in."

Amca said, "I'll go with you," as my aunt pulled me toward her, holding me to her as if she would never let go.

CHAPTER 4

Gabriel

THE FRONT door slams as I go inside, leaving Kerem to go to his own house. I toss my backpack onto the floor by the door and head to the kitchen. I'm starving. That chicken sandwich was good, but it wasn't enough to fill my perpetually empty gut. I usually scarf down a huge lunch in the school cafeteria, and on days I have swim practice, I take snacks to have before and after. That thing that moms say, that you can't swim until thirty minutes after you eat, is a fairy tale. I could eat three Whoppers and then go swim and never have a problem. And believe me, my swimming's a strenuous workout.

Mom's sitting at the kitchen table, perusing one of her forty thousand cookbooks. Hearing me come in, she looks up.

"Oh, it's you," she says.

"Who did you think would be coming into the house unannounced at this hour of the day? Your boyfriend?" I give her a conspiratorial wink, then smile broadly.

She gives me that Mom look, like she's having none of my jibes at her. But she's just playin'. "My boyfriend, young man, is at his desk right now at American Mutual Insurance."

"So no afternoon delight?" I love teasing her, and as I've gotten older, I've gotten bolder with my jabs.

"Not today or any day. *I* am a good Christian woman. And don't you forget it." She *is* a good Christian woman, but you'd never know from the laugh in her voice when she said it. "I guess I was startled it was you because A: I was engrossed in this wonderful new cookbook I got this morning, *Perfect Afternoon Tea for the Modern Brit*, and B: I'm so used to you staying after school for swim practice that I didn't realize the team probably hasn't started their workouts yet."

"Well, A: Does Dad know how much you love your Amazon Prime membership? And B: Coach says next week. Nice guy. Kid I met yesterday says his team really likes him. I'll miss my coach at home"—she raises her hand to stop me, but I don't miss a beat when I continue—"I know, this is home now. Anyway, I'm truly looking forward to getting back into the pool and working out. My trunks are so dry, they'll probably melt at the first drop of water. I haven't been in them for five days now."

"The Y has a pool, I'm told. Your dad joined this summer for the whole family. Maybe your friend—Kerem, isn't it?—would enjoy going over there now with you. Muslims swim, don't they?"

"The topic hasn't come up." I think of all I've learned in such a short time, and I'm surprised it didn't come up. My guess is that yes, they do swim. "I've got some homework I want to do before I forget what the teacher said, so I'll pass on the Y." I grab the bread, undo the twist tie, take out two slices, and then raid the fridge for sandwich fillings.

As I make my sandwich, piling it high with—yes—ham, turkey, salami, pickles, tomatoes, lettuce, three kinds of cheese, and mayo, Mom says, "I'm thinking of doing some baking. I thought it would be nice to take goodies to the neighbors to introduce us. What with moving and getting the house ready to live in, I haven't had a moment's rest all summer. Now I have some time, I want to try some of these new recipes I've found this afternoon. There's a yummy-looking one right here for bacon maple scones. What d' you say? The neighbors would like those, don't you think?"

I turn to her and shake my head. "Not Kerem's family. No pork for Muslims. And you'd better check to see if any of the other neighbors are Jewish. A lot of them don't eat pork either."

"You mean Muslims and Jews never get to have a nice baked ham? What a strange world they live in."

Mom can be a bit dense sometimes.

"You know, Gabriel, I suddenly realize that in our hometown, we never came into contact with any Jewish people. And I certainly don't think there were any Muslims anywhere near. I don't remember any women in those scarves they wear, and most of the men in town didn't have beards."

"Mom, you've got a lot to learn. The scarves aren't required, and Kerem doesn't have a beard, so I'd bet that's not a requirement either. We—you, I, most Americans—are brainwashed by the stereotypes that flood the news. They show us Muslims in Iran, Iraq, Afghanistan, and all those other countries, and we believe they all look like that. Or worse yet, act like the terrorists."

"Well, I certainly know that's not the case. I will never believe that all Muslims are terrorists. But I guess I have a lot to learn about how they appear and how they act. It's high time I got my baking done so I can meet the neighbors and find out how they really are." She gets a stricken look on her face. "Oh, I just remembered. Dad says there's a family named Chen at the end of the block. What will I bake for them?"

I laugh at her. "Cookies, Mom, cookies. Everybody likes cookies. Especially *your* cookies." I lean over and kiss her forehead. Then I grab my sandwich, wondering if I will be able to get my mouth around it to take a bite, and head up to my room.

I am finishing my feast and deciding that I really need to go down for a glass of milk, when my phone chimes. I look and see it's Shaun.

"Shaun, my man. Whuzzup?"

"Nuttin'. Jus' tryin' to keep it real."

"Missed you today, guy. You weren't playing helicopter coz like yesterday."

"I figured you knew the lay of the land by now and didn't need me anymore. I'm like an old sock with a hole. You can throw me away, no more use possible." I hear a fake pout.

"Shaun, I'll never toss you away. You weigh too much for me to lift."

He laughs. I'm glad. Despite the fact that he's rough around the edges, Shaun has been a big help to me. And he *is* my cousin. Like the old song goes, "We are famil*eee*."

"Where were you at lunch? I looked for you. There were some guys I wanted you to meet."

"Guys?"

"I hear ya. No, not guys as in date material, just guys I hang with that I think you'd like."

"Oh, I get it. 'Cept for Lou yesterday, you don't know any nancy boys. Or maybe you think your cousin isn't good enough for your gay friends." I'm ragging him, and his reaction tells me he knows it.

"Stop it, Gabe. Truth be told, I don't know many gay guys. Hell, I don't even know if Kramer is gay, but I figured you'd know—gaydar and all."

"Gaydar is not all it's cracked up to be, Shaun. You can't always tell."

"Well, I'll keep a look out. There's bound to be a bunch of guys who'd like your skinny butt, and I might uncover 'em if I try."

"Thank you so much, dear cousin. I don't know how I'd get a date without your help." I laugh.

"So where were you at lunch?"

"I was in the library."

"The library? You got a research paper assigned this soon?"

"No, Kerem invited me."

I hear a slight, almost inaudible huff.

"What? You two plotting the overthrow of the school already? Why were you talking to *him*?" Disgust pours into my ear. "He may have a lot of the other seniors fooled, but not me. *I* didn't vote for him. The last thing Compton needs is a reputation that Muslims are taking it over."

"You're wrong, Shaun. First of all, Kerem is the only Muslim, so Muslims, plural, can't be taking over the school. And taking over is the last thing he would want to do. He's a good person, coz."

"So you've known him only a day, and you're defending him already? You've barely had time to say hello and shake his hand—"

Without thinking, I say, "From what he told me, Muslims don't shake hands."

"See! I told you. My dad says a man who won't shake your hand has something to hide."

"Shaun, get over it. Ker is a really good person. I know because I've talked to him. And apparently a majority of our classmates think so too, or he wouldn't have been elected class president."

"So you two're so tight now you call him Ker? I've never, ever, heard anyone call him that. You guys must be *real* close now." He picked up on the nickname I invented, I guess, and now he's really worked up, wound up tighter than a yo-yo.

"What's next? You gonna sleep with him?"

That's a low blow.

"Cut it out, Shaun. You're my cousin and I love you, but you've crossed the line. It's none of your business who I sleep with, but to answer your question, sleeping with Kerem's not likely. He's very religious, and I don't know if Islam even permits homosexuality. And what's more, I doubt that Kerem's gay. I just find him very nice, he's teaching me a lot about Islam, and he lives across the street from me, so I'll be seeing him a lot."

"Across the street? Well, isn't *that* nice."

"Tone it down, Shaun, or I'm hangin' up. Change the subject."

There is a long pause. I hear breaths. Finally he says, "A couple of guys on the football team are giving a party after the game Friday night. The guy whose house it's at—his parents're going out of town. Should be a blast. I hear they're gettin' a keg, and a bunch of people are bringin' bottles. You game?"

The thought of a drunken party was not on my radar, but I don't want to set him off again. "I'll think about it."

"Don't just think, do. We'll book it to the game together, then head to the par-tay."

"Maybe. I'll let you know what Mom and Dad say."

"Well, that means you won't be going. I know your folks, and Mr. Goody-Goody, the guy to whom I'm speaking, will probably spill the beer beans."

"Shaun, I'm new. I don't know if a booze bash is the best way for me to meet people." I'm trying to let him down easy.

"Can't think of a better way. You convince Mary and Ken of that." I hate that he calls my parents by their first names without using aunt and uncle. The family upbringing my dad and my mom gave me wasn't the same as Dad's sister and my uncle gave Shaun. Or, as often happens, they taught and taught and taught, but he refused to learn. "Tell 'em it's a pizza party. That sounds innocent enough."

"Like I said, we'll see. I gotta go now. Homework." And I end the call before he can say anything more. After that, I really need that glass of milk. I might even sneak a little Amaretto in it to rev me up a bit. I deserve it.

Mom and Dad keep all sorts of liqueurs in the house. Mom has them mostly for cooking, but Dad indulges sometimes after dinner. A tiny glass of Bailey's is a far cry from a keg of beer.

But the sneaking of liquor is not to be. Mom has a couple of globs of batter dripping off her apron when I get to the kitchen. Great cook, but a bit of a loose cannon when it comes to keeping the kitchen—and herself—spotless during the process.

"Let's see." She points to each item on the counter. "I have the almond cookies for the Chens—"

I cut her off. "Hold it a minute. Almond cookies for the neighbors with the Chinese names?"

"Yeah. They have almond cookies in Chinese restaurants all the time."

"Mo-om." I roll my eyes at her. "Don't you think that might come across as a racist thing? You're trying to make friends, not show your deep-seated prejudice."

"You know I don't have a racist bone in my body."

"I know that. But do the Chens know that?"

I see the light bulb go on over her head.

"Okay, my little pop-culture scholar. I'll box up the almond cookies for the Martins, and the red velvet cupcakes for the Chens, the Dillingers, and the Uzuns." Looking stricken, she asks, "Did I say it right?"

"Yeah, it's *red*, rhymes with *head*, and *velvet*, rhymes with, *well pet*," I deadpan.

"You are so, so funny." She narrows her eyes. "The neighbors' name, smartass." Mom calls it as she sees it. "I don't know how to speak Muslim."

I laugh at her. "You can't speak Muslim, Mom. It's not a language; it's a religion. People's names come from whatever country their families came from. Ker's last name is Turkish. His dad immigrated from there. And yes, you said his last name right, or as right as you'll probably ever get it. I've only heard it once, and you sounded pretty much like Ker did."

"Ker? You're already shortening his name? In my book, that means 'close friendship.'" A sly look.

"Whatever. Yeah, I like him. His friends at school always call him Kerem but you know me. That's too much work. So I shortened it, and I guess he's okay with that. He hasn't told me otherwise."

"Don't kill me for asking this." Uh-oh, it's never good when she starts that way. She either has a criticism or a probing question. Either is never fun. "Are you interested in this boy?"

"Interested? I like him. I said that. I like that he's nice. I like that he's different. I like that he's teaching me about Islam. I like that I found a friend on my second day in town. I like that he's my neighbor." I pile it all on to shut her up. But it doesn't work.

"Don't play coy with me, Gabriel Franklin Dillon." Why do moms always reference the birth certificate when they get serious? "On the grave of my grandfather Solomon Franklin, I promise I don't want to hear any bullshit right now. I asked you a question." Woo! She's really worked up. She only swears on her grandfather's grave when I've truly irritated her. Normally she's a pussycat.

I hold up my hands defensively. "Okay, okay. If he were interested in me, I could be interested in him. But like I told Shaun on the phone a few minutes ago, I don't even know if that's possible. Two guys together might be totally forbidden in his religion, you know? I'm just gonna take it nice and slow and see what happens. Right now, I'm probably only interested because he's the most beautiful man I've ever come into contact with." It's nice when you don't have to pussyfoot around your parents. They made it perfectly clear when I came out to them they were totally okay with it. "Lust is not the same thing as a relationship. You know as well as I do that I'm looking for a mate. Maybe not a lifetime mate, but someone I can cuddle up to, tell my secrets to, and really feel connected to. And that sort of thing takes time. If getting to know Ker leads to that, and he's willing to be open and honest—I won't love a guy who's in the closet—then I'll be happy. Meanwhile, I'm going to take it one step at a time."

Mom rushes to me and grabs me into a hug that's claustrophobic and comforting, all at the same time. "I raised a wonderful man, I tell you what."

"Uh," I say, trying to talk with very little air coming into my lungs, "didn't Dad have something to do with that, also?"

She breaks away. "Maybe. A mother's love trumps a dad's love any day." Suddenly she shouts, "My scones!" and she leaps to the stove, grabs a hot pad off the stove top, opens the oven door, and pulls out a perfectly baked pan of what I can only assume are bacon maple scones. Thrusting them in my direction, she says, "Are these not the most gorgeous things you've ever seen? When they cool a little, you and I are going to eat 'em all. Don't tell your dad."

I just look at her, waiting for what I know will come.

"All right, we'll save him one, maybe two. And yes, he was a big factor in the man you've become." I smile. "You knew I'd cave, didn't you?"

The scones are fantasmagorical. It's like the bacon in them is having sex with the sweet maple flavor, producing a gushing orgasm in my mouth. Mom's found a winner. I beg her to make them again and again. I don't know how she remembers which recipe is in which cookbook, but she remembers everything, and these will be put into regular rotation in the Mary Dillon kitchen.

I haven't done my homework, but I give up. I'll get to it later. All this talk has given me a powerful urge. I look at the time on my phone. It's long before sunset, so I text.

Free? Meet you. Sidewalk my side of the street. OK?

I had barely sent the text before Ker answers back.

Two seconds.

I head outside and he's already waiting.

"*Salaam Alaykum.*"

"Huh?" I look at him, wonder in my eyes, I suppose.

"It's a greeting. It means 'peace be upon you.' You respond, '*Wa-Alaykum*,' 'and on you.' We use this for hello and goodbye."

"Wahleekum," I try.

"Wa—" He motions for me to try it.

"Wa," I say.

"Ah—"

"Ah."

"Lay—"

"Lay."

"Kum."

"Kum."

"Now, all together: Wa-Alaykum."

I say it, perfectly this time.

"Wonderful," Ker says. Now I say, 'Salaam Alaykum,' and you say?"

"Wa-Alaykum."

He smiles so big that if it were a shout, you could hear it clear across town. Before I know it, he hugs me tight and says, "You are a good student, my friend." His warm breath in my ear turns me on. I pray that he doesn't notice.

When he breaks away, he says, "Now you try greeting me."

Hesitantly I say, "Sa-la-am Alaykum."

"Wa-Alaykum." He spouts it out with such joy that for a moment, I love him. "Now, you teach me something Methodist," he says.

I have to think. What is "something Methodist"? I'm racking my brain when something comes to me. I hope he doesn't think I'm making fun of him. He may have to get used to my twisted sense of humor. "Okay, repeat after me: puh."

"Puh."

"Ee."

He looks at me like he thinks I'm crazy. "Ee."

"Suh."

"Suh."

"Now." I look him straight in the eye. "Put it together."

Haltingly, he says, "Puheesuh." Then he adds, "Are you putting me on? That doesn't sound like anything I've ever heard."

"Now, say this very quickly: buhwitya."

"Buh wit ya?" He says it like a question, like I'm teaching him Greek, and he is totally confounded.

"Now, we put it all together. Puheesuh buh witya."

"Puh ee suh buh witya." He stops. Takes a breath. "Puh ee suh buh witya."

"Say it faster. All together this time."

"Puheesuhbuhwitya." And then he stops and stares. He's trying to mask a smile with fake anger. "Peace be with you?"

"You got it! An old Methodist saying. Or at least I've heard it said in church. Sometimes."

He shoves me with his hand. Not hard. Not angrily. To me, it feels like love. I say, "You see? We're not so different after all."

He begins to laugh. It is joyful. I've made him happy, and he's made me happy by just being here.

"You wanna walk?" I ask, not wanting to break the spell. But we can't just stand here on the sidewalk and stare at each other.

"Sure. There's a pond with benches a couple of streets over. Have you been there yet?"

"I've been nowhere. If it wasn't on my route into town or on the way to school, then it's been off my radar."

"So let me introduce you to a new pleasure. I will love doing that." The way he says that sounds affectionate, but I chalk it up to his being from a very different kind of family than I'm used to. Maybe they talk that way.

We walk and talk. I'm determined not to invite any more lectures. That last tutoring session brought out something I was not expecting. I have to be careful. But I'm fascinated by Islam and all it entails—especially him, so I do want to keep learning. Just not right now.

"It's so beautiful this time of year, don't you think?"

"If you like hot and dry," he says.

"I do. When you spend three-fourths of your life in water, you enjoy dry sometimes. Besides, this is a beautiful neighborhood. Look around. Flowers're in bloom despite the heat, and these're some nice houses. I don't have a clue as to how big the raise was my dad got, but it must be enormous if he can afford to move us here."

Ker laughs. "It's not like these are mansions and everybody has maids and drivers."

"I know, but your folks are both doctors. Mom says it's not right to talk money, but they must make a lot to afford this."

"We are very lucky. Baba and Mama work hard, and their income is plentiful, praise Allah. Pride is sinful, so I should not be saying this. I will anyway because it's just between two friends." He looks toward heaven. "Forgive me, Allah, if I offend." Then he cuts his eyes back at me. "I have no idea the extent of my parent's income, but I suspect we could live in a much grander house than the perfectly lovely one we have now. But Baba and Mama give far more to the poor than the prophet, PBUH, advises. They are generous souls." I wonder what PBUH means, but I figure it will come up eventually.

"They must be good people. But, of course, I know that because they have such a good son. I'm looking forward to meeting them." I also love how his speech pattern changes a bit when he talks of his family. Like they deserve a formal delivery.

"And you will. Soon, I hope. Perhaps you can join us for dinner sometime."

"And you at my house. I've already warned Mom that ham is off-limits. She's an amazing cook. She collects cookbooks, and she not only finds the best recipes in each one, but she adds her own touches. You'll love her cooking."

"I look forward to it."

We turn a corner, and at the end of the street, I see the park area he'd spoken of.

"Race you to the pond?" he challenges. And I love a good challenge.

I start running, and he yells from behind, "No fair. You didn't say ready, set, go."

Despite my head start, we arrive at a park bench right at the same time, both of us huffing for breath. I collapse onto the bench, and he follows suit.

For a moment there is total silence, except for the sound of our breathing going back to normal.

Finally I notice. "You didn't tell me there were swans." A pair of magnificent snow-white birds glide on the water.

"Oh, yes." He chuckles. "If they come toward us, run. They can be mean motherfuckers."

I gasp. Is this the same kid who was so Queen's English just seconds before?

"What? I'm a red-blooded American teenage guy. We sometimes say stuff like that."

I laugh at him, and he joins in. But as he laughs, his eyes roll to heaven and "Forgive me, Allah" comes forth. That makes me laugh even harder.

I want to take his hand in mine. It's so peaceful here, hearing the ripples of the water and watching the swans, laughing with my newest friend, this beautiful man beside me. If only.

"You settling in at school?" he asks.

"Yeah. Easy-peasy. Not a bad teacher on my schedule, and I'm keeping up. Swim practice starts next week, and that always makes me happy."

"There's something I want to ask you. You can say no. But I'd really like you to say yes. It would be a good way for you to meet some great people, and you and I—" He stops.

"Ask away." I don't know why he stopped, but if I can encourage him to talk, maybe I'll find out.

"You know I'm class president, right?"

"Right."

"So the senior class has a class project. Which really means the class officers and a few others have a project. Throughout the year, we'll be raising money for the victims of this past summer's floods and tornadoes. When the year's complete, we tally up our earnings, announce the total at graduation, and then we donate it all. The first fund-raiser is Friday night."

"But Friday's the first game. Won't everybody be busy?"

"We decided to get started right away. We'll be having a bake sale at the game. The concession people're willing to let us sell after the game, as people're leaving. We'll have a table right outside the stadium, with signs and people trying to steer buyers to us. We figure we can make five hundred dollars or so if we have enough baked goods. You could help us, if you want."

"I want." The look on his face is like sunshine breaking through clouds. "And I'll even hit my mom up to donate baked goods. She spent all afternoon in the kitchen baking today, so doing it again on Friday won't be a problem."

"What was she baking?"

"You name it, she baked it. Offerings for the neighbors. She's trying to buy their love. By the way, expect a knock on your door this evening. If you see a beautiful blonde woman through the peephole, it's not a Jehovah's Witness. It will be Mary Food Network Dillon."

"Wonderful. But don't forget we pray at sunset, then again later. Steer her over around eight. That would be perfect. And—"

"I know—no pork."

"I was going to say no alcohol flavorings. We stay away from strong drink too. And I ask you, who puts pork in cookies?"

"My mom. Well, not cookies, but she was planning bacon maple scones for you. Which, in case you're wondering, are delicious."

"I'll take your word for it. And thank you for warning her."

"You, my friend, will be getting a basket of red velvet cupcakes."

"Yum. Now, back to the bake sale. You wanna go to the game together? I may cut it close getting there after prayers, but we should be able to make the kick-off."

"Sounds great. I hear there's a party after. Shaun told me."

He grimaces, and it's very noticeable. Was it the mention of Shaun or the party that triggered it?

"Those parties are always drunken messes. Not my cup of tea, which is an odd metaphor to use when speaking of beer parties. Everybody gets tanked and does things they wouldn't do otherwise. I would stay clear of that even if my religion permitted me to drink."

"Me too. There's nothing worse than an idiot choking on a beer bong. Shaun wants me to go, but I'll tell him I have a higher calling—raising money for a worthy cause." I can only hope that appeases Shaun.

"Fantastic. It's getting late, and sunset will be here before we know it. We need to start back."

We rise from the bench in tandem, and we walk. We don't talk. Something tells me it's okay not to. We enjoy. That's all. Two friends walking.

When we get back in front of our respective homes, Ker starts to speak. I put my finger on his lips. And feel a rush, by the way.

"Salaam Alaykum," I say.

"You remembered. Wa-Alaykum." He smiles.

And he *has* brought peace unto me.

CHAPTER 5

Kerem

CHOCOLATE CHIP cookies, oatmeal raisin cookies, chocolate cupcakes, lemon bars, peanut butter fudge, and much more fill half the table with second and third containers awaiting as our stock depletes. Gabe's mom has outdone herself. And the other officers have baked goodies themselves and gotten their mothers, grandmothers, and even dads to contribute to the sale as well. My vice-president's dad owns a restaurant, and he's had his pastry chef whip us up some amazing napoleons and eclairs. Our fund will start off with a bang. I can feel that five hundred in my hand before a sale is made.

As I expected, the only other volunteers are my fellow officers, and two of them, even, are missing. My secretary turned her ankle at her dance lesson this afternoon, and my historian was committed to a trip to her grandma's in the country. So while the remainder of my cabinet drums up sales, steering people to us, Gabe and I man the sales table.

"That'll be five dollars even." I take money from Ms. Hunselman, one of the assistant principals, and hand over a baggie of the infamous bacon maple scones. "You're gonna love these. I've heard they're incredible." I smile as I conclude the sale and put the fiver in our stash.

"Mom'll be so happy. Her stuff's selling like hotcakes. Those are the last of her chocolate chip cookies, and we're low on those cherry chip cookie bars too. And I figured the napoleons and eclairs would go first."

"Having the restaurant logo on them helped. Everybody knows that Le Gran Eiffel is the best restaurant in our city."

I straighten our wares and reach down for items to fill the empty spots from sales Gabe is currently making.

I look up to see Gabe's cousin Shaun hovering over us.

"Well, well, well," he says, contempt dripping, "so this is the charity you blew me off for? And where's Mary? I guess telling me she would be with you was a lie, huh? She'd cramp your style, now wouldn't she?"

"Not that it's any of your business, Shaun, but my mother—your *Aunt* Mary—baked a lot of these things. That was her contribution to a very worthy cause."

"What cause? Funding the Taliban?"

"Low blow, coz. You can read. The sign says we're raising money for flood and tornado victims." Gabe's voice has an edge to it.

"So it does. But don't fool yourself. Johnny Jihad here will siphon off all or part for his own devices. You can be sure of that."

I'm surprised that Gabe is holding his temper. I'm used to doing that. Luckily most everybody at school knows me, knows my family, and they are great. But out and about, sometimes, prejudice can rear its ugly head when you least expect it. My looks alone can set someone off. Baba and Mama have taught us to walk away, turn the other cheek, as the prophet Jesus, PBUH, teaches.

"C'mon, Shaun, you wanna buy something, or do you wanna just stand there being a butthole and block everybody else from buying?" Gabe challenges his cousin, and I wait to see how this plays out. *Please, Allah.*

Shaun shakes his head from side to side. "I spent my entire summer trying to acclimate you to a whole different world. Not only do you not appreciate it—witness the fact that you blew me off; you couldn't even go to the first game with me—but you betray me by hanging with"—he nods to me and stares at me like I'm pond scum—"*him.*" There is so much hate in his voice that I feel it coat me like a barrel of motor oil overflowing.

Gabe moves from behind the table and steps so close to his cousin, Shaun's dragon breath must be enflaming him. He looks Shaun straight in the eyes and is about to raise a fist when—

"What's going on here?" It's our principal, Mr. Zynco. "Shaun, Gabe, you two have an unresolved issue?"

Amazingly Shaun instantly backs down. "No, sir. I was just buying some cupcakes for our pizza party we're having."

I can't imagine how someone who had, a moment ago, been so angry, so hateful, can switch to Mr. Kiss-Up so quickly. And lie through his teeth, because both Gabe and I know Shaun is heading to a drunken blowout, not an innocent pizza party.

Shaun turns to me and says, "The strawberry cupcakes, Kerem, please." He pulls a ten out of his wallet and hands it to me for the five-dollar container of cupcakes I hand over. I reach down to get his change but I hear him say, "Keep the change. It's for a good cause." And he walks away.

Gabe looks at me with relief and apology, and then he once again joins me behind the table.

"How's the sale going, guys?" Mr. Zynco asks. "A lotta delicious things here. My wife has a sweet tooth. Tell you what, what can I get for a fifty?" He pulls out a fifty-dollar bill. He must have planned this because he had it right there in his front jeans pocket.

"Ten items. You name 'em," I tell him.

"Let's see: got any more of those strawberry cupcakes?" I reach down and pull up the last container. "Wonderful! And I'll take those and those and those." He points to three more things, then stops a moment, pondering. "If you have it, I'll take three of the fudge. Peanut butter fudge is my daughter's favorite. And let's top the order off with one each of the lemon bars, the oatmeal raisin cookies, and the scones. There's an older couple at our church who are from England. I'd bet they'll love those scones with their afternoon tea tomorrow."

Thank goodness I brought some large grocery bags. I fill two of them with all he's bought and hand them over.

"Thank you very much, Kerem. And Gabe, I'm glad you're helping. Jumping right into the deep end I see. Charity is always a blessing."

As he walks away, I say, "I wonder if he planned that metaphor, you being on the swim team and all."

"I'd bet my weekly allowance he did. He strikes me as a very smart man."

"He got here just in time from what I was seeing. Did you plan to deck your cousin, Gabe?"

"If he didn't shut up, I suppose I might have. It's good the bomb was defused by our very insightful leader. I didn't see him lurking nearby, but my guess is he was. That's what principals do. They're always on the watch for an uprising. At least the one at my old school was. She could smell a fight brewin' before the fighters knew."

"Is Shaun always that volatile? I don't know him very well, and apologies if I offend you, I'm not sure I like what I see."

"Shaun's a good guy. With a blind spot. I don't know why. And, of course, lots of times, there's never a reason why someone's prejudiced. They have their reasons, and you can poke a zillion holes in their arguments and never make a difference. People are going to believe what they want to believe. With Shaun, though, I've seen the goodness in him, and I'll keep working on his attitude about you. Or I'll die trying."

"What he called me—Johnny Jihad. I hate that for one reason only. I told you this before, but it bears repeating. The haters think a jihad is a hostile act, but it's not. The Quran teaches that we spend our lives in jihad, a search for meaning for our lives. What we're doing here, charity, is a jihad."

"Well, then, let's get this jihad restarted. I think your cowboys have herded another group of cattle our way." And indeed, five or six people are approaching the table.

In the end, we sell almost everything we have, and my cabinet members, sweaty from all that herding they've been doing, show up to devour the one remaining container of cookies. We celebrate, Gabe saying, "I wish we had some milk to dunk these in." Everybody agrees, although I'm sure one or two of them will end up at the big party where milk will not be on the menu.

They fold up the table and put it in one of their cars while Gabe guards me and the money as we head to my car.

Hiding the money box in the center console, I start the engine and leave the stadium parking lot.

On the short drive home, Gabe says, "Starry, starry night. Reminds me of that famous painting. What artist was it? Van Gogh? But *this* magnificence. Better than any picture. Allah is a talented artist. Look at those stars twinkle."

I smile at him. "You know, God and Allah are the same. We may be in my car, but you don't have to call Him by his Arabic name. God is perfectly acceptable."

"I know. I just like saying it. There's something very special about it."

"Not *it*, *Him*. Allah is indeed quite special. But a warning, when you attend your Methodist church on Sunday, you might not want to lead the congregational prayer by starting with 'Allahu Akbar.' You might start a holy war." I laugh.

"Thanks for the advice."

I pull into our drive. "Want to come in and count our plunder?"

"Don't you have evening prayers?"

I look at the dashboard clock. "Not until about an hour from now. Come on, you can meet Baba and Mama."

We head into the house, and three-fourths of my family is sitting in the family room.

"Baba, Mama, Tim, this is Gabe, our new neighbor."

Mama leaps up from her recliner and rushes Gabe, enveloping him in a hug. "So good to meet you, Gabriel. I met your mother the other day. What a lovely woman. And those cupcakes—they didn't last long around here. Timur ate half of them." She nods toward my cousin.

"They were very good," he says, staring at Gabe like he is appraising him.

"Tell your mother that she can bake for us any day," Baba says. "We are quite grateful for her gracious gift. Please thank her. If I know my wife, though, a written thank-you note is on its way to your house." He looks at Mama with the love he always showers down on her.

"It probably arrived today, Aram, my love. The prophet, PBUH, teaches us to be grateful, and my own mother taught that a written thank-you note is required when a gift is given."

"Don't I know it," I spout. "You've had me writing thank-you notes since I was old enough to spell."

"And you're a better person because of it," Mama says. "But enough, have a seat, boys."

"Can't. We're heading up to my room to count our loot before evening prayers."

"How was the sale?" Baba asks.

"Very successful. We sold out. And believe me, there was plenty of baked goods. Gabe's mom must have spent hours in her kitchen."

"Mary said she was contributing, but I figured she'd simply do a batch of cookies or something. Now I feel like Aysel's and my contributions were meager. Forgive me, my son."

"Nothing to forgive," Gabe answers for me. "My mom loves to bake, and you will soon learn that she goes overboard with everything." He laughs.

"Never laugh at your mother, Gabriel." I can't believe Mama is admonishing a virtual stranger. But mothers are like that.

"Of course, Mrs. Uzun. Thank you for reminding me." Gabe's upbringing certainly outshines his cousin's.

"Where is Aysel? I'd hoped to introduce her to Gabe too."

"Her first official date with Hasan," Baba says. "She was giddy. But I don't know how it will go. Apparently his grandmother is chaperoning."

"As it should be," I hear Tim mutter.

I turn to Gabe. "My sister has a new boyfriend, and he is orthodox. Dating alone is not allowed." I sigh. "So let's head up. I wanna see how well we did."

We climb the stairs to my room.

"Nice room," Gabe says. He walks to a framed piece of calligraphy I have hanging above my bed. "What's this?"

"A verse from the Quran. You know how Catholics hang crosses above their beds? Sort of the same thing."

"My gram has a portrait of Jesus above hers."

"Forbidden. We do not believe in making images of the prophet, PBUH. In our mosques, there are no statues, no portraits. But you will find calligraphy like that one."

"What's it say?"

"I seek protection in the words of Allah from the evil of which He has created."

"You believe He created evil?"

"Of course, everything in the world was created by God. Without evil, we would not know what good is."

"Makes sense. I like that verse."

"I'm glad. It's comforting to me." I sit on the bed and pat the place next to me. "Sit."

He does. I open the box of money, and hand him half of it. "Count."

There is silence as we each tote up our piles of cash. I look to make sure he is not still adding in his head. He nods. "I've got two seventy-five. You?"

"Three fifty."

"Wow! More than we hoped for. And there's still a ton of change at the bottom of the box." I look over at my alarm clock. "But that will have to wait. Almost prayer time." I stand, and he follows suit.

As we descend the stairs, I say, "I really enjoyed tonight. I hope we spend a lot more time together." I feel so awkward. I want to grab him and kiss him, but I don't know if he feels the way I do. And I certainly don't know how Mama and Baba would take it if they caught us.

"I do too," he says. At the front door, he touches my shoulder and says, "Sunday?"

My heart skips.

"After afternoon prayers," I answer.

As I shut the door after him, I am startled by Tim's "You two have fun?" The question has no emotion in it.

I look at him. "Yeah. It was a great game, and the sale was a success, so, indeed, it was a lot of fun."

His face is set. No emotion whatsoever. "Prayers?"

"Sure." And I join him and Baba. Mama often skips evening prayers, but Baba says that is between her and Allah. She was brought up differently than Baba. Her family was much more lax in their practices. But Baba says everyone has his or her own relationship with Allah.

At the end of the prayers, when it is time to offer up our own requests and such to Allah, I pray silently, not wanting Baba or Timur to hear. It's not that I'm ashamed of what I beseech; it's that I am not ready to reveal my innermost self to my family.

I pray that Allah bless this friendship that's formed so quickly with Gabriel, and selfishly—*forgive me, Allah*—I pray that Gabriel will become interested in me in a closer way.

As we finish prayers, Aysel comes bounding in the front door. Mama greets her at the foot of the stairs.

"I heard the car and figured it was you. How was your date?"

"It was fabulous," Aysel says as she and Mama come into the family room.

"Sit, sit. Tell us all about it," Baba commands. And we all sit, Timur, Baba, Mama, Aysel, and me, eager to hear an account of my sister's first date.

"Well," she says, "Hasan is just the most beautiful man ever." I think that can't be true, because Gabe takes that prize. "He is a gentleman in every sense of the word. His grandmother's nice too. We went to a Middle Eastern buffet downtown. I guess they are used to chaperoned dates there because they seated me and Hasan at one table and his grandmother at another. I kinda felt sorry for her, being alone, but she didn't seem to mind, and I wanted to be alone with Hasan."

I bet you did. I look to Timur to try to read his thoughts on this, but he is silently appraising Aysel's story, not revealing himself in any way.

"So—the food was amazing. And I learned a lot about Hasan's family. Yes, their ways are stricter than ours, but one of the first things he told me was that I didn't have to wear the hijab on his account. He hadn't said that when we'd had coffee the other day, so I figured he was glad I was wearing it. I must have looked disappointed because he quickly added that he was pleased I was wearing the hijab. He said his mother and father were no doubt very happy that he had found an obedient Muslim girl."

"Obedient?" I laughed.

"Hush, Kerem," Mama said. "Aysel, darling, what did he mean by that?"

"I guess I frowned when he said that, because he quickly rephrased his comment, careful to make sure I understood. 'That was a poor choice of words. Even in our family, we don't demand that a wife be subservient. That's not in the Quran.' Then he went on to say he used the word obedient because in the old country that's what the culture would demand. His mother seems to me to be very independent. She has her doctorate and teaches at the university—in the pharmacy school."

"I wonder if I know her," Baba says. "I've been to the pharmacy school to speak on the latest advances in meds for my heart patients. What's her name?"

Aysel rolls her eyes. "I guess I'm just the ditz you always say I am, because I don't remember if Hasan ever said her name."

"Love, you may be a ditz, but you are *my* ditz, and I love you," Baba says.

"I know, I know, Baba."

"And besides," Baba adds, "I've never seen a Muslim woman there. I assume she'd be wearing a hijab, at least."

Aysel nods. "I think so. I haven't met her personally yet. But a hijab would probably be right. His grandmother certainly was covered from head to toe."

Mama nods at that.

"What else happened? Did Hasan take you in his arms and plant a big smackeroo on your lips while performing a to-the-floor dip?" I rib her.

I hear a slight *hmmph* from Timur. Is it an amused reaction or disgust?

"Kerem! Nothing like that. I'm not sure Hasan has that in him, and certainly not on the first date, not with Grandmother training her eagle eyes on us." She looks at Baba and Mama, who have smiles pasted on their faces. "Besides," she reassures them, "I was brought up right. There will be nothing heavy going on until after I'm married."

"Which will be a long time off, inshallah," Mama says prayerfully. Inshallah means God willing, and I know Mama is hoping God's will is that Aysel's marriage is several years from now.

"Of course," Aysel mumbles, not very convincingly. I think she has fallen for this guy. "Well, I am exhausted, so I think I'll go up to bed." She stands, inquisition over.

As she kisses Baba's cheek, he intones, "Sweet dreams, benim küçük kızım."

Somehow I think those sweet dreams will be filled with Hasan.

Aysel says good night to me and Tim. He nods, not showing any emotion.

She kisses Mama, who offers a similar benediction, and then my sister waltzes out, caught up, like Cinderella, in the memories of her night at the ball.

"I'm turning in too," I declare. "Night, Baba; night, Mama."

"Good night, my love," Mama replies and Baba nods to me.

As I begin to nod off, I'm aware that a dream is just beginning. And playing the starring role in this night movie is Gabe. I guess Aysel won't be the only one with sweet dreams tonight.

CHAPTER 6

Timur

MY AUNT and uncle are good to me. They are not as devout as my parents were, though. They have tried to make me a part of their family, but life here is not like home. They are good Muslims, I tell myself—try to convince myself. Not as strict as my family was, but good nonetheless. This is something I repeat over and over in my mind.

But they are not my parents. Kerem is not my brother. Aysel is not my Delal. And they could never be.

I miss my family all so much. Their lives here in America were so hard. My father was not a doctor like Uncle. In the old country, my father was a master stonemason. He was sought out. He worked for the rich, the powerful.

But my brother got sick. Zeheb contracted a rare blood disorder. The doctors in Turkey did what they could for him, but Mother felt that care in the United States would far surpass the care Zeheb was getting at home. She and Father pled their case to Uncle Aram.

After years as a citizen, Uncle was able to bring my parents to America. At first Zeheb responded to treatment. Life was good, I've heard, for I was not born yet. It was not as good as the life Uncle and Aunt had, but Father did start a business. He was not lauded for his stonework here, but he was able to put a crew together and secure contracts for bricklaying. Mother stayed home, caring for Zeheb, and later Delal and me.

But things took a turn. Zeheb got weaker and weaker. His kidneys began to fail. Because of his blood disease, dialysis was not an option. At first he spent a few days in the hospital, then a few weeks, and as his condition worsened, the months before his death, Mother never left his side.

Father would take us to visit, and Mother would come home to shower and change clothes, but that was while Delal and I were in school. I missed her so much.

As Father spent more and more time on the job, trying to make money to pay for Zeheb's treatment, my sister and I were left alone.

Delal was getting older, and she was out of the apartment more and more when Father and Mother weren't there. She was supposed to be watching over me, but she knew I would not tell, so she left for hours at a time.

On our visits to the hospital, even *I* noticed that Mama was not well. She winced in pain sometimes when she thought I wasn't looking. But she never said a word to any of us.

At last, at the age of seventeen, my brother Zeheb—which means "gold" in Turkish—died. My parents had lost their golden boy.

As is Islamic custom, Uncle and Father prepared my brother's body for burial, and he was buried within forty-eight hours of his death. Father was heartbroken. His eldest was gone.

Mother returned to the apartment in mourning. She tried to take care of us. She tried to correct the failings she saw had developed in her daughter during her absence. She tried to pour her love on me, her youngest. But in the end, she was not up to the task.

She was diagnosed with stage 4 breast cancer, a cancer that could have been stopped had it been caught early enough. But she was too devoted to my brother's care to tend to her own. She passed away, and a part of me went with her.

Delal acted out more than ever after Mother's death. And Father had no idea what to do with his rebellious fifteen-year-old daughter.

That was when he arranged the marriage.

CHAPTER 7

Gabriel

THE LOUD pounding on my bedroom door startles me from a white-hot dream.

"Gabe, get your lazy butt up! You plan to sleep the whole day? Did you forget about the lawn?"

Dad insists I be the official groundskeeper of his vast estate. I groan, trying to wake up, wishing I could turn over and go back to Kerem's arms—even if they are only dream arms.

"Do I have to come in there?"

I yawn.

"I'm talking to you, son. Answer me."

Dad's great, but he can be an overlord sometimes. I smile, realizing he had to do his own grass cutting all summer long. No wonder he's rousting me out of bed now. He wants to reestablish his authority in all things lawn care.

"I'm awake," I shout. "Why do you have to raise such a ruckus at dawn on a Saturday?"

"Check your watch, son," he yells through the door. "It's ten already. You could have had the job done by now. Get up and open this door. I want to make sure you are among the living."

Cursing him for interrupting the only kind of sex I will ever have with Ker, no doubt, I haul myself out of bed, go to the door, and open it, rubbing my eyes, standing in nothing but my briefs.

"I may have changed many a diaper on you in my day, boy, but I don't need to see your naked butt now," Dad says. "Put some clothes on."

I turn, grab a pair of gym shorts, and slip them on.

"That's better. Your mother could have been lurking out here. She doesn't need to see that."

I yawn again, wanting him to go away so I can slip back into paradise.

"You do realize I let you sleep in?" Dad smiles.

I want to say, *and do you realize you ripped me away from the man I love?* TMI. Instead, I simply answer, "Yeah."

"But the lawn needs cutting, and it's your job. Just because we live in a fancier neighborhood now, I'm not about to hire a lawn service when my son can do the job much cheaper."

"Like for nothing?"

"Like for a roof over your head and food in your belly. Besides, pushing the lawn mower was my job growing up, and now it's yours. Just be glad mowers are gasoline powered now."

I laugh at him. "Dad, they haven't made a push mower since 1874, the year of your birth."

He smiles slyly. "Now you got me. And for your information, wiseass, I was born in 1974, not 1874. You got your centuries wrong." He suddenly pulls me into a hug.

"What's up?" I say, trying to break away.

"I just realized I haven't hugged you since the other day when you pulled into the drive from Mom and Pop's. This new job's eatin' my lunch. I don't have a moment to think, much less spend time with my only son."

I love my dad. And I let him hug me for as long as he wants after that explanation.

Hug over, he asks, "So how's school? You gonna like your new swim coach?"

"School's great, and yeah."

"A man of few words." He smiles. "Your mother says you've already made a new friend, the neighbor boy? He gay too?"

Gotta love 'em, my parents. They get right to the point.

I think about that question. With regret. "Nah—at least I don't think so. He's Muslim."

"Your mother said that. Really strict, is he?"

"Only sorta. Not as strict as some, but stricter than I've read they can be. At least American Muslims, that is."

"Doing your research, huh?" My dad loves that I'm not content to just sit around and wait for knowledge to come to me.

"Reading up a little. Plus, Ker's been teaching me." I must have smiled a little too much when I said Kerem's name. God, I hope my dick isn't *smiling* too.

Dodged that bullet. Dad continues his interrogation. "Sweet on him?"

Sweet on him? What am I, a thirteen-year-old girl? Dad's lingo definitely needs some work.

"Let's just say that if something develops—and I doubt it will—I wouldn't be unhappy."

"Go for it, son." Dad and Mom's support is incredible.

"Now, get out of here so I can get downstairs to the lawn. No more questions. Especially questions you probably already knew the answer to because you and Mom talk all the time."

Again, that sly smile. "I just like to catch up with my boy, not always hear everything secondhand." And he leaves.

I pull on a T-shirt that's slung over the chair, and I search for jeans in the pile of dirty clothes on the closet floor. Mom long ago stopped doing my laundry for me. Or at least that's her edict: do your own washing. I wait until I have nothing left to wear before I cart it all down to the laundry room. When I hear the washer going. If I put it on the laundry room floor while she's doing her and Dad's stuff, she will usually do mine. That's my mom.

As I finish dressing, I think of my dad's question. Yes, I've been doing research. That's the way I am. I haven't found out a lot yet—certainly not anything about Islamic attitudes about homosexuality—but I do now know that PBUH means "peace be upon him." So I don't have to keep wondering about that—or ask Ker what it means.

My cell chimes, and I run to the bed table to get it, hoping it's Kerem. So sure that it's him, I answer, "I was hoping you'd call."

"Well, isn't that nice?" I don't recognize the voice and quickly glance at the Caller ID: Lou Kramer.

"Lou, I thought you were someone else."

"Apparently. But I don't blame you. You couldn't have known I have your number. Shaun gave it to me. Last night. At the party. He was drunk out of his skull, but he managed to pull up your digits so I could put 'em in my phone."

I roll my eyes. Shaun's on a path he shouldn't be on. I've got to find a way to turn him around. Muslim-bashing, being on the verge of having your cousin punch your lights out, and getting plastered are not good things.

"I hope you don't mind," Lou says, breaking my immediate concern for my coz.

"Nah. It's okay. Whuzzup?"

"Thought we could hang together for a bit. Today. About one? We could get a burger. Or something else. Whatever you want."

Since Kerem's the only friend I've made so far, I guess I really should meet him, even though I don't know if I care.

"I saw a Fuddrucker's outside Dornabrook Mall. Meet you there?"

"Great," he says, "see you at one o'clock, sharp. I'll be wearing a white carnation in my lapel so you'll know it's me."

I laugh even though I roll my eyes at his lame attempt at humor. "Right," I say and end the call.

The lawn hasn't grown a whole lot since Dad cut it last, so that task, thankfully, doesn't take long.

I shower and find some reasonably clean clothes for my "date," a term I use loosely, because if Lou Kramer is gay, like Shaun seems to think, I'm not sure I want to lead him on. Then again, my abstinence is making me horny. That dream was not just a tribute to Kerem; I know it was fueled, too, by my need for release. Kramer might be willing for a one-off. Who knows? If he's willing and his parents aren't home?

He's waiting outside when I get there, and—wonder of wonders— he does have a carnation pinned to his shirt. He points to it as I approach.

I shake his hand, do the shoulder-bump thing, and we go in. "Nice touch, that flower."

"Didn't want you confused as to who you were meeting." He laughs.

We each order, and then we get our drinks. We maneuver to a table. There aren't many people there, but I guess it's a little late for lunch.

As we sit, I say, "So tell me about yourself, Lou."

"First of all, I hate being called Lou. Sounds like a girl. My friends call me Kramer."

So Shaun *is* a friend of this guy. Or at least enough of a friend to call him by his preferred name.

"Kramer it is."

"Thanks. Okay, about me. I'm in the band. Tuba. I like Stephen King, cheeseburgers, and hip-hop. And I'm gay."

He looks at me like he is begging for a reaction. I give him none. I don't know what to answer. As far out of the closet as I am, I'm not ready for the rest of this meal to be about gayosity.

"What? You homophobic?"

"No, no, no," I say. "Not at all."

"Then why are you sitting there with a shocked look on your face?"

I thought I was deadpan, but I guess he sees otherwise. So I take the plunge. "I'm gay too."

"I knew it! My gaydar never fails me."

"I'm glad yours is working, because mine's on the blink. I had no idea about you," I say, ignoring what Shaun had said about Kramer.

"There're four or five of us at Compton. I could introduce you."

"No, I'm fine."

"Closet?"

"Not at all. I simply prefer to let things come naturally. It's that 'you tell people when you want to' thing."

"I respect that." Suddenly both our buzzers start buzzing, lights flashing. We pick up our food and head to the condiments bar. I'm seated before he returns with his tray.

He grabs his enormous burger, squishes it down, and takes a gigantic bite. He is still chewing when he says, "So have you read any King?"

I'm confused. I expected him to go on and on about gay this and gay that. That's been my experience when I meet a new guy, but Kramer is more into his cheeseburger and reading.

"I have," I answer. "I loved *The Stand*, and the two books he wrote with Peter Straub are way cool. In fact, I like Straub more than King."

"No way. Straub's good, but not as great as King."

"Each to his own," I say, taking another bite of my burger.

"Meet the coach yet?" Kramer asks.

"Yeah. Like you said, he's a nice guy. I can't wait to get full-on into working out. I've missed it."

"There's a gay guy on the team."

"I know—me," I counter.

"No, I mean there's another gay guy on the team."

"Well, don't tell me. I want to see if my gaydar gets any better. And maybe he doesn't want you outing him." I finish my last bite.

"He wouldn't mind, but I'll let you discover for yourself. And I'll keep your secret." He slathers the last fry on his tray with ketchup, then stuffs it in his mouth.

"Brownies?" I ask. "I love Fuddrucker brownies."

"A man after my own heart."

We rush to the counter and get two brownies. He gets the plain; I get the one with cream cheese frosting.

Sitting and enjoying our brownies—a little too much for Kramer; he keeps humming the whole time he chews—I ask, "What's your favorite TV show?"

"Streaming or otherwise?"

"Either."

"*Empire.*" A bit of brown goo spits from his mouth. He grabs a napkin and masks his "Sorry" as he wipes his mouth. "You watch it?"

"I've seen it. That Cookie is something else. Hell on wheels."

He laughs. "Sure is. I like Jamal. Cute and sings like an angel. I'd tap that any day."

I ignore that comment, and say, "What about *Walking Dead?*"

"Yuck. Not while I'm eating. I can't stand that show. I've only seen it when I've been forced to watch it. My ex made me watch it. He watched the old episodes on Netflix over and over. I tried to avoid his marathons, but sometimes he'd insist, and I'd be stuck."

"But it's so good. A real metaphor for life, if it's okay to sound like an English teacher."

"Maybe, but I can't stand the walkers. They creep me out. And Daryl? He's so Mr. Macho with his hairy chin, his motorcycle, and his perpetually dirty body that I want to puke every time he's on the screen."

Daryl's my favorite of all. "Well, it takes all kinds to make a world," I say, "or a TV audience, as the case may be."

We finish and say our goodbyes. Kramer's a nice enough guy, but anybody who doesn't like *Walking Dead* and Daryl is not for me. I don't think we'll be besties, and I *know* he's not boyfriend material. I'll just have to stay horny.

When I get home, I start upstairs.

"How was your date, dear?" Mom's voice stops me. She's dusting the hallway table.

"It wasn't a date, Mom. Just some guy from school. Shaun intro'd us the other day. When the guy called this morning, I didn't really want to go, but what could I do? I didn't want to be rude."

"I'm glad you went. It's important to make new friends."

"Right," I say, and continue upstairs.

I go to my computer and bring it out of sleep mode. I then text Kerem: *Skype. One minute?*

Instantly he replies, *Two. Have to get to the computer.*

I impatiently look at the clock in the corner of my PC screen. I've already logged in. Two minutes pass.

Magically his beautiful face appears. And the horny feeling returns.

"How's it going?" I ask.

"Great. I saw you mowing the lawn this morning."

"You should have come out. Brought the laborer a glass of water so he didn't pass out from the heat."

"Mama had me helping her clean the house. Aysel usually helps, but she was meeting Hasan for breakfast."

"Didn't she just have dinner with him last night?"

"She's falling head over heels. Can't get enough of the guy. Or his grandmother either, I guess."

"Grandmother? What does she have to do with anything?" I ask.

"In orthodox Islam, dates must always be chaperoned. Even that's a bit progressive. Poor Hasan at least is getting to choose who he dates. And apparently his family doesn't consider a coffee or quick lunch a date. So he's lucky. He could be roped into an arranged marriage."

"They still do that?"

"Oh, yes. Fairly common, even in this day and age," he says.

"Even here, in the US?"

"You don't have to be in Pakistan or Palestine or Saudi Arabia to be a strict Muslim. And strict Muslims follow the old customs. Score one for Hasan that his family is allowing him to pick his bride himself."

"Bride? Has he already proposed to Aysel?"

"Not yet, but if I know my sister, she's already hoping. Mama tries to keep her on an even keel. My sister is a hopeless romantic. But enough of this. What you been doing?"

"Went to lunch with Lou Kramer. You know him?"

"Plays tuba in the band, right?"

"That's him."

"I don't *know him*, know him. But I know who he is. Some say he's gay." There's a hesitancy in his voice, a funny look on his face when he says that word.

"He is," I answer, and leave it hanging in cyberspace.

"So why is he meeting you?"

It's right then and there that I decide I can't keep it from him any longer. It's not fair for my new best friend not to know. Not in a world where I believe in openness.

"You feel like a walk?"

He doesn't react to my ignoring his question; his face lights up instead. "Sure. The pond and back?"

"Sidewalk, your side. Ten seconds."

He's already waiting, because despite the fact I'd said ten seconds, I realized I needed to pee, and I certainly didn't want that weighing on me for this maybe monumental revelation.

"Sorry. Nature called," I say as I cross the street.

We walk, making small talk along the way. He tells me more about Aysel's dinner date with Hasan. I make a joke about the old crone sitting at the next table, her evil eyes gazing upon them. He likes that and laughs.

We sit on the bench, and the motherfuckers are swimming across the pond. I smile, remembering how Ker had called the swans that.

A moment. I'm leading up to it. This could break our relationship. I have no idea how Muslims feel about it all, and more to the point, how Kerem personally feels about queer sex.

"You asked a question," I say, starting slow.

"No, I didn't. Are you crazy? I haven't said a word since we sat down." He punches my shoulder to say he's kidding me.

"Before."

"Before?"

"You asked, 'Why is he meeting you?'"

"Kramer? Doesn't matter. His reasons, your reasons. Not my business."

"You deserve to know."

"This sounds ominous."

"Not really. I just don't know how you'll react." I take a deep breath. "I'm gay."

He immediately crosses his arms, like he's had a pain, like he's protecting his heart.

"You okay?" I ask, concerned.

"No prob." But something tells me there is a problem.

I plunge into the deep end. "I've been out for a long time. Everybody at my old school knew. And nobody cared. At least nobody I cared about cared. But I'm new here, so I've been a bit discreet about it.

"Kramer is indeed gay," I continue. "But we didn't meet to hook up. At least I didn't." I feel guilty, thinking about how I had considered a little afternoon session if we'd both been willing. But that didn't happen, and I'm glad. "I don't know what his intentions were, but it didn't seem he was putting the moves on me. Shaun introduced us the other day. He gave Kramer my number. And I didn't want to blow him off."

He cuts his eyes toward me wickedly.

"I said 'blow him off' not 'blow him.'" Kerem laughs, and I know that things are going to be all right. "Get your mind out of the gutter, Ker. I went to lunch with Kramer because I thought it would be good to get to know somebody other than you, you dork."

"I understand. See what the community outside Islam is like," he jokes.

"I believe it's a much bigger community. At least in my world, since you and your family are the only Islamic community I know."

"We'll have to do something about that. Maybe I'll convert you. My father has a ceremonial sword. You'll kneel before him, and he'll tap you on the shoulder and dub thee a Muslim of the realm."

"Uh, I believe that's how King Arthur makes you a Knight of the Round Table. So how *do* you convert to Islam?"

"You planning?"

"Give me a break and just answer my question."

"It's easy. You state, 'I believe in the one true God, and in his Prophet Muhammad.' It must be a true and sincere declaration of faith. You can speak only to God, or people can be in attendance. And it must be spoken in Arabic, the language of the Quran."

Again, his speech takes on that formality. It tells me he's quite serious about his religion.

Then he adds with a smile, "Let me know when you are ready."

"Not any time soon, but thanks for asking. But we've taken the wrong road that diverged in the woods. I believe we were talking about my being gay. It doesn't bother you? It's not against Islamic law?"

He smiles at me. "Bother me? No. Against Islamic law? No. Against Muslim customs? Yes. But like I said, Islam has developed many variations over the years, as people and cultures evolve. Although there is still the idea that marriage is between a man and a woman, many modern Muslims accept homosexuality and allow gays to pray in their mosques."

"What about your family?"

"Tell you the truth, the subject hasn't come up." There's a catch in his voice. "But I'm sure as loving as Baba and Mama are, they would accept gays. They already love you, and that's half the battle. But I don't think there would be a battle." Again I hear something I can't identify in his voice.

"So we're okay with this? *You're* okay with this?"

"You can be anything you choose, Gabe." He stops, pauses. "Wait—it's not a choice, is it?"

"Nope."

"Then you can simply be. Now, if you decide to be a Jehovah's Witness or an ax murderer, there might be a problem. I'll let you know after I've thought about it."

I laugh at his joke, and he joins in.

We walk silently back home. I've given him a lot to think about.

When we reach his house, I say, "Salaam Alaykum," and he answers "Wa-Alaykum" with what only can be described as love in his eyes.

CHAPTER 8

Kerem

THIS CAN'T be happening. Gabe is gay. Did Allah send him here just for me? And now, what do I do?

I'm eighteen. I'm a man. I can act on my feelings. I can be who I am. As much as I've prayed on it, I know Allah will back me up here.

But Baba and Mama? How will they feel? I told Gabe I thought they'd be okay with it. But I really don't know.

We don't live in one of the old countries where the idea of being gay is looked upon with disgust. I don't know how people in Turkey feel, but I certainly know that in Iran, a gay man can be put to death. Islam and the government are all tangled up in Iran, but over there, that happens in a lot of countries. And even if Islamic law is not civil law, people can have some very strict beliefs. Gay people can be harassed or killed even if it's not against the law.

At least things are different here. It's not perfect and gays still have to be cautious, but the law is on our side, mostly. That's the law. It's not Baba and Mama.

They taught Aysel, Timur, and me that we must obey all the laws, but they also have standards based on their beliefs, and some of those beliefs are stricter than the government's. So how do they stand on gay rights? Especially the gay rights of their son?

I shudder to think. Not because I'm afraid they will not love me—their unconditional love for each of their children, Timur included, is proven each and every day. No, I'm simply afraid they will not approve. And then where will I be?

I don't know how to tell them.

And Gabriel might not even be interested in me in that way. Do I tell him? That I want us to go for it? Is it too soon? Do I want him because I'm sick of waiting? Tired of not knowing what it's all about? Or do I really like him in that way?

What if he rejects me? I lose a good friend. How awkward would that be, with him living right across the street? Going to my school? Running into him constantly?

Maybe it's best to just let it lie. Things will work out, inshallah.

How is it possible to say sunset prayers with all this rolling around in my brain? Forgive me, Allah.

Prayers ended, Mama serves the dinner she'd prepared earlier.

We gather at the table, and before you know it, Aysel is babbling. Hasan this, Hasan that.

"Aysel, dearest, eat your dinner," Mama says. "Let us have a little peace."

My sister is offended. "Peace? I've met the love of my life, and you find it stressful to hear about him?"

"Not about him, love," Baba says. "It's just you're a bit shrill. The family is trying to eat in tranquility. It's important for the digestion." He smiles at his cleverness.

"Baba," Aysel scoffs, "what is all this talk? We've never had one of your *tranquil*"—sarcasm spills from her lips—"meals ever. You and Mama have always encouraged us to share everything."

I think of the latest news I could share and feel guilty. It's true that we are a sharing family. But I am keeping quiet on this. At least for now.

Maybe someday.

Timur speaks up. "You just met the guy. It's impossible to be so much in love already. Have a little dignity, cousin."

"I think what your cousin is trying to say is that perhaps you are moving too quickly, love," Mama says.

I refuse to weigh in on this for fear the topic will end abruptly and someone will ask about my day. As long as Aysel is babbling, I don't have to talk.

I grab another piece of *ekmek* and stuff Mama's heavenly bread into my mouth. Before my Aunt Sila, Timur's mother, passed, she shared her recipe with Mama.

"I am *not* moving too quickly, Mama. Didn't you know Baba was the one for you the moment you first laid eyes on him?"

She had her there. We all three know the famous Aram/Maria love story. Baba might joke about how he first saw Mama in a burqa and fell in love instantly, but the last part is true. They passed in a hospital hallway, and as she tells it, sparks flew.

"Your father and I are an exception, love. And it's not only the moving fast thing. Hasan's family's ways are much different from ours. You need to get to know him so you can adjust. It's romantic right now to embrace their traditions, but will you be able to live with them for the rest of your life? Your father never practiced the strict ways of his family, of your aunt and uncle, may they rest in peace, but I still had adjustments to make our marriage work. My family was not as devout as your baba is. It was hard to change."

"No one asked you to change, Maria, my most cherished," Baba adds. "You well know your relationship with Allah is between you and Him, but I kiss the earth that you were willing. It was a blessing to me that you put up with me and my ways. I'm not perfect, and I don't follow Islam perhaps as perfectly as I should."

Timur is stuffing his face with food, but I hear him say under his breath, "You surely don't."

"But with you by my side and supporting me," Baba continues, "I feel I have a clearer path to heaven, inshallah." He leans over and kisses her cheek.

"That's exactly what I'm trying to say. I feel a connection to Hasan like the one you two have. I would do anything for him."

"All we're asking is that you keep your emotions in check and engage your brain," Mama says. "Give it a bit more time to grow. If a marriage with Hasan is meant to be, we will support you. After all, our teachings tell us that marriage is a sacred bond between a man and a woman, and it is to be sought."

I almost wince at that statement. Is Mama saying that a marriage between me and Gabe or whatever man I end up with is not sacred?

Baba adds, "And besides, I'm an old man." Baba is only forty-eight, hardly ancient. "I am eagerly awaiting my grandchildren." He looks at Timur and me, making sure we know we are included in this statement. "Don't wait too long, but wait long enough that you truly know your heart's desire."

My heart skips, thinking of how I will ever give Baba those grandchildren he is demanding. Will I, as a gay man, be allowed to adopt? I know some have, but some are not granted that privilege. And being Muslim might be a barrier. Who knows?

I help Mama clean up after the meal. Aysel goes upstairs, waiting for a call from her beloved Hasan. Tim, I assume, goes to his computer, for that is where most of his life is spent.

I'm putting a serving bowl in the dishwasher when Mama says, "Your sister is something else."

"That she is."

"I so hope this match she is intent on is the one for her. Allah has always smiled on all my children, even the one I didn't birth but took to raise, and He will continue to show us the way. If Hasan and his orthodox ways are right for Aysel, Allah will let her know. And who are we to question Allah? He makes us all in infinite varieties, and we must accept all those."

But what about a gay son? Could you accept that, Mama? Will you feel Allah made me the way I am?

"Aysel certainly has never gone along to get along, Mama. She makes her own path, and we've always had to walk it alongside her if we wanted to be with her. This newfound belief in the orthodox ways is just like her. And I don't think we can chalk it all up to her infatuation with Hasan. She's too smart for that. I would venture to say, this has been coming on for quite some time. I look back, and I see her transformation into the perfect Muslim wife was begun long before she met Hasan."

"How so, love?" She hands me a towel and her mother's crystal bowl. We learned long ago that it was not to be put in the dishwasher.

"It's hard to pinpoint. Little things. So little that I don't even remember most of them. But I can tell you one thing: the hijab? She's been fiddling with that scarf since she was in middle school. I'd pass by her room, and she'd be arranging it on her head oh so perfectly. Then she'd admire herself in the mirror. And from the look on her face, she wasn't playing around. Not one bit."

"I never knew that. But I'm not surprised." She takes the bowl from me and puts it safely away in the cupboard in its special spot.

"If she was doing that, she may have been fantasizing about what an orthodox life might be like. And you and Baba always brought us up to make our own decisions about everything, especially Islam. If I've heard it once, I've heard it a thousand times: 'It's between you and Allah.'"

She laughs at me, not realizing that I'm not only talking about my sister but also feeling her out, should I decide to come out of the closet right here, right now.

"Kerem, my darling, it's true. Only you and Allah need to approve your innermost feelings, how you think, how you live."

I take a deep breath. Start to speak. Hope that the words come out right.

"But marriage is the most important step in life." She stops me before I can say anything. "How you choose to spend the rest of your life and with whom you choose to do it cannot be taken lightly. It requires much prayer before a decision is made that will bring happiness, inshallah."

Not knowing what God's will is for me, I instantly fall deeper into my closet.

"Well, it appears we're through here." She kisses my forehead. "Thank you, love, for helping me. And now, I must take a nice bath before evening prayers."

I look at her with wonder.

"You may think you know your mother, but you don't know everything. Just because I don't pray standing behind you, your father, and your cousin doesn't mean that I don't pray. Yes, I fail sometimes and skip my prayers. But most evenings, I pray in the privacy of my bedroom."

She leaves me in confusion. I never knew that. And I'm not sure Baba even knows.

I spend an hour or so reading; then I go find Baba and Timur in the family room, waiting.

"Why is it you can't be early for prayers instead of rushing in at the last minute?" Timur asks, with that disdain that is so often on his tongue.

"Isn't on time better than late?" I spit back at him.

"Boys, let's prepare and stop this bickering."

We cleanse ourselves, unroll our prayer rugs on the marble floor, slip off our shoes, and perform the ritual. At the end, the personal prayer part, I silently pray for guidance on this issue that's been plaguing me since I saw Gabe this afternoon. And I selfishly ask Allah to make Gabe fall in love with me.

Prayers finished, we roll up our rugs. Timur says, "You'd think Aysel and Aunt Maria would join us sometimes. When I was young, we prayed as a family."

"We've heard this so many times, Tim. We could recite it with you."

"Kerem, be kind. Your cousin grew up in a much stricter family than I've brought you up in. Your Uncle Sivan was very devout and believed in following all the old ways. I suppose I could be a better Muslim, like my brother was."

"Your brother k—" I put the brakes on my wayward tongue immediately when my brain engages. We never, ever talk about Delal's death or the fact that it was her own father who killed her. Especially not in front of Timur. That is a family secret left buried. I think quickly. "Your brother, my Uncle

Sivan, kind of went a bit overboard with religion. I like the way we practice Islam much better, Baba. Uncle Sivan, I'm sure, was a good man...."

I look at Timur when I say this, hoping to make amends for what I almost said and hoping he doesn't pick up on the fact that I don't believe any man who could kill his own daughter could be a good man. But judgment is only for Allah. I truly believe that.

"And he brought up his family in the way he saw fit, but there is so much love in our house, there is no way Allah could possibly find fault with you."

"Thank you, my son," Baba says. "From your lips to God's ears." He smiles at me. "Now, I have an appointment with a soft bed. Good night, Kerem." He kisses my forehead. He turns to Timur. "Good night, my nephew." And he kisses Timur as well. There is no pleasure on Timur's face from the kiss.

In my room, I punch in Gabe's speed dial digit.

"I didn't expect a call from you tonight." His voice warms me, but there is hesitance in it. "After what I laid on you today, I figured you'd need time to process. Or time to delete me from your phone and Instagram." He chuckles, but I can hear he is just nervously trying to make light of his revelation.

"I admit what you said surprised me. But it doesn't bother me at all. I told you that."

"Yeah, but that's what you say when someone lays something heavy on you."

I desperately want to tell him I'm not bothered because I'm like him. But I can't. It's too soon.

"Look, do we live in a world where a Muslim can get elected class president in a school that has no other Muslim students?" I ask.

"Well, yeah. I think you know that."

"Then we live in a world where said Muslim's best friend can be gay, and it's not a big deal."

I hear him expel a giant breath. "It makes me feel so good to hear that. Now, why are we on the phone when we could be skyping?"

I laugh. "Because I figured it was so late you might already be in bed. And I didn't want your naked ugly butt filling my screen."

He laughs back, not knowing that looking at his naked ugly butt is exactly what I'd like to be doing right now.

"For your information, I have a very nice butt. But I will make sure you never get to see it." There is challenge in his voice.

"Oh?" I ask, wishing I could rush across the street and gaze upon that butt right this minute. "I may have to pants you the next time we're together if that behind of yours is that special." It feels so good to be tossing innuendoes about like we're lovers—even though I know that Gabe would probably never take a Muslim lover. Too much baggage involved.

"You just try. And speaking of, when are we getting together next?"

"Well, we go to mosque on Sunday mornings."

"Sunday? Like us Methodists go to church?"

"Not quite. There is no sermon, no promises of hellfire and brimstone. We go to pray. Traditionally Muslims gather for noontime prayers together at mosque on Fridays. But that's hard in the dog-eat-dog world we live in here in the US. Baba and Mama have a hard enough time seeing all their patients as it is. If they had to leave to go to mosque for Friday prayers, they'd never get caught up. And I, of course, am in school. They accommodate my praying at lunch, but I'd miss my calculus class if I had to leave campus for mosque. So for us and all the other modern Muslims, there is Sunday prayer at mosque, a chance to make up for missing Friday prayers and a chance to commune with others like us. Used to be—and in a lot of tiny mosques—the prayers are said, visiting is done, and people go home. In our mosque, there are hundreds of faithful. So we pray and visit. Then there's a big potluck lunch. Not everyone attends, but we usually do. It's fun. You wouldn't believe how much good food is there."

"Oh, yes, I would. Methodists do the same thing sometimes. Not every Sunday, but when they do, there is an enormous spread of everything you could imagine. Mom always takes her prize-winning ham, of course."

"Not a lot of ham at the mosque."

"Not any, I'm betting."

"You got it. Anyway, I have a proposition. Aysel's spending the day tomorrow with Hasan, and Baba and Mama are going to the theater—to see *Fiddler on the Roof*, no less; sort of an interfaith experience, wouldn't you say?—and Tim is always holed up in his room. That means the family room is totally free and clear, so we can get our *Walking Dead* fix. What say we stream a few episodes? I have my favorites, and you no doubt have yours. We could put a playlist together and wallow."

"I'll bring my spear in case the walkers invade. I've learned a few techniques from Michonne."

"Somehow I don't think we'll need any protection, but if we do, I'll let you do your thing while I scream like a frightened little girl."

"Oh, I'd bet you could wield an ax as well as Glenn." He pauses, then laughs. "Can you imagine what someone would think if they'd just tapped into this conversation and didn't know *Walking Dead*? The cops would be at our doors before we knew it."

"Yep." I involuntarily yawn. It's been an exhausting day. "Come over around two tomorrow, 'kay?"

"You got it."

I smile as I put my phone on my bedtable.

My dreams are sweet ones.

I WAKE up for morning prayers. I ask Allah to make two o'clock come as quickly as possible. I'm pumped about this—what do I call it?—do I dare call it a *date*?

I can barely wait to get home from mosque and shoo Mama and Baba out the door to their theater date. I pop some microwave popcorn, and it smells enticing, when my phone chimes. It's Gabe. Oh, no, is he canceling?

"I'm at your front door," he says.

"We do have a doorbell," I say as I open the door to let him in.

"I know. Phone's better." He steps inside, and we head to the TV.

"I like Episode 5, Season 1; Episode 2, Season 3; and Episode 9, Season 5," he says, settling on the couch.

I beam. "Those are three of my favorites too." I sit next to him. I reach for the remote and hand it to him. "You know how to work this thing?" I ask. I reach around to the sofa table, where I've left the popcorn. "I made us a snack."

He gets everything going expertly, and within minutes, we're watching Rick and the gang.

I sneak peeks at him as he watches. He's so cute, sitting there totally engrossed in our favorite characters. He makes little noises as he watches, of fear, of fun. I want to lean over and kiss him, but I know that is not going to happen. Too soon.

The second episode starts, and about fifteen minutes in, I can't stand it. I have to do something. I hesitantly put my hand on his. He doesn't seem to notice. I squeeze, gently. Lovingly, I hope.

He looks at me. "I thought you didn't shake hands." A wicked smile. "A Muslim thing, you said."

"We don't. But I never said it's a Muslim thing. Actually, it's a Dr. Dad thing. Too many germs. But I'm not trying to shake your hand," I say. I'm trying to make these sound like words of love, but I don't know a thing about how to do that. This is all so new to me.

He turns the palm of his hand up and clasps my hand in his. "I thought this would never happen," he says. He starts to lean toward me.

"What you guys watching?" It's Timur. How long has he been standing there? I quickly pull my hand away from Gabe's, praying Timur has seen nothing.

Before I can answer his question, Gabe's phone chimes. He pulls it from his pants.

"Whuzzup, Mom?"

I look at him. His smile vanishes. His face turns dark.

"Is he okay?" A beat. "Hospital?" He listens again. I'm worried now. Has Gabe's dad been in a car wreck? Has his grandfather had a heart attack?

"Are you there now?" he asks his mother. "Wait! I'll go with you. Be right there."

He jumps up. "I gotta run. It's Shaun." Thank Allah it is not his father or grandfather. Then I immediately hate myself for thinking it's better if it's Shaun, especially since Gabe is showing such concern for his cousin. "Mom didn't know all the details, but Shaun was in a pickup game at the basketball courts at the park. He popped off to a guy, and the guy beat him up. It's pretty bad, Mom says. We're headed to the hospital now." He says all this as he makes a beeline to the door.

"Is there anything I can do?" I ask.

"No. Probably nothing *we* can do. But family is family, so we need to be there."

"I'll pray for him," I say.

"Do that. Please. I know God listens to you."

"Text me if you can."

"I will."

Just as he is going through the door, I grab him and turn him around. "I enjoyed this afternoon. Before we got such horrible news."

From the way he looks at me, I think he knows what I'm trying to tell him.

About us.

CHAPTER 9

Timur

I DON'T blame Father for what he did. Delal, as much as I loved—love—her, dishonored us.

I'm a pretty good lurker. Aunt and Uncle never discussed it with me, but they had their own discussion. When Uncle returned, hours later, from accompanying Father to the police station, he spoke with Aunt. I overheard it all.

The man who'd brought Delal back, her new husband, was angry. He told Father that she had not bled. Her hymen was already broken. She was not a virgin. He wanted no part of her.

Aunt told Amca that there were many reasons why a young girl wouldn't bleed when penetrated, but I know of only one. And since Delal had spent so many afternoons out of the apartment, leaving me alone, it was obvious what she'd been doing.

Funny, I was a ten-year-old, and I should not have understood. Perhaps I didn't. Perhaps I've filled in the gaps as I've grown older. The one thing I know is that Delal had been returned and that she had brought shame to Father and his family. *My* family.

My brother was dead, my mother was dead, my sister was dead, and my father, no doubt, thanks to US laws, would soon be dead. Or at least put in jail forever.

It wasn't long before I learned that we lived in a death penalty state, so the very government that decried the death penalty in so many Islamic countries put my father to death. For defending his family's honor.

And in some ways, they executed me, as well. I was to live with a family that didn't follow my family's customs, that didn't live the pure life I had been taught to live. A family that would bring up a daughter they were trying to turn away from her religious ways and a son who might be planning a life that would be one of grievous sin.

I saw them. It was disgusting. Sitting there. Hands clasped. Like young lovers.

Aunt and Uncle might be lax in their practices, too modern in their ways, but surely they cannot condone this. It is an abomination.

No family should have to put up with this.

It is an unforgivable act of dishonor.

JANUARY

CHAPTER 10

Gabriel

I GRAB my phone and text: *MFs?*

Sure. Bundle up. Cold out there, he replies.

Ker and I haven't walked to the pond in months. Three, in fact. Life got in the way.

I burst out my front door. I don't care if it is thirty-six degrees outside. It's been ages, and I've missed my friend. He stands on the sidewalk, waiting, gloved and hoodied.

I almost leap across the street, my mom screaming in my brain that I didn't look out for the cars. Thank God we don't live on a busy street. I'm too filled with seeing Kerem right now to remember Mom's basic life-preserving rules. There is so much I hope I can say to him.

"Nice outfit." His beautiful smile invades his voice. "You look like the Michelin man. Or maybe an Iditarod spectator."

"You're pretty covered up yourself."

"It's colder than a witch's tit out here, thanks to the wind."

"You want to go back inside and visit? We could save the walk for a warmer day."

"Not on your life. Our friends the swans are probably wondering where we've been. For their lonely sake, we need to get back to our walks. I've missed them. And you. So we can brave a little cold. I'm up for the icy challenge if you are."

I'm definitely game. I'm not about to give up this chance to be with Kerem after all these months, despite what's lying heavily on me. I gesture for him to lead the way.

As we stroll, shivering, we talk, catch up. Our breaths freeze in front of us, it seems. The cold, crisp air smells fresh. It's the aroma of renewal. With our walks back on track, our bond is sealing its crack, the crack of nonattention. Which is my fault.

"Shaun leaves tomorrow, thank God, and I'm ready for normal. I'm glad we could help my cousin, but I'm an only child, and I like it that way."

"It was nice of your parents to take him in while he recovered." His breath forms little clouds that linger on his beautiful lips, lips that may never be mine.

"Well, Aunt Evvie was a total wreck over this, and Uncle Don has been working tons of overtime, trying to keep the family from going under. Seems their insurance was not the best in the world. And with Shaun doing daily physical therapy, there wasn't much left over in the family coffers, money or emotion-wise. My cousins, Shaun's brother and sister, were going to starve, literally, if Mom and Dad didn't step up to help. And as under pressure as Shaun's folks have been, I know if they'd had to oversee Shaun's care, my young cousins would have withered from neglect. Aunt Evvie and Uncle Don are frazzled. But now that Shaun's on the mend, Mom and Dad think they can handle it."

"So how is Shaun doing? Really."

"Better. Much better. His PT says he's about as good as he's ever going to get. He's walking with a cane, and that's probably going to be for the rest of his life. As for his attitude, it's positive. He's pumped about going home, and he'll be back in school very soon. As soon as the new routine at home sets in, he'll be good to go."

"I'm glad. For Shaun. And for you."

Ker's a good guy. I know he has no love lost for Shaun, but he does care, which doesn't make my impending revelation any easier.

"Thanks," I say, not adding anything else. I've missed Kerem so much, and I don't know what he's really thinking. About us. Is he glad that the pressure of Shaun's care is off me now? Or is he glad that we can be together again, now that I'm back to being alone? And how does either impact me?

"I've missed you so much, Gabe. Seems like we've been a thousand miles apart forever. Right across the street from each other, but so far away. The texts were great, but I missed our regular skyping, our walks, and our being together."

My heart breaks when he says this. Why did I neglect him? And just when we were getting closer. I couldn't do anything else. With school and swim practice and swim meets, I barely had time to breathe. And Mom needed my help with Shaun. She moved him right into our house so she could nurse him while my aunt and uncle tried to keep their family afloat. With all that going on and helping Mom entertain my aunt and uncle and cousins when they came to visit Shaun—which was just about every day—I was overwhelmed.

Who am I kidding? That's all bullshit. I talk a good game about being so open, so out of the closet, so *I'm gay and don't care who knows it.* But that moment when things between us started heating up was not so tiny, especially when the phone call came from Mom about Shaun. Yes, if there'd been no call, I would have let anything happen to see where it led. Then I heard what happened to Shaun, and suddenly I worried about the shit that having a Muslim boyfriend might bring. Yes, Shaun brought it on himself, but what if the attacker had been the aggressor who hated Muslims? It happens. And it scared the piss out of me as I sat in the emergency room that day. All-American Methodist Gabriel Dillon, head over heels in love with Muslim Kerem Uzun, was a coward. A lily-livered pansy who was having, deep down, doubts.

But not making any time for Ker just about killed me. It ate at me. I had to face it all. My fears, my prejudices. I had to decide who I was. Was I someone who could face the world no matter how it treated us? Could I deal with the prejudices that Kerem deals with every day of his life? Did loving him mean that much to me? And I had my answer.

"I know what you mean, Ker. I'm sorry. I should have—probably could have—squeezed in time for you." I'm afraid to go further, explain why I treated him like I did. I want my friendship with Kerem back on track, and confessing now could ruin this walk. And ruin my life. "You know you mean the world to me, don't you?" I say, trying to keep emotion out of my voice.

"I think back to that afternoon, the day that happened to Shaun, and we were making a connection. It's been hard being apart so much, but what you said, that you think the world of me, is something I know very well, because I feel the same about you."

"And you understand the pressure I've been under? When Mom stepped up to the plate and took charge, she was run ragged. It's been three full months, and Aunt Evvie still is not herself entirely. She's barely able to take care of the two younger kids. Mom knew right away that Shaun would not get the care he needed unless she took him in and made sure of it. I'd rush home from swim practice so I could give her a couple of hours of respite from dealing with Shaun and his needs. Some days, I don't know how I had my head in the game—at school, at swim—because I worried so much about Mom."

And so I—*chickenshit Gabriel Franklin Dillon*—tell the half-truth, the half that weighs so little compared to its 50 percent omission.

"Your mom is a good person. To take on all that extra responsibility."

"Well, as she says, somebody had to do it. She was on constant vigil while Shaun was in the hospital, and then she rented a hospital bed for the family room and moved him there. Little by little, he got stronger. Then she carted him to PT every day. And of course, she fed his family almost every time they came to visit. My mom's a saint."

Why can't I come out with it?

"She sure is," Kerem confirms.

The pond looms ahead. There is a bench farther away from our usual place. It is surrounded by a small grove of trees which will block the wind. It also provides more privacy than our other bench. We head for that.

As we sit, I say, "You see the motherfuckers?"

He shakes his head and laughs at me. "You'll never let me forget that, will you?" He points. "See the tall rushes over there? They're hiding in there, staying away from this wind."

"Like we're hiding here, on this secluded bench?"

"Exactly. The pond never freezes. It doesn't get cold enough here. So as long as there is protection from the wind, they survive."

"And as long as we have protection, we survive. I've prayed a lot during these last months. For Shaun, for Mom." I pause, then add, "For me. For us." I look into his eyes and see them tear up.

"And Allah has heard from me as well. Not only did I pray for Shaun and his family and your mom and you, but I prayed for the strength to endure our separation. I hated every moment we couldn't be together, but Allah saw me through."

I want to kiss him right now, but I don't know if he's ready for that. The last—and first—bit of physical affection we had was holding hands. Dare I progress from that to a kiss? And do I deserve it? And do I understand and accept what a kiss would mean for us?

Maybe it's too soon. Maybe, deep down, he harbors resentment that we've not seen each other all these months. I know I do, but my resentment is not for him. It's not even for Shaun. I hate myself for not making time for Ker. For my doubts. How can I tell him I love him when I've had such thoughts? When I've neglected him for so long? What am I thinking? I should have banished those negative thoughts, trusting only in what I was feeling—what I feel now—and made the time. That's what people in love do. If nothing else, we could have skyped. But no, I told myself I was bound up in swim team, the Shaun thing, and the worry I had for my mom. But I was really bound up in my own fears. I wouldn't blame Kerem if he just stood and walked away.

"Shaun finally told me exactly what happened that day," I say, distracting myself from my thoughts.

"I thought he didn't remember. That's what you told me in one of our infrequent skypes." Do I hear a tiny bit of resentment? Or is it that I want to hear it so I don't feel so guilty?

I trudge on, trying to clear the negatives in my brain. "I wasn't lying. His memory was a blank. But little by little, it has come back. Here's how it played out: he and his buddies were shooting hoops at the park. You know that already. It was hot, and one of the guys pulled off his T-shirt and had it hanging on his head. Shaun kept calling him 'raghead.'" I look for a sign that I've offended Kerem. Somehow—it's weird—I want to offend him, if only to punish myself.

He sighs. "Go on. I'm not surprised. Your cousin has a way with words."

"Just so you know, this isn't me talking. I'm repeating what he said."

"I do. You would never say such a thing otherwise."

A thunderbolt of guilt sends its voltage through me.

He puts his gloved hand on mine, and even through my heavy wool gloves, I feel his warmth. How can he be so even-tempered? So forgiving of me? And will he still be forgiving if....

I babble on, telling the story so I don't have to say what I need to say. "So this guy they'd never seen before came up and asked if he could join their game. The guy was friendly, Shaun says, so they let him play. As the game progressed, the guy got more and more frustrated because his every shot was getting blocked. He was trying to make a successful layup when Shaun shouted at his buddy, the one with the tee on his head, 'Raghead, nine-eleven his butt.'

"Well," I go on, "the stranger went ballistic. He lunged at Shaun, screaming 'What'd you say?' Shaun says angry flames were in his eyes. The other guys were so startled at what was happening, they held back, frozen in place. Shaun's friends are mostly pussies, so I'm not surprised. After all, all these months and they kept this shit to themselves. I had to wait for Shaun to remember it to hear what happened. Anyway, the guy kept raving, 'My uncle was in the Twin Towers that day. It's not a joke, you shitass.' And he threw Shaun on the ground and began stomping him. And as he stomped, he sobbed and said, over and over, 'It's not a joke, it's not a joke, it's not a joke.' Finally one of Shaun's friends grew some balls and pulled the guy off Shaun.

"Shaun says his friends told him later it was like a light bulb went on in the guy's brain. He stood stock-still with a stricken look on his face. Then he ran.

"While two of Shaun's buds hovered over him, the third dialed 911. The rest you know."

"Did they catch the guy? I never saw a thing in the newspaper."

"He was long gone. May have been a drifter. May have had family who put him on a plane. Who knows?"

"That's quite a story. I prayed to Allah for Shaun's recovery."

After all Shaun said and did, Kerem could still pray for him. That's what his religion does for him. And it's what mine should do for me. They're one and the same, after all, only different expressions of the same feelings. I pray that God, that Allah, strengthens me and gives me wisdom, courage, and the words I need right now. But my prayer's not being answered.

"Well, Allah listened. So I know Shaun thanks you."

He huffs. I look at him. "I'm sorry, Gabe. I would never have wished that on your cousin, and I'm very glad he has made his remarkable recovery, but the Shaun I know would never thank a Muslim for praying for him. He'd probably be pissed because I pray to a different God from his. Or at least he thinks Allah is not the same as his God."

"Ker, you know and I know whether we call Him God or Allah, He's the same guy sitting up there watching over us all." Just speaking those words gives me insight, a tiny bit of inner strength. "And Shaun knows that too, now. I was not about to babysit him without making sure I set him straight. I put him on a path to enlightenment, I tell you what. But I have to say this: he was already right at the edge of the path once he remembered the whole incident and understood he brought it on himself. You won't be hearing Shaun calling you raghead, towelhead, Johnny Jihad, or anything else derogatory again."

"That's good to hear. For his sake more than for mine," Kerem says. He's such a good person. But I guess forgiveness is part of every religion.

"After Shaun admitted the error of his ways, he was open to understanding. We talked after he came to live with us. He wanted to change. And I helped him understand Islam, that it has nothing to do with the terrorists. Those cowards clothe themselves in your religion, Ker, because they can't justify the evil they do any other way. I won't say it was a quick reversal of Shaun's thinking, but because he was willing to change, I was able to get through to him. Thank God. Shaun now knows that Islam is good." And indeed it is. It is only the bad seeds in this world who rail against it or are too ignorant to know that.

"Would that it were that easy with everyone." There's sadness in Kerem's voice, and I feel for him. I don't think he's experienced a huge amount of prejudice in his life, but I'm sure he knows those who have. And he faces that every day; the threat is there every moment. How he does it, I don't know. I do know that if he can do it, so can I. I have to tell him that if we are to be together. But something still holds me back.

"But enough about Shaun. Catch me up on the Uzun clan. I feel like I'm totally out of the loop. I haven't caught an episode of *All My Days of Our Guiding General Lives of Aysel and Hasan* in years, it seems."

That elicits a belly laugh. I love hearing that laugh. The icy wind that whips past us in our little barricade here is a warm one as long as I can hear Kerem's laugh. "Oh, you've missed a ton of stuff, my friend. There is a wedding to be in exactly one month's time."

I look at him incredulously. "Have I been out of the country? How do I not know this?"

"Aysel sprang it on us! And the date is looming because Hasan's grandparents are coming from Lebanon for a visit—the first ever—and she and Hasan want them to be there."

"You have to hand it to your sister. She makes her mind up fast."

He puts his hands under his arms to warm them.

"You want to go back?" I ask. "You must be freezing." I kick myself for even suggesting we sit out here in the cold. But I don't feel it. Kerem is my warmth.

"No, I'm fine. I'm enjoying this too much to cut it short."

I put my arms around him and draw him to me. "Let me warm you up some."

As soon as my flesh touches his, I feel it. Under all the layers of down quilting, my body becomes vibrantly alive to the warmth that is Kerem. It's not a body warmth; it's a soul warmth.

He looks into my eyes with more love than I've ever seen before. I'm content. More content than I've been in months. How could I have blown him off, barely communicating, letting my doubts overtake me, and blaming my cousin? I don't deserve Kerem's love, but oh, how I want it.

And right now Kerem and I are back together, huddled against the cold, and life is more than good. I want to hear all about Aysel, the sprite who makes us both smile, just to bask in Kerem's joyous laughter. Before *it* pulls us apart.

"So," I say, "fill me in."

"Aysel is in a dither right now."

"When is she not in a dither?" I quip.

He laughs, a gentle tinkling sound that could shatter in this cold but brings life to me. "This is worse. The wedding is fast approaching, and she doesn't have a dress. She found pictures of three different dresses with features she wants to combine, but she can't sew and neither can Mama. And especially not a fancy wedding gown. Mama has asked every friend she has and even some strangers at the mosque, but so far she's found no one. The really good seamstresses are totally booked up and laugh at the idea of having so little time, especially when they see Aysel's pics."

"I know someone."

"Huh?"

"I *know* someone."

"You, a man who has only been in town a few months, can steer us to someone who can make an elaborate wedding gown in three weeks. Not believing it. Unless you've managed to squeeze in a part-time job at a bridal shop between nursing your cousin and winning swim medals. Congrats, by the way."

I had won gold at our last swim meet. "Thanks, by the way. Now, it's true I haven't scoured the city from top to bottom. It's true I've been consumed with Shaun and swimming—and a senior research paper that ate my lunch. But I tell you, I know someone."

He swats me. It's a caress to me. "Quit playing with me, Gabriel Dillon. Spill it."

"Mary Dillon, Empress of the Needle."

"Your mom?"

"My mom. With Shaun gone, she needs a new project. And I'm telling you, she can whip up that dress in a flash. I've seen her work miracles." God, it feels good to be back here, back simply conversing, making each other happy.

"Would she do it? How much would she charge?" The excitement in his voice crackles in the cold air.

"Yes. And zero."

"Baba and Mama would insist on paying her. Especially because she'd be working with Aysel. No amount of money is enough for that."

We both laugh, and there is diamond dust in his eyes.

"If I know my mom—and I do, intimately—she will refuse any money. But she will want an invitation to this shindig. She cries at weddings, FYI."

"Done deal. As soon as we get back, you ask her and get back to me. I won't say a word to Mama until I hear from you."

"You got it, but I'm telling you Mom will be happy to do it. Okay, that covers Aysel." I pause at my joke. He chuckles. "Now what about Timur. He still his sullen self?"

"You picked up on that, huh?"

"Yeah, you never liked my cousin, and I never warmed up to yours."

"Well, he's better, actually. There was a turnaround somehow. I've never told you how he came to live with us, but that's for another day. Suffice it to say that he's harbored resentment ever since Baba and Mama took him in. No matter how they showed their love, he resisted."

"I could tell."

"Well, about a month ago, Baba had a scare at his office. All the data went missing from the office computers. His office manager was frantic. It's a big deal. Medical records getting stolen can be the end of a practice. Baba called in Timur, the family computer guru. I always knew he spent a lot of time in front of his monitor, and I knew he did computer stuff for a living, but I had no idea how good he was. That's a failing on my part, so I take some responsibility for his not fitting into the family. After all, I was supposed to be a brother to him, and I cared so little I didn't know what he really did with his time."

"Don't be so hard on yourself," I say as I stroke his cheek. My fingers tingle, touching him. I want more. But I probably shouldn't even dare this bit of intimacy.

"Easy to say, not easy to do. Anyway, he found the problem and recovered the data. It wasn't stolen; it was just hiding. Baba was so grateful that he bought Timur a new car."

"Awesome. Your baba's a generous man."

"Yeah, Baba has always told us that when we are old enough to drive, we use the family vehicles until we can buy our own. That's why I walk to school and back most of the time. I can't believe I never told you that. And Aysel? Would you believe she took the city bus to college until Hasan started picking her up each day? So—Tim was driving this old clunker he bought as soon as he saved a few bucks from his job. I don't know how it was holding up, because, believe me, it was a bucket of rust, literally held together with bailing wire and duct tape."

I laugh. "I've seen it parked in your drive. I was surprised the homeowner's association didn't raise a fuss. I wondered where it went when it finally disappeared. I've been out of the loop."

"You wouldn't believe the change in Tim when Baba presented him the keys to his new car. I know that love that's bought and paid for is not really love, but this wasn't like Baba was buying Tim's love. It's as if Tim finally feels appreciated and a part of the family, like that car has validated him, honored him, placed him on an even playing level with Aysel and me. I'm telling you, that sullenness is pretty much gone. You can't make a silk purse out of a sow's ear overnight, but it seems Baba may have done that with Tim."

"A good Muslim boy making pig jokes?" He smiles at my chiding him. "But what you told me is amazing. All it took for Tim was a simple act of kindness. For Shaun, it took a stomping to get through to him. I'm glad Timur came around without any violence."

"I am too. And our relationship, his and mine, is healing, inshallah."

"I'm glad."

I'm still caressing his cheek, and he wraps his fingers around my hand, pulling it close to his lips. I want him to kiss it, but he doesn't. He just holds it there. I can feel his warm breath. And it drives me crazy.

"Okay, now I'm dying to know what you did your senior research on," he says. Is he teasing me with the hand thing?

I don't want to continue this line of conversation. What I want to do is smother him with kisses, feel every part of his body, let him take me. I smile at my ultraromance-novel thoughts. But I can't have these thoughts. Not as long as I keep from him my secret. The secret that could bring this all crashing down. I can't let that happen, so I get back to the research paper thing.

"That's an abrupt change of subject. We go from wedding dress to happy cousin to research paper?"

"Just thought we could use a respite from family, family, family. My research paper kicked my butt, but I got it done."

"Topic?"

"'The Importance of Early Testing and Treatment for Breast Cancer.' My mother is not a lady-parts doctor for nothing."

"So Mommy wrote her baby's paper?" I tease, glad to be back on solid ground.

"She certainly did not," he answers with pretend indignation. "She may have been a valued resource, but I sweated blood over that thing."

I smile at him.

"Why are you smiling? Are you finding comfort in my pain?" There is play in his voice.

"Nah. I was thinking about what you said. I think I'm rubbing off on you. I'd bet before you met me, you would never have called your mom a 'lady-parts doctor.'"

"Don't make fun of me just because you're a bad influence. You're right. Before I met you, I was pretty straitlaced. I was a good Muslim son who would never have called his mother such an unseemly thing." I hear false formality.

"Or—I'd bet—call a couple of swans 'motherfuckers.'" I let out a huge belly laugh that would wake those MFs if they weren't huddled far across the pond.

"You're just a bad influence, Gabe, a bad, bad influence." But he doesn't mean it. I know. I feel it. Ker and I are made for each other. Now if only I can quit playing around and lay my cards on the table. But it's hard to get serious when you fear the response.

"So what'd you get on this magnificent treatise?" I ask, trying to make myself change the thoughts plaguing me.

"I got an A."

"Good for you! Is now when I tell you I got an A-plus?"

"Rub it in, rub it in. And what, pray tell, was your topic? Wait. Let me guess. Continuing the mommy theme: 'How To Sew a Perfectly Straight Seam Without Puckering.' Or how about, 'The Way to Bake a Perfect Six Layer Fudge Cake.'"

"You're cruisin' for a bruisin'. My mother was no help whatsoever with this one. I chose a topic that I've recently embraced. Near and dear to my heart." I add the last because it's part of my "working up the courage" thing.

"And what is that, pray tell?"

I sit. Waiting. Not knowing how he will take it in. Hoping he will like it.

"Are you going to tell me or not?"

"Don't get your panties in an uproar. I'd tell you, but I'd have to kill you."

"Would you please get on with it? It's freezing out here."

It's now or never. I lay it on him. "'Homosexuality in Islam.'"

He's speechless. The silence is a frozen cloud between us.

Say something. Please. I need a reaction here.

He puts his hands on either side of my head, leans in, and kisses me. A beautiful, long, loving kiss that tells me I've honored him.

It's now or never. He's revealed himself to me. Now it's my turn.

"Ker...." I hesitate, staring into his eyes. "You may take that back when I tell you what I need to tell you."

I see hurt.

"No! That was wonderful," I say. Then I pause to formulate my words. Confession may be good for the soul, but it's gut-wrenching. "I've wanted you to do that for almost as long as we've known each other. Hell, who am I kidding? I wanted to kiss you from the moment I saw you across the commons that first day of school."

He caresses my cheek, which makes this even harder to say.

"But here's the reason why we've barely talked in the last three months. It wasn't Shaun, it wasn't swimming, and it wasn't my research paper. That fucker taught me a lot, but it only fueled my irrational fears. I was afraid, Kerem. Terrified."

"About what?" he says quietly and gently.

"Of loving a Muslim. Horrifying thoughts would form and keep me awake at night. Me—who's never cared one whit about what people think—would fantasize all sorts of scenarios where we'd be out together, and some idiot would want to stab us, shoot us, obliterate us from the face of the earth. And I didn't know if I could deal with that."

He listens. I see nothing in his face. No questioning. No judgment.

"And so I let Shaun's stay at my house be my excuse. I could cool it with you. But my fears drew me to that research topic. In many ways, it scared the shit out of me. But it also made me realize something: I could face whatever crap the world dealt us, if I were with you. I need you to give me life. That's sounds like romance novel bullshit, but it's true, Ker. I don't think I can live without you, and I hope you feel the same way. That's why I wanted this walk today. To clear the air. To see if there's hope for us. To confess. And now that it's all out in the open, I wouldn't blame you if you cut me out of your life."

"What? And lose a good dressmaker? Aysel would kill me if she found out I tossed out her seamstress just because her son had doubts." He smiles.

And then, once again, he pulls my face in and kisses me.

Life.

CHAPTER 11

Kerem

MY FIRST kiss.

My first actual kiss—if you forget about that time after mosque when Selimah Abdul grabbed me and smacked my lips so hard with hers that it hurt. She thought we were making love, but her lack of technique was brutal. What does a seven-year-old girl know? I backed away in horror. She definitely offended my sensibilities. Boys that age don't want to even think a girl can be so bold. And Muslim girls never are. Except for Selimah.

But here I am, the icy wind whistling around us, huddling with Gabe, holding on for life like the swans hiding in the rushes, and my first amazing, beautiful, comforting, warming, rapturous kiss happens.

And *I* kissed *him*. Not the other way around like I had imagined it would happen. Three months of virtual separation had produced countless fantasies. Gabe was always the initiator. He would lean into me, whisper some sweet thing in my ear, and then press his lips on mine as I melted.

I never, ever thought that I would be sitting here, with the courage I never thought I could muster, now having done the deed and immediately wondering how he'd react.

Then that revelation. Poor Gabe. Agonizing all these months. Over something I face and know is real but can be dealt with.

And so I kissed him again. This time for reassurance. And because I wanted to feel his lips again.

I wait for his reaction, wait to hear an affirmation. Have I just shown that I'm with him, that I will protect him, that his fears can be conquered?

I get my answer as he kisses me back. His tongue touches mine. It is electric. Forget that this is something I've never felt before. It is something I never knew could happen. How can I be as old as I am, as gay as I am, and not have at least read about this? I'm a gay Muslim, and Gabe knows more about being gay and being a gay Muslim than I do, thanks to that paper he wrote.

I banish all these thoughts and tell myself to shut up and enjoy. He wants me.

His hands caress my face, and each touch of his fingertips leaves me wishing for more. I wonder when he had the chance to remove his gloves. Again, I will myself to stop thinking and continue feeling.

He kisses my forehead, my eyelids, the tip of my nose. I am on fire.

He kisses my gloved fingers, and I feel the warmth of his breath through the layer of wool between his lips and my skin. I feel *it* rising in me, wanting to burst forth.

He returns to my lips, and his tongue probes deeper. It leaps inside me.

Still with our lips locked together, I begin to moan, tiny little yelps at first, but as the eruption starts, my cries get louder.

"Oh, oh, oh," I shout, louder and louder. Somewhere deep inside, I fear that my voice is being carried by the wild wind, across the pond, through the freezing cold, alerting the neighbors, Gabe's mom, Baba, Mama, Timur, Aysel, that Kerem Uzun is breaking out of his shell, enjoying life for what seems is the first time, and feeling the call of prayer. Thank you, Allah.

"Salaam Alaykum," Gabe whispers.

"Wa-Alaykum," I answer back.

Then there is silence. We sit. Perfect contentment.

Finally Gabe brings us back to reality. "Uh, is it noticeable?"

I look at him, wondering what he is talking about. "Huh?"

"Your jeans. Is there a wet spot? That was quite an orgasm, my friend."

I panic. Everyone will know. I hide my head in my hands.

Gabe laughs at me. "Don't worry. I don't see anything. Your secret's safe." He pulls my hands down. And kisses me again. Lightly this time.

"All's right with the world," he says. "And with me. I can't say my fears are totally gone, but I can say that I will face them with you. And this? Do you know how many times I wanted this to happen? Probably since that first day I saw you, standing like a god across campus. But the new boy wasn't about to make a move on the Muslim boy anytime soon. I waited, keeping my dick in check. We got to know each other, and I thought, 'Now. Now it will happen. I'll finally get to taste those gorgeous lips.' Then Shaun happened, and our lives were put on hold. I felt, just now, that we were connecting, but I was riddled with guilt. I couldn't make a move without my confession. So I knew I'd wait to give you that first kiss, wait until you knew me before I made my move. But you made the move for me. Whatever possessed you? I know from my research that being gay, generally, is frowned upon in Islam."

"That's why," I say quietly.

"I don't understand, Ker." He leans in and honors me again with a tiny kiss.

"You cared enough about me to find out how my religion felt about it all. You didn't brazenly jump in and let the consequences happen, you wanted to know how it all might play out. And it gave you doubts, but you told me of those doubts. That's love."

"But my research told me there was no way of telling how you'd react. Like I said, Islam frowns upon it, and modern Muslims have a mixed reaction, as do Christians and Jews and probably even atheists. And don't forget, what happened to Shaun and then my research confused me."

"But you quashed your confusion. Told me all about it. And you cared enough to try to find out how Muslims would react. And for the record, in theory my parents are okay with it. The world is changing and so are Muslim attitudes. I'm not like you, though. I've never told them about these feelings I have. Your parents embrace you and your homosexuality. I don't know if my parents would be okay with mine."

"I told my mom not long ago I refused to love a man who wasn't open and out in this world. I really believed it at the time. But having gone through my own coming-out experience, I know how personal it is. So I will wait for you to find the right time. Your family needs to know, but I won't be the one to tell them."

"I promise I will tell them. Soon. When the time seems right. And they will be fine with it, inshallah."

"All I can tell you is that God will be willing for them to be fine with it. But what God wills and what man does can be two different things entirely. Be prepared."

And he kisses me again.

"Well," I say, rising from the bench. "I must get home. Mama probably needs help for tonight before sunset prayers."

"What's tonight?" Gabe says, now beside me, walking.

"Big, big dinner. The meeting of the parents. Hasan is bringing his father to discuss the *mehir* with Baba, and we will meet Hasan's mother and the infamous grandmother for the first time. She's the maternal grandmother. The paternal grandparents are the ones coming from Lebanon."

"Mehir?" Gabe asks.

"Usually called *mahr*. Mehir is the Turkish word for it. You know what a dowry is?"

"Yeah. The girl's father pays the groom's father to get the girl married."

"Uh-huh. Only in Muslim culture, the groom pays the bride. Supposed to be insurance if he dies young. Sometimes the groom negotiates the payment; sometimes the groom's father. Tonight, it will be the battle of the patriarchs."

"I'd like to be a fly on the wall for that." Gabe laughs.

"Could get bloody," I quip.

At my front door, Gabe says, "Salaam Alaykum."

"Wa-Alaykum," I answer. "I wish I could kiss you goodbye."

"It'll happen eventually. Your parents will approve. You'll see."

I nod. But I'm not very convinced.

"And Gabe, I'm not sure Salaam Alaykum is approved for *after*-talk."

He looks guilty.

"The imam might frown on it." I smile at him.

"You'll have to teach me some Muslim bedroom talk sometime," he says.

"I'll have to read up on it," I say. "Oh, don't forget to ask your mom."

In the seclusion of my doorway, he touches my cheek. "Will do."

Then he runs across the street.

My thoughts are in the clouds as I enter the house. Soon, hearing Mama and Aysel chattering in the kitchen and Baba's conversation with Timur wafting from the family room, I return to earth. How will they react, when and if?

Those grim thoughts are broken by Gabe's ringtone.

"It's on. She not only said yes, but she started across the street immediately to discuss it with your mom and Aysel. Don't worry, I held her back. Told her about the big shindig tonight. She agreed that your mom could phone her in the morning. Or tonight after evening prayers is okay too."

"I'll tell Mama right now. She and Aysel will be ecstatic. And Gabe—thank you. For this, and for before. I love you." I whisper the last.

"Thank *you* for loving me, despite my myriad faults. Now get in there and break the big news. You'll be the hero of the Uzun clan, my man."

I stuff my phone in my pocket, look down to make sure there's no trace of what happened before, and then head for the kitchen.

Mama sees me. "Where have you been, love? Your sister, here, wanted to file an Amber Alert. She is so afraid everything won't go perfectly tonight."

"I was taking a walk with Gabe."

"How is he doing? You haven't mentioned him in weeks," Mama says.

"He's been helping his mom nurse his cousin back to health, and between his swim team and that, he hasn't had much free time."

"His poor cousin. How is he doing?"

"He's almost recovered and moving back to his own home. That's why Gabe had some free time this afternoon."

"Well, I'm so happy all is well. Gabriel's mother has had her hands full with all this. I inquired early on, asking if I could help, and Mary said she was fine. I worried, but then all this with your sister came about, and my own plate became full very fast. I'll have to phone Mary and have her over, now that she has more free time."

"Actually you'll be phoning her for a different reason."

"Kerem," she says, scrutinizing me. I present a solemn face, a mischievous *holding back*. "Is something going on I should know about?"

I break into a grin. "Gabe's mom has agreed to make your wedding dress, Aysel." Aysel's eyes get very wide. I turn back to Mama. "Gabe says she's an amazing seamstress and can look at a picture and make a dress at warp speed. He just asked her if she'd do it, and she said yes. She wants you to call her tomorrow. Or after evening prayers tonight, if you want. The only payment she wants is an invitation to the wedding."

Mama grabs me and hugs me for dear life. "She would have gotten that anyway, love. You've saved the wedding. My prayers today will be filled with praise, thanking Allah for my beautiful son. And for His bringing this wonderful family into our lives."

"So she can do everything I want? She can combine my pictures?" Aysel asks, still not believing.

"Yes, yes, yes." My sister pulls me away from Mama and envelops me in her own hug. "Show her the pics, Aysel, and she'll work miracles, inshallah."

"Allah better be willing," Aysel spouts.

"Hush, daughter. That is no way to talk. I'll phone Mary this evening. Now, Kerem, can you lend a hand with this dinner? Daughter here's afraid everything won't be letter perfect."

"Have no frets, benim küçük kızım; all will be well." Baba has entered the kitchen, and he obviously has heard the last comment.

"Oh, Baba," Aysel gushes, "Gabriel's mother's going to make my gown."

"Is she now? I surmise from your happiness that she will meet all your demands?"

"I'm not demanding, Baba," Aysel counters. "I just want everything my way."

Baba's belly laugh fills the room.

"You could be marrying in our living room, you know," Timur, who has followed Baba, says. "A simple statement of vows is all that is needed."

"I know, Tim." There is a bit of disgust in Aysel's voice. "But what's needed and what's wanted are two very different things. I want to say my vows in the mosque, with family and friends surrounding me, and a giant party afterward. Hasan's family agrees, even if they are orthodox. Even orthodox Muslims enjoy a party."

"I'm just saying you don't need all this stress," Timur says.

"It's not stressful; it's fun." Aysel actually says that with a straight face.

Mama gives Baba a "she's your daughter" look.

"So what can Timur and I do to help? Sunset prayers are fast approaching. We need to finish the preparations so we can get this party tonight started."

We all scurry about. The table is set with Mama's finest crystal, china, and silver. In Mama's cherished bowl from her mother, Timur arranges the flowers Baba hastily purchases on a run to Kroger's flower department because Mama had forgotten to go earlier. The arrangement is lovely, and I discover one more talent my cousin possesses.

At last all is ready, and we say sunset prayers. As promised, I thank Allah for bringing Gabe into my life.

Prayers completed, we await the onslaught, Aysel on pins and needles.

The doorbell rings, and the royal family arrives.

After a round of introductions, we sit. Hasan's father looks exactly like him, only a grayer, more wrinkled version. They both are bearded; they sport the same short black hair. Hasan's mother is a handsome woman, not beautiful like Mama, but certainly not ugly. She is dressed in a hijab and flowing robes that cover her from shoulder to toe. The grandmother is not the old crone Gabe and I joked about. She actually is more beautiful than her daughter. Hasan's mother must have taken after her father.

Mama serves the *meze*, the Turkish hors d'oeuvres, she has prepared. She has a plate of wonderful fritters Aysel made, plus a plate of cheese and meats. She also has a tray of glasses of *Şalgam*, a Turkish drink made from turnips and purple carrots. Sounds awful, tastes great.

"The fritters are delicious," Hasan's mother says.

"Aysel made them," Mama says. "Our daughter knows her way around a kitchen."

"Thank you, love," the grandmother says to Aysel. "These are quite good."

"I'm glad you like them, *teta*," Aysel says lovingly.

I'm starving as more and more small talk ensues. I don't hear much of it because my mind is on Gabe. All I want is another of his kisses. In fact, as hungry as I am right now, I would forego Mama's fine meal for a taste of his lips.

"Shall we have dinner?" Mama asks.

Everyone rises, and Baba shows them into the dining room.

We consume the delicious meal with everyone oohing and aahing. Dinner conversation is constrained a bit. Hasan's father dominates most of it, and he is anxious, without seeming ungracious, to know just how strictly Mama and Baba follow Islam.

Baba is wise and intelligent. He makes sure the man understands we are an observant family without going into much detail. Hasan's father seems pleased.

With dinner finished, the women retire to the living room, while the men retreat to the family room. I would much rather hear Aysel bubble over her wedding gown, but I know I must forego the distaff side of the family and join the movers and shakers for this powwow.

Baba motions for the patriarch to sit in the recliner that is usually reserved for Mama. Baba takes his own throne.

Hasan, Timur, and I line up on the couch, three blind mice in a row. Like I said, the groom can negotiate for himself, but it is clear that Hasan's father runs this family.

"So shall we begin?" Baba asks. I know personally that Baba's only doing this for tradition's sake. He long ago established trusts for each of us. Aysel, in the event of Hasan's death, would have plenty of money. But Baba doesn't want to spoil Aysel's marriage by declaring what he really believes: that this is old-world claptrap.

"How much do you feel is fair?" Hasan's father inquires.

Playing the game, Baba counters with "How much are you offering?"

And the game is on. After a while I quit listening. I'd much rather be across the street.

I'm startled by Timur's "Do you really think my cousin is worth only that?" Tim has entered the fray.

"Timur," Baba says, "Let the man talk. I'm sure we can come to an agreement."

I don't know what the offer on the table was, but apparently Tim was not happy with it.

I retreat into my romantic netherworld.

At last, Baba and Hasan's father stand. The negotiation is over. The price is set. Aysel has been purchased. At a premium, if the smile on Tim's face is any indication.

In a normal negotiation, a handshake would be in order to seal the deal. But Baba doesn't shake hands. I'm surprised to see them each lean over to the table between the recliners and sign a document. This thing *is* important.

"It has been a pleasure," Baba says. "Now let's join the ladies for dessert, shall we?"

Nothing's said of the contract when we join the women. Mama serves dessert, and at last Hasan takes his family away.

Hasan's happy, Aysel's happy, and Baba's happy—that it's over.

As soon as the horde of people departs, Tim turns to father and exclaims, "You got a fair price, Amca."

"Timur, you make it sound like I was marketing cattle. My benim küçük kızım is not for sale. I was playing a part, and I played it well."

"That you did," Tim says. "And perhaps this family gave you a taste of how we Muslims should live."

"Do you feel we are not good Muslims, Timur?" Baba asks.

Timur's face darkens. "No, not that at all. I'm just saying that we might take lessons from Hasan's family."

"They're very devout, Baba," Aysel chimes in. "I'm learning so much, and I feel much closer to Allah."

"Your relationship with Allah is between you and Him, love, and mine is between *me* and Him." He smiles at her, then looks at Tim. "Timur, you'd best remember that. We strive to be the best Muslims we can be in this house, and no external practices will make us better."

"Yes, Amca," Tim says. "May I help you with the dishes, Aunt?"

I'm surprised. Tim never offers to do what he considers "women's work."

Aysel and I gather up the dirty plates and take them to the kitchen, where Timur's loading the dishwasher, Mama beside him.

"The mother was a very nice woman." Tim states this matter-of-factly, and he doesn't seem to need a response.

"I did enjoy meeting her," Mama answers, nevertheless.

"She reminded me of my mother." The volume in Timur's voice lowers, as if he has revealed a very personal thing, and he's not sure he wants us to hear it.

"Sila was a wonderful person, Timur, love," Mama says to him. "She was very devout, and she loved all of you very much."

I expect Aysel to chime in with something like "oh, Mama, you're devout and love us too." But even my ditzy sister senses when it's time to keep quiet.

"She left us far too soon, Timur, but she gave me a second son, and for that, I'm grateful." Mama kisses his forehead.

I scold myself silently for not seeing the real Timur. The heartbreak he lived through had to have scarred him. And yet, for years, I've let myself be caught up in my own world.

"And now," Mama says, "what say we honor Sila by all joining together for evening prayers?"

Tim has a larger smile on his face than I ever thought he could muster.

Aysel and Mama stand behind Timur, Baba, and me as we pray. Tonight's evening prayers somehow seem more meaningful to me. Baba has confidently done the negotiation he'd been dreading, Mama has comforted Tim during his time of need, Aysel is supremely happy with Hasan, and I—well, I have Gabe.

Prayers finished, we all disperse. I know Mama will be phoning Gabe's mom, Mary, with Aysel hovering over her. Baba will no doubt spend a quiet hour reading the Quran. Timur will retreat to his keyboard and monitor.

And I can skype with my love.

"Whuzzup?" he says when he sees my face and I, his.

I love the way he says that. I love the way he says everything. I love the way he sometimes doesn't talk at all. Voluble or silent, he is ecstasy.

"Everything went well."

"So how much is your sister worth?"

"Would you believe I spaced out and missed the final showcase?"

"So she could be a $3.99 bottle of Suave shampoo, huh?"

"For all I know. But judging from how pleased everyone was, I'm thinking she fetched thousands."

"Good for her." He laughs. "Are we horrible? Talking about your sister like she's a prize on *The Price Is Right*?"

"Allah will forgive." His laughter fills me, and I laugh along.

"I've been thinking about you," Gabe says. "You're some good kisser."

I'm sure he can see my blush, but I don't care.

"You're not bad yourself," I flirt.

"Well, if you had not plunged in and taken charge, we might still be waiting. I was afraid."

"Let's talk about that for a moment," I say. I really want to erase his fears.

"You're sweet. What I meant was I was afraid you didn't want me. Not the other thing. Your loving me has taken care of that."

"So easily? I hope. But never, ever be afraid to discuss it with me. As for that other fear, you never have to be afraid of me, Gabe."

"It seemed like things were leading up to this, but then the three-month hiatus happened. I lost momentum. That's putting it mildly," he adds, an aside. Then he continues. "I started to doubt. About the prejudice we might face. I also worried the Muslim thing would get in the way just generally speaking. You may not have noticed, but we have been raised differently. And then, too, maybe I was moving too fast. And finally, maybe you weren't even gay, much less want me."

"Look, Gabe, my love, my only love, I can help you with your fears. I can guarantee that we were not raised all that differently, because we've both been raised in houses full of love. And full of God's love. Whether we call Him Allah or God, he is among us, in both our families. And that too-fast thing? I admit I'm glad we took it slow, but there was a moment, that day on the couch when we were watching the walkers, that I wanted to kiss you so bad I couldn't concentrate on the TV. Oh, I wanted you, all right."

"Me too. And these last three months, I shoulda stuffed my fears and made more time for you. I wasted so much of our time together. I'm sorry about that."

"No need. We're together now. And that's all that matters."

We fall silent, gazing into each other's eyes. He seems so happy. I'm beyond content.

At last he speaks again.

"I guess we both need to get some sleep," Gabe says hesitantly.

"I know. I just don't want to leave you. I don't ever wanna leave you again."

"Walk to school tomorrow together?"

"Do you think we'll make it? I know a clearing in the woods. We could ditch school, and—" I pause, leering at him. "—you know."

"Kerem Uzun, supreme leader of the senior class, I'm surprised at you." He flashes a wicked grin. "Besides, that clearing is where you pray. We shouldn't defile a sacred space, and at this moment, I want to defile you, over and over and over and over and over...."

He's still talking when I say, "I love you."

I hear a noise in the hallway. Why didn't I shut my door when I came in? I was so intent on seeing Gabe that I forgot a basic tenet of covert operations. Who was out there, lurking? And did he or she hear anything?

CHAPTER 12

Timur

I DO a Google search for mahr. I feel like Amca has gotten a fair price. I hope to find examples of what other brides have gotten. But my search is in vain. I suppose it is a personal thing that is not broadcast all over the internet. But what's not broadcast these days?

I like Hasan's family. They appear to be wonderful Muslims. Very devout.

I know Amca and Aunt are good people, that they are devout followers. I only wish their practices matched more closely those of my father and mother. Before everything happened, our family was so happy. I miss that.

But I have a new family. It felt so good for Aunt to say what she said, to call me her son. More and more, I feel that. For so many years, I think I didn't let them in, Aunt and Amca. I shut them out of my life, somehow thinking that would bring my own Baba and Mama back. I was a kid. A kid when Zeheb passed, when Mama died, when Baba did what he did to Delal. And for all the years since, I've stayed that kid.

But now I am a man, and I must act like one. I saved Amca's practice with my computer skills. And he rewarded me far more than he has rewarded his blood children.

And now Aunt Maria has proclaimed me her son, equal to Kerem.

Kerem, the magnificent. The golden child.

I must get to bed. But first, I must brush my teeth. I go to the hall bath.

I hear him. There is another voice. Gabriel. What are they talking about? The mahr.

I position myself hidden outside Kerem's door. I want to hear if my cousin credits me for the magnificent sum we negotiated. He does not mention my name at all.

But what is this he's saying?

To Kerem, the magnificent; Kerem, the golden child; I can add another thing:

Kerem, the sinner.

CHAPTER 13

Gabriel

I'M BEING goofy. Defense mechanism, I guess. Joking about sex seems as good a way as any to ensure I don't get hurt if Kerem is not as serious as he seemed to be earlier about us. His words say he's serious, but this is happening so quickly. I feel total guilt. My fears are real, but there are a lot of fears in this world. If everyone gave in to them, the world would not turn. Then, too, I felt us heating up that afternoon Shaun was beaten half to death, and I got scared. Scared that I was reading too much between the lines. Scared that this was something that couldn't be, even though we both wanted it. That cliché: two different worlds. It certainly applies. My senior research didn't provide the comfort I'd hoped for. It just left me in the dark about how Kerem's family would accept us as a couple—how Kerem would accept the idea. So I bury my feelings in humor. That's me.

But his "I love you" stops me, sets me right—thrusts me instantly back into the romantic mood of this afternoon. I will never get tired of hearing that. Not from him.

I open my mouth to say *I love you* back at him, but his face vanishes from the screen. Suddenly I'm looking at his backside as he rushes away.

That's it. I blew it. I came on too strong with the teasing. I should be treating him with the proverbial kid gloves, metaphorically speaking. He's newer at this than I. I, at least, have been out of the closet for years.

"Ker," I call. "Ker! Where'd you go?"

I hear him say, "Just a minute."

Then he returns, a stricken look on his face.

"What's wrong?" I am genuinely concerned. One moment we are whispering sweet nothings, the next he is trembling. Did I cause this?

"I think someone heard us. I was so anxious to skype with you, I forgot to close my bedroom door. I think I heard something out there, in the hall."

Before I try to calm him down, for a millisecond, I thank God that I didn't cause this. "Don't panic," I reassure him. "It could have been anything. Did you look? Was anyone out there?"

"I didn't see anyone. I hear the bathtub running now—the pipes in this house are very noisy. Maybe it was just Aysel heading to her nightly bubble bath. I shut the door, so we have privacy now."

"Well, don't worry about it. I know you're concerned about your family's reaction to us, but I've met your family, and I can't imagine your folks being upset—especially since, as you say, they are okay with the general idea of gay Muslims. It will be all right."

"I hope you know what you're talking about." The fear's still in his voice, but it's less. Like he's accepted that the immediate threat was nothing.

"Listen to me, Ker. I know what I'm talking about because I've gone through the whole tell the parents thing. I agonized over coming out to my family, and when I finally worked up the courage, they were like 'no big deal.' I don't know your mom and dad well, but I think that will be their reaction to your revelation too." It feels good to be covering familiar territory.

"Inshallah."

A knock. "Hold on a minute," I say, then swivel my chair toward the door.

"Gabriel, can I come in?" It's Mom.

"Sure."

She opens the door and waltzes in, happy as a clam. I don't know why or how clams can be happy, but that's what I've heard, and Mom is very happy now, so she must be happy as a clam.

"I just talked to Maria. She and Aysel are as excited as I am about the dress." She glances toward the computer. "Oh, I interrupted." She leans over toward the desktop camera.

"Mom," I plead mockingly, "how do you know who I'm talking to? You might be interrupting a very important call."

She pushes at me with her hand. "Oh, poo! I know it's Kerem. Who else would put that smile on your face?" Then she stares at the screen and adds, "See? Was I right? Hi, Kerem. I was just telling Gabriel how excited I am about your sister's wedding gown."

"Not half as excited as she is, Mrs. Dillon."

"Now, you call me Mary. We'll be seeing a lot of each other, what with fittings and the wedding and such. Your mama told me she's cleared her afternoon schedule for the next month to deal with all the prep for the wedding. I told her I'd be happy to help her with all that, after I get the dress done. She sounded like she figured I'd have no time to help, what with the dress being a big job and all, but I told her, 'Maria, you just wait. You'll see.' Gabe will testify: I'm like a house afire once I get started."

"You tell him, Mom," I chime in, having to crane my neck over her shoulder to be seen by Ker. "Tell your mother that Mary Dillon's unstoppable."

"I'll tell her that," Kerem says, then adds a hesitant, "Mary."

"Well, I'll leave you boys to whatever you were doing. Enjoy!" And Mom waltzes back out, pulling the door closed.

"Your mom is a powerhouse, Gabe. My mama and Aysel don't realize what they've unleashed—Super Mary!"

"She has a big yellow *S* under her Mom dress at all times."

We laugh. "Now," I say, "where were we?"

"I think we've exhausted the coming out thing. My parents don't know, I'm afraid to tell them, and you say it will be okay. Am I missing anything?"

"No, babe. You'll know when the time is right."

"I hope the time is sooner rather than later." He stifles a yawn, then says, "I plan to have very sweet dreams tonight. And BTW—now you've got me saying 'by the way' with only the initials; I'm becoming a typical kid instead of 'that Muslim'—I liked you calling me *babe*."

"You go night-night, *babe*"—I punch it for his sake—"and I'll see you tomorrow. If not at school, then certainly after school. I don't have swim tomorrow, so I'll come with Mom for the big meet. I want to hear all about this fantastic dress Aysel has ordered."

"Oh, really? You're into wedding dresses? I was hoping you were coming just to see me."

"That too, babe, that too." I flash him my patented wicked smile. "Sweet dreams."

"I hope yours are sweeter. Although I don't see how they could be," he counters.

"Enough. Gotta get my beauty sleep. We all aren't naturally beautiful like the neighbor boy."

He giggles at me, and then his face leaves the screen.

I can't stop thinking of him as I lie in bed. His piercing black eyes flash in my brain. They are like black diamonds. Although, I've never seen a black diamond. But if they are supposed to be the most exotic of jewels, Kerem's eyes must put them to shame.

My thoughts roam back to earlier. The pond. The kiss. There were others after it, and there will be thousands more to come. But none will compare to that first one.

I feel that kiss, deep, deep down. It makes me so happy. And so turned on.

I reach down. Slowly I caress myself. I usually jerk and jerk and jerk until I get off, using whatever fantasy comes to mind.

But tonight I don't need fantasy. I have reality. And I stroke, gently and slowly. His eyes, his lips, his voice, his whole being fill me, and the eruption begins. Electricity sparks within me. Over and over and over. I feel the lightning strikes within will never stop. I hope this feeling never ends.

Thank you, God. Thank you, Allah.

I fall asleep, spent—and wrapped in a cocoon, a cocoon spun by Kerem, my beautiful god.

NEXT DAY, school goes well. But I'm distracted the entire day. All I want to do is find Kerem and kiss him all over. But that's not cool. So I continually check my watch, waiting for the final bell.

He's already on the path home when I catch up to him. When he stops in the woods for afternoon prayers, I stand and watch him, gazing at this now familiar ritual performed by this beautiful man. A man who is mine. I pray myself, thanking God for bringing me to him.

Finished, we head straight home. No dawdling. I'm looking forward to the big wedding gown conference. The Uzun women have never met a force like Mary Dillon.

A quick "Salaam Alaykum/Wa-Alaykum" between us, and then Kerem goes into his house and I into mine.

Mom's standing there, tapping her foot, her tape measure around her neck, her pincushion on her wrist—although I don't know why she would need pins at an initial planning meeting—and pencil and notebook on the kitchen counter, waiting to be scooped up.

"Where have you been? We're going to be late. I don't know why you want to go anyway. This will be strictly girl talk. You'll be bored, I predict."

"Believe me, Aysel's never boring. And I'm not late. I have it on good authority Ker just got home for the big meet and greet."

"Whose authority? Your own? Have you two finally made your connection?"

I love the way she asks her question that way. So refined; so detached. Inside, if her upbringing would allow it, she wants to scream, *did you two finally hook up?* "Maybe," I answer coyly. "I don't kiss and tell."

"That means 'yes.' I'm so happy for both of you. Kerem's such a great kid. And he's quite a looker." For all her enthusiasm about sewing, cooking, and the like, when it comes to my love life, she plays it calm, cool, and collected.

"Don't I know it. But he's not out to his family yet, so don't spill the beans. 'Kay?"

"What happened to 'I won't date a man who is not out and open'? I knew you'd wind up eating your words."

"And very delicious they are. I'm giving him time. It's a hard thing to do, coming out."

"Nothing I don't already know. I can't recall how many times I wanted to shout at you, 'okay, tell me already.'"

"Moms know everything, don't they?"

"Not all, maybe, but this one does," she says. "Now, let's get our butts across the street."

It's like Aysel's been at the door, peering out the peephole, wondering when we'll arrive. I no sooner punch the doorbell before she opens the door.

"You must be Aysel. I've heard a lot about you. I'm surprised we haven't met before," Mom says.

"I spend a lot of time at the college, but I'm glad we're meeting now," Aysel says.

Yeah, a lot of time at the college where Hasan works, I almost say.

Aysel leads us into the family room.

Kerem jumps up from the couch as we come into the room. "I know you," he says to me. "Long time, no see."

"Yeah, right. How long has it been? Seven minutes?" He motions me over, and we sit together on the couch.

Maria Uzun arrives from the kitchen, drying her hands on a dish towel. Aysel has gone for her, and from the shrug she gave before she left the room, Aysel's a little pissed that her mother was not there waiting.

"Forgive me," Mrs. Uzun says as she goes to Mom. "My children are prone to leave unwashed glasses in the sink. I was just tidying up. Sit, sit." She motions to one of the recliners. Mom sits, and Mrs. Uzun sits in the other chair. Aysel takes the chair to the left of Mom, but she drags it close to the recliner Mom's in.

"Aysel, love, you don't have to crowd Mary. Give her some breathing room, dear."

"I'm fine," Mom says. "I've got tons of questions, and I want a lot of feedback, Aysel. This is your dress we're creating. A girl's wedding gown is the most special garment she'll ever wear. I understand you have some pictures to show me."

Aysel reaches into her pocket and pulls out a balled-up mess. She unwads it all, then presses each clipping against the edge of the coffee table.

I poke Kerem in the side and look at him sideways. He rolls his eyes. I stifle a laugh.

Kerem's mom says, "Aysel, love, how is Mary going to make much out of that mess?" She's speaking with a touch of anger and a whole lot of love.

"Don't scold her, Maria," Mom says. "I don't blame her for keeping something so precious near her. Now, let me see these, and you explain what features you want in your gown."

Aysel points as she shows Mom each of the three pictures. "I want the headpiece of this one, the arms of this one, and the skirt from this dress."

"Aysel, love, Mary's doing this as a favor to you. Could you give up just one thing to make her job easier?"

Aysel looks as if she's about to cry. Her mother jumps up and puts her arm around Aysel's shoulder, comforting her. "I didn't mean to upset you, love. I simply don't want Mary to think you are so demanding."

"Brides are supposed to be demanding, Maria." Mom leans over to Aysel and speaks directly into her face. "This is not a problem at all. I can do everything you want." And Mom begins sketching while Aysel and her mother look on.

I'm fascinated by this whole interchange. I'm so proud of my mom, I'm amused by Aysel, and I'm impressed that her mother can remain so calm amid all this turmoil her daughter brings on herself.

But my fascination's quickly dispelled, because Kerem, obviously seeing that the ladies are distracted, starts making light circle eights with his finger on my upper thigh. A tingle wells inside of me. I brush his hand away. All I need right now is a stiffy. He puts his hand right back. I push it away, and mouth, "Stop it." He cuts his eyes to me and imitates my wicked smile I'm so proud of. Again his finger's back. I grab his hand and stuff it under my leg and sit on it.

I guess my movement's distracted Kerem's mother, because she glances our way. She gives her head a tiny shake, and a wisp of a smile crosses her face.

At that point, I hear, "So have you figured out this one is hard to please?" He walks across the room toward Mom. "I'm Timur, Aysel and Kerem's cousin."

"Good to meet you, Timur." Mom puts out her hand for him to shake, and she's left hanging.

I quickly throw out, "Mom, I forgot to tell you. The Uzuns don't shake hands."

She smiles and nods at Timur, then returns to her sketching. My mother is unflappable.

Timur turns. "I'll leave you to it." As he walks past Kerem and me, he looks down and sees me sitting on Kerem's hand. He shakes his head in what I can only believe is disgust, then walks past us.

Mom finishes her sketch, and she presents it to Aysel. Kerem's mom's still standing above her.

Aysel lets out a yelp. "Oh my God, this is exactly what I wanted. Mary, you're a genius!"

"Mind your manners, love. It's Mrs. Dillon to you," her mom admonishes.

"Mary is perfectly fine," Mom says. "I was telling Kerem just last night that he should call me Mary."

His mother looks at him questioningly.

"Gabe and I were on Skype, Mama. Mary came in Gabe's room, and she joined our conversation. That's when she told me." He turns to Mom. "I could tell by my mother's expression she was wondering when we met last night."

"Oh, Kerem, my love," his mother answers, "you know I'm almost helpless with computer things." She then turns back to Mom. "It appears that my daughter is in love with the beautiful dress you've designed. What is the next step?"

"How about we take some measurements, and then we can discuss a trip to the fabric store."

"Can we go tomorrow? I don't have a class until eleven. Fashion Fabrics opens at nine thirty." Aysel is bubbling over with excitement.

"Aysel," her mother says, "I have appointments until 2:00 p.m., and those will most likely run a little late. If I hadn't cleared my afternoons, I'd be working until six or later, so be glad, my love, that I could make time for us." To Mom, she says, "I spend far too much time with each patient, but I love each and every one of them." She adds, to her daughter.

"Now, not only do I *want* to be with you at the fabric store, but if you want me to pay for it, I will *have* to be there. You know your baba won't let you have free rein with his credit card."

Aysel is suitably contrite.

"Let's just say my lovely progeny here is a bit loose with her father's money," Mrs. Uzun says to Mom. Then she laughs. "But darling—and Mary—he won't be there, and I will authorize the funds for the finest finery money can buy." She laughs again, a hearty laugh that is aimed at herself, it seems.

"Wonderful," Mom says. "Shall we head out about three thirty?"

"Perfect. That will give me time to get home from the office and Aysel home from school. We will do our afternoon prayers and then pile into my car."

"Okeydokey. Now the measurements." Mom turns to Kerem and me. "You boys must be bored stiff, and it's only going to get worse. The hens're gonna be clucking here for quite some time. Why don't you two skedaddle? Do some guy things."

"But, Mom, we haven't seen the sketch yet. That's what we've been waiting for, and now you're trying to get rid of us before you show it to us."

"Like you two care about a wedding gown. But if you must see it, here it is." She passes it to Kerem, who is nearest to her.

He holds it so we both can examine it.

"This is exactly what my sister has been talking about for ages. No wonder she's so happy. You're a magician."

Aysel sits, beaming.

"Mom, you're a true artist. I've seen things you've made before, so I know you can pull this off. But none of your creations has ever been as elaborate or magnificent as this."

Mom gleams with happiness, and I am bursting with pride.

"My finished product will echo that exactly, God willing."

I smile, thinking of how Mom has just prayed inshallah in English. Our two families are not as far apart as some might think.

"Allah *will* will it, Mom." I look to see how Mom reacts to my using Allah instead of God. She flashes me a look of love.

"Listen to you, Gabriel. My son's rubbing off on you," Kerem's mother says.

"How could he not, Mrs. Uzun? You've got quite a son here." I smile at Ker, and in a flash, I think, I hope my face is not as full of the love I have for him that's welling inside me right now. If so, the jig's up if his mother notices.

"Now, now, now, you may call me Maria," she says. "No more Mrs. Uzun. I'm not *that* formal."

"Very well. Maria it is. And, Maria," I say, using her name again on purpose, "if you don't mind, your son and I could benefit from a walk." Kerem, almost motionlessly, pokes me.

"How very polite you are, Gabriel," Maria says. "You are excused." And she gives us a queenlike dismissal with her hand.

Outside, I immediately pounce. "Kerem, were you trying to out us? What was with the finger thing?"

"I couldn't help it. You were so close to me, and no one was watching, so I took the chance."

"Well, don't think for a minute that no one was watching. You don't know what they were seeing from the corners of their eyes."

He looks at me, deadpan. "Do you think for even a millisecond that Aysel saw anything? She was glued to your mom and her sketch pad. And my mother was intent on appeasing Aysel, keeping her in check."

"And what, pray tell, do you think Timur was thinking? I saw that look he gave when he saw me sitting on your wayward hand."

"Timur can think what Timur wants to think. He and I have never been close, and a newly formed bond is not likely. Although, lately, I have been thinking more highly of him—or at least, seeing him more clearly."

"How so?"

"I'll tell you at the pond, when we're on our bench. It's a long story."

"Well," I say, looking ahead, "we'll be there before you know it."

We arrive at the pond and sit on the secluded bench, the one where we are not likely to be seen as easily as the one at front. The weather is much milder today. The bitter cold windchill has left—at least for one day.

"Okay, give me the scoop," I say.

He fills me in on all things Timur.

"Your uncle actually killed your cousin with Tim looking on?"

Ker nods. "It's called an honor killing. It happens a lot in the old countries. Not so much here, but every so often you see a news item that makes you think 'honor killing.'"

"And your uncle turned himself in right afterward?"

"That's the custom. The perp, as they call them on TV, goes straight to the police to tell them what he's done."

"It's always a dad who does it?"

"No, it could be a brother, a cousin, an uncle, sometimes even the mother, but they always turn themselves in. Well, I take that back. I heard of a case in Houston where the police had to investigate to find out who did it. That father was a coward, and he certainly wasn't following the old customs."

"So the daughter who's killed? What does she do to deserve this? I know you said your cousin had been roaming the street and her new husband didn't think she was still a virgin, but are there other reasons?"

"The virgin thing is usually why. But girls have been decapitated, shot, stoned to death for things as innocuous as having men's phone numbers in their cell phones."

I can't believe what I'm hearing. "So the guy who does the deed. He's executed, right?"

"That's the thing. In a lot of those countries, they are given light sentences because the poor girl, now dead, had brought dishonor to their family. And honor is everything in those crazy countries. But this is the US. In some states, the death penalty is very much alive." He chuckles at his oxymoron. "My Uncle Sivan was tried, convicted, and died of lethal injection. And that was that."

"Not really. Your poor cousin must still bear the scars of what he saw. And of his mother's death, his brother's death, his sister's death."

"I've had years to come to that conclusion myself. And I guess because Tim's not one of my favorite people, forgive me, Allah, I never thought of it that way. And here that's your first thought. I'm such a bad person."

"No, you're not, babe." I touch his cheek. "You've just been too close to the situation. If I know you, you will set yourself on a path to redemption as soon as we get back to your house."

He takes my hand and kisses it.

"But first, I think we need to take advantage of our time, here, on our bench. The bench where yesterday's dirty deeds were done." I twirl the ends of an imaginary mustache. He looks at me like I'm crazy. I guess he's not into old-timey *mellerdrammer*.

I grab him and make him forget all about his cousin Timur and his woes. At least for now.

CHAPTER 14

Kerem

SUNSET PRAYERS completed, Mama and Aysel, with Mary trailing along, have gone to meet Hasan and his mother at a bakery for a cake tasting. I'm not sure why the mothers are needed. No doubt Grandma, who tagged along as chaperone on the first date, could be there for her official duties—to keep the young couple pure and chaste. But nevertheless, both mothers are going. It's the bride and groom's cake that is being chosen, so no input is needed from the mamas, but I suspect the women will be there to referee if a fight breaks out between Hasan and Aysel. If you ask me, Hasan already knows that he needs to just go along with whatever Aysel wants.

Amazingly, in the two weeks since she took measurements, Mary has finished Aysel's gown. Neither Gabe nor I have seen it, for Aysel has declared it will be a surprise reserved for the wedding.

Baba and Timur have gone to get a burger. Mama, Aysel, and Mary will get dinner after the tasting. I'm left to fend for myself, but since Gabe's dad is working late, I'm skipping dinner in favor of dessert. Special dessert.

I head over to Gabe's house for our happy hour. Well, two hours, we're hoping.

He greets me at the door by yanking me in, slamming the door, and planting a long, wet, hard, probing kiss on me.

"Hold up, cowboy. Slow your horses," I say. "I like this a lot, but we've got two hours. I don't want to be thrown from the bull too quickly because the operator has run out of power."

"Listen to you with your country and western bar patter." He kisses me again, this time more gently. "You hungry?"

"Yeah," I say. "Hungry for you."

"I was hoping you'd say that." He cradles his arms around my chest and fakes trying to sling me over his shoulder. "Damn, I was going to take you to my cave, Neanderthal-style, but you're too manly man for me to lift."

"Go on with your crazy self." I smack him gently across the cheek. "Ah'm just a wee wisp of a boy." I bat my eyelashes at him.

Gabe rolls his eyes. "Enough. Let's get going. I've got moves for you you've never even imagined. And Dad might get home early, so we need to get crackin'."

We get up to his room. We've spent a lot of time at the pond the last two weeks, but this is our first time truly alone, in private, together. I cross the threshold of his bedroom, and instantly I'm apprehensive. It's easy to joke in the entryway downstairs, but this is push-comes-to-shove time. Will I please him? Will I know what to do? Will I be a good student for all he plans to teach me?

He turns to face me, pushing the door shut. He looks into my eyes. I know he sees the fear I'm experiencing.

"It's okay. I won't do anything you don't want me to. All that talk downstairs? Bravado. Translate: bullshit. Pure, unadulterated BS from someone who's as scared as you are. Yeah, I have some technique that you, inexperienced you, don't have. But all I want is to make you happy. And that's a lot of pressure." He begins to unbutton my shirt. A simple act. How can it provide so much pleasure? I start to tingle all over. "Slip off your shoes," he commands.

"I'm taking this nice and slow," he says as he unzips and unbuttons my jeans. I lift each leg as he pulls them off me. "If you want me to stop at any time, say the word." He buries his nose against my brief-covered crotch. Instantly I grow. "Hm," he hums. "I love the way you smell. It's not just a man smell. It's a Kerem smell, and it's intoxicating," he whispers.

He stands. "Slide under the covers. I'll be right there." As I head for the bed, I hear him behind me, securing the lock on the door.

This is it. What I've waited for, longed for, thought about for years. This is what I've fantasized about ever since the strange new kid spied on me at prayer in the woods. Please, Allah, allow me to please him.

Gabe slides under the covers, and he takes me into his arms. For a moment, we lie there, cheeks touching. Tears flow down my face.

He breaks away. "What's the matter? Are you not ready for this?" There is naked, raw alarm in his voice.

I shake my head. "These are tears of joy, not sorrow." He smiles as the visible tension falls away from his face.

He kisses me. A kiss full of meaning. Full of "I love you" and "I want you" and "I need you."

His head disappears under the covers. He plants tiny little spark-making kisses down my body. I feel him remove my briefs. His breath is hovering over me, there.

I shudder as his lips take me into his mouth. His softness is warm and enveloping. His tongue is masterful. He begins to draw me out.

I try to hold it back, but I feel it rumble from deep inside me, and suddenly I burst, shouting, "Allah! Allah! Allah!" over and over. At last there is nothing left. I relax into the mattress, and silently pray. *Forgive me, Allah, if using Your Name was inappropriate. But oh, Allah, thank you for this.*

Gabe, by now, is lying beside me. We are both staring at the ceiling.

"That was amazing. *You* are amazing," he says. He adds, "Babe, you make me so happy."

"No, you make me happy. Now I will try to please you as much as you've pleased me," I say, adding, "inshallah." I start to dive under the covers.

"Whoa!" He pulls me back. "We've got time for that. Right now, let's just enjoy each other's company a minute. Build our strength back up." He kisses me; then he pulls his legs from under the covers. "Is it hot in here?"

"I'm hot. Hot for you," I say, not believing that I even know that phrase.

He laughs. "You're a quick learner, babe."

Several probing kisses later, and we are both ready again. It is my turn to pleasure him. A bit of apprehension hits me as I lean down toward his middle. Will I be as good at this as he is? Have I learned enough already to try this?

I pull his stained and wet briefs off him. His penis is pointing toward the ceiling, rigid.

"You're circumcised," I say, without even thinking. Anatomical talk could kill the mood, I instantly realize.

"So are you," he says.

"But it's a Muslim thing."

"Babe, it's a lotta men thing. Jewish men are always cut. And doctors used to believe that it was healthier to be cut, so parents had their little boys trimmed soon after birth. I was one of those lucky cherubs."

"I can't believe it. I'm supposed to be smart. And I thought only Muslims were circumcised."

"Another lesson learned. Now could we quit talking before I lose my mojo?"

Uh-oh, what I feared was happening. Why can't I learn to keep my mouth shut? Speaking-wise, that is. For, staring at Gabe's root once again, I have no plan to close my mouth.

I take it into mine, and instantly, as I run my tongue down it, stuffing it farther and farther into me, I wonder if I will gag. But I don't. Because this is the most exquisite feeling I've ever had—next to the previous feeling Gabe pulled from me just a few minutes before.

Feeling totally inadequate, I try to work the magic that Gabe worked on me.

"Yeah, babe, yeah. Slower. Slower. That's right. Uh-huh. Oh, oh." Gabe seems to be in a trance as he guides me, and I keep doing what I'm doing. I'm sure there are techniques I can study up on, but for right now, it seems like I know what I'm doing simply by instinct.

I really don't want to stop, but Gabe has had all he can stand. It feels good to know I've brought him to this. I kiss his abs, all the way up to his neck. I nibble on his ear, and then I kiss his lips, over and over, gently, lightly. At last, I rest my head on his chest.

"Babe, you've been taking lessons, now, haven't you?"

What? He thinks I'd cheat on him? That I'd do this with someone else?

Then he laughs. "Just funnin' you." My heart starts slowing down from the race it was running. "That was fucking awesome."

I look up at him. "You really think so?"

"Not much I can teach you in that department, babe. You're a master already."

"So no more lessons, huh?"

"We-e-e-el-l." He draws it out seductively. "There's some more I can teach you, but that's for another day, another time." He whispers into my ear.

"Normal people really do that?"

He nods.

"I thought it was just something that porn stars did. Doesn't it hurt?"

"It can. But not if you're prepared for it. And we're talking Nirvana when two guys are totally into it. But you always use a condom. Big risk if you don't."

"You're clean, aren't you?" I ask.

"Sure, but you don't know if everybody else is."

"But I don't plan to do it with anybody else."

"Nor do I." He kisses me again. "But you never know. If your life takes a different path, stop by the drugstore first."

"Okay," I say, knowing my path has been laid right here, right now.

We spend more time together, here in bed; then reluctantly I say, "I guess your dad could be home any minute, huh?"

With disgust in his voice, Gabe answers, "Yeah. Time to get back to the real world."

He gets out of bed, grabs a clean pair of briefs from a drawer, slips them on, and then he starts to dress. I do the same thing.

"Thank you," I say.

"No, thank *you*," he answers.

We go downstairs and after a goodbye kiss, I say "Salaam Alaykum."

"Wa-Alaykum." There's devotion in his eyes.

I'm floating across the street, wishing I could have spent the entire night in his arms.

I enter the family room and Timur says, "Where you been? It's almost time for evening prayers."

"I was over at Gabe's house."

"Good time?" Baba asks.

With lips closed, I nod and hum a mute version of *uh-huh*. I don't trust myself to speak.

We perform the prayer ritual; then Tim and I head up the stairs together.

"What do you two do? You're over there all the time these days, it seems."

I quickly think. "Homework, watch TV, visit."

"Well, don't forget our family needs you to help prepare for this wedding," he says.

I want to say *my family*, but I realize how hurtful that would be to him. And after all these years, I suppose it is *his* family too.

"Aysel knows she can count on me. And Mama too."

"It's not right for a non-Muslim like that Mary woman to be nosing in on a Muslim wedding."

"That Mary woman, as you call her, is a very nice person, and she only wants to help. Besides, without her, Aysel wouldn't have the dress she wanted."

"Whatever. I just pray the wedding goes off without a hitch. Hasan's family is very traditional. This wedding will please them, inshallah."

"Quit worrying. Pleasing Aysel is more important. It will be her big day. You know how she is."

"I do, I do. She's changing, though, thank Allah. She is becoming more and more devout each day."

"Don't kid yourself, Tim. A lot of that is a show—for Hasan and his family. Yes, she is embracing their traditions, and it will be good for her, for if she's marrying into that family, she has to become a part of it. But our family's ways are just as much a path to heaven as theirs. As Baba says—"

"It's between you and Allah." And in a rare display of humanity, Timur laughs at that. His laugh is not one of derision; it is one that shows he loves and respects Baba. Is Tim more human than I ever imagined?

This conversation has been taking place outside my closed bedroom door, so I turn the knob as I say, "Good night, cousin."

He says good night also, and we retreat to our rooms. He, I'm sure, will be googling whatever the hell he googles incessantly. I, however, plan to instantly fall asleep so I can dream of Gabriel, my angel.

I must remember to tell him that he is named after the angel Gabriel, from his Bible, the same angel who brought Islam to Muhammad, PBUH.

An appropriate name for someone who has brought such happiness to me.

I SPEED through school the next day, doing all the right things, I hope. I wouldn't know because my mind is filled with Gabe, Gabe, Gabe. I even look for him in the hallways between every class. I go to places I never go in my quest just to catch a glimpse of him. Once or twice, our paths cross, and he flashes love to me as we pass in the hall.

He doesn't follow me to afternoon prayers because he has swim practice. I thank Allah for the gift He has given me.

When I get home, Mama is sitting at the dining table, tweaking the seating chart for the reception. I'm not sure how she's doing that because all the RSVPs aren't in yet. But Aysel has been working with that chart for at least a week already. She seems to think she knows just who will accept and who will decline.

"Where is everybody?"

"Your sister is still at school, Timur is at work, and your father took a much-needed afternoon off to golf with Dr. Hill. Your baba works far too much. I'm so glad he managed to get away for a few hours."

"What ya doin'?" I ask, to make small talk more than anything else. It's obvious what she's doing.

"Trying to make sure your Aunt Àgata and your Aunt Octàvia are seated across the room from each other. You know how my sisters are. Ten minutes together, and they are at each other's throats. The latest argument involves who has the most luxurious car, for Pete's sake."

"Anything I can do to help?"

"Not much, but I would love for you to make me a cold glass of water. And then sit and visit while I review the entire chart. I'm good at multitasking."

I get her water and bring it back to her. I sit at the end of the table, she right next to me at the side.

"How was the cake tasting?"

"It was scrumptious. Aysel liked the chocolate malt cake. Hasan liked the carrot cake."

"So they're getting chocolate malt, right?"

She looks at me and smiles. "You know your sister well."

"And Hasan is smart, giving in to her. His family may be orthodox, but I have a feeling that he's already figured out Aysel will not be a subservient wife."

"Poor Hasan. I love my daughter, but she can be a handful."

"And Mary. Was she amused by Aysel last night?"

"Gabriel's mother is a jewel. She just smiles and seems to understand Aysel's every mood."

"She does seem nice. And wow—did you ever figure she'd get the dress done in less than two weeks?"

"Heavens no. I figured she'd be fitting it on Aysel right up until she met Hasan for the vows. And that was not an easy dress to make. The details she put into it are incredible."

"I can't wait to see it."

"I'd bet. Brothers *always* are eager to see their sisters in their wedding gowns. My theory is that they are glad they are finally leaving the nest."

I laugh at that. "I have been thinking of converting her room into a home gym."

"Sure, sure, my son." She looks at me wistfully. "You'll soon be leaving yourself. First college, and then you'll find someone to love."

I feel the blush rise in my cheeks.

"But that last has already happened. Hasn't it, love?"

How do I answer that question? I stare at her, speechless.

"You've been spending a lot of time with Gabe lately." *What?* "And you come back always looking so contented, so much in love."

My eyes grow wide. There has to be terror in them. I can't believe what I'm hearing. From my own mother's lips, no less.

She smiles slyly. "What? You don't think I know?"

Again, I'm so not believing what I'm hearing that I can't answer her.

"Kerem, love, I knew long ago that you were gay."

Finally I find my words. I have to respond to this revelation. "How?" is all I can muster, though.

"A mother knows, love."

She lets that sink in; then she continues. "When I first met Gabriel, I thought, 'Now there's a boy my Kerem could love.' Oh, I didn't know if he was gay, but as you two seemed to bond, my heart swelled, knowing I'd made the right match for you. I was overjoyed when his mother agreed to make Aysel's dress, for I knew that would give you and Gabriel more time together, with the families bound together at last. I have to tell you, it was a dark time for me when his cousin was hurt and you and Gabriel quit seeing so much of each other. I prayed."

Never in my short gay life would I have predicted I would be listening to my mother say these things.

"So tell me, love—I'm right about it all, correct?"

A weight lifts and suddenly I want to talk. "Yes, you are right. Gabe is the most wonderful person I've ever met, and we are very much in love."

She throws her hands in the air and proclaims, "Praise Allah!"

Then my apprehension floods in again. "But how will Baba take this? His son homosexual. And not only that, in love with a non-Muslim."

"He will embrace you and Gabriel both and tell you 'that is between you and Allah.'"

Will he? I don't really know. I hope so. I expect so. But I don't *know* so.

"But, love, let me ease those fears I see in your eyes: we won't say a word to him until after the wedding. Okay? He has enough on his plate, giving away his daughter. If he has any misgivings—" She quickly adds, "and I know he won't have any—about his son being gay, then he will be more receptive when the stress of all this hoopla is over."

I want to accept her affirmation that all will be well with Baba. I feel it will, but I won't know for certain until I tell him. And I'm glad I have a two-week reprieve from that task. I can enjoy attending Aysel's wedding and loving Gabe without worry. Inshallah.

Then I will have mustered the courage to tell Baba. And he will be as overjoyed as Mama.

He will.

Won't he?

CHAPTER 15

Timur

THEY THINK I don't know. About them. What they do.

Like I said, I'm a good lurker. I've followed them to the pond. They sit in the shadows of the trees, kissing. It's disgusting.

I can't get close enough to hear what they say, but I can imagine. If Amca knew, he would be so angry. He would be so very hurt as well. What father wouldn't be?

His son, a sodomite.

If this becomes known, it will ruin Baba. It will destroy our family.

The golden boy is a filthy homosexual. Allah will rain down fire on him. It may not be soon, but it will be—eventually. If not in this world, in the next. My perfect cousin will never sit with the virgins in heaven. He will burn eternally for this.

I fear this has gone far past the kissing. Homework? TV? Visiting? Who does he think I am? Some gullible fool? They're visiting all right. The two of them were alone over there last night. There is not a doubt in my mind what they were doing.

I have no personal knowledge of what those people do. But I've researched it. It is vile. It defiles the body that Allah has given us. The Quran forbids tattoos, and this defilement of the body is far worse. There is no way Kerem can cleanse his mouth enough to be worthy to taste the food that Allah provides.

It is an unholy act.

And I don't want to even think of the other. Surely they are not doing that. Unclean, unclean. And dangerous. Kerem is setting himself up to die a wretched man. Broken and condemned.

And he is taking our family with him. Dragging us into the dung. Burying us in the garbage of his sin.

I pray for him. I pray that these urges are taken away from him. That he steps back onto the righteous path.

I fear he has already strayed too far.
May Allah strike him down before this family is lost.
Because of him.
Because he sins.

CHAPTER 16

Gabriel

"YOU WOULDN'T believe how happy Mom was when your mother and Aysel declared her co-wedding coordinator." I lightly run my fingertips along his perfect body.

One week to the wedding, and Kerem and I are stealing more time together. In my bed.

"Mama told Aysel, 'if Mary is going to be with us, helping us make decisions and doing all this work, she deserves the title.' And then she added, 'I'm surprised a woman of her many talents isn't doing this for a living. She is the complete package: exquisite seamstress, insightful planner, and if people wanted it, she could even bake the cake, I'm sure.'"

He shivers as he touches my hand, brings it to his lips, and plants tiny kisses on it.

"It feels good that Maria—it's weird calling your mom that—has such regard for my mother. I've always known she is extraordinary. It's great hearing her praised by someone else."

And lying here, enjoying this, is a side effect of that *high regard*. This close to the wedding, Mom's spending more and more time away from home. And Dad works late an awful lot, leaving me to my own devices. Devices like what's taking place right now.

And I adore those devices and Kerem. If he's as turned on as I am right now, I can't imagine how we can keep up this conversation. But prolonging it can only make what comes after sweeter.

"Well, believe me, Mary's been a big, big help." He caresses my face. "When Aysel sprung this wedding on Mama, it seemed like it would be a simple thing, so Mama didn't hire a coordinator." He kisses me, a gentle angel kiss. "That was foolish on her part because she knows my sister all too well. But anyway, once she realized she was in over her head, it was too late to find anyone competent. Then Allah, via one of his precious angels—the Angel Gabriel—sent Mama a coordinator who is far more incredible than any hired hand could be." He gives me two more of those light as air kisses.

I'm ready for more, and I can't help myself. I reach down and play, gently, and he is getting aroused again.

"Stop it, Gabe." He takes my hand and forcibly moves it away. I leer at him. He smiles. "You devil. Quit thrusting temptation on me. You know we have no more time for that. Oh, how I wish we did, but your dad will be home soon, and our moms could pull up any minute from their trip to the reception hall."

He slides away from me and out of my bed—away from my grasp. I sigh. As he dresses, he says, "Timur has gone off the deep end with this praying at Hasan's mosque thing. He even has Baba over there tonight, saying evening prayers." He looks heavenward. "Forgive me, Allah, if I'm late with mine. I promise to do them as soon as I get back home." He continues his banter to me. "Baba even canceled some appointments last Friday to do noontime prayers at Hasan's mosque because Timur insisted. Baba never does Friday prayers at a mosque, much less someone else's mosque."

"Why all the sudden devotion?" I ask. Kerem is tying his Nikes as I languish in bed. I don't want to lose the feeling, but I do need to lose the erection. And watching Kerem go from naked to dressed is a turn-on, rather than a turnoff.

"For Baba, I think it's just a way to show unity with Hasan's family. My baba is a nice guy, and he wants to reassure Hasan's father that his son's marrying a girl from a good Muslim family."

"And for Tim?"

"Tim, I think, is rediscovering his roots. His family was so ultradevout. He's missed that, I'm sure, since mine's very modern in their Muslim ways. And, too, recently Timur has seemed to embrace our family more deeply. Perhaps he thinks he can pull Baba into being more orthodox by exposing him to Hasan's family's ways."

"Sounds like Timur's confused, wanting to be more a part of *your* family, yet migrating to another family's ways and customs."

"You know, my friend," Kerem says, giving me a sly look as he dubs me "friend" as if to say "that was a misnomer, wasn't it?" I smile at him.

"Friend? I think we are much more than that, babe." Finally I feel his grip loosening. I've never had that happen before. Usually the stiffy just goes away, doesn't linger. But then again, before I was not in love.

"Whatever," he declares, with fake annoyance. "My cousin has to be conflicted. After all that happened to his family."

"True, true."

"Aren't you going to be a gentleman and show me to the door?"

"You've drained me," I say. "I don't have an ounce of strength left in me. You can show yourself out. After all, both my parents know everything about us, including this. Out of respect, I don't think we should do it when they are home. And yes, if we forgot to lock the door, one of them might barge in on us, so there's that. But I have no secrets from them." I let that hang on the air. I don't know if I said that to reassure him or if I said that to encourage him to come out to his folks.

He sits on the edge of the bed. I can tell he's struggling to tell me something.

"I haven't mentioned this." He stops. I can almost see the words formulating in his brain and trying to burst out.

"You can tell me anything, babe." For a brief moment, I am gripped with fear. What if he's saying goodbye? What if he's decided we aren't meant to be? *No!* I scream deep inside. That isn't it. It can't be. He's not breaking up with me. It's something else. Inshallah.

"Remember that first time for us? Last week?" Again, he pauses, gathering his words, gathering courage.

"Of course I do. It was the most magical time I've had since I moved here." I stroke his arm, hoping to give him courage to continue.

"When I went home that day, Mama was there alone. She wanted me to sit and visit. I thought nothing of it."

Oh, no, oh God, no. His mother figured it all out and does not approve. She wants him to end it with me. I feel a tear form in my eye.

But if that's the case, why today? Kerem would not disobey his mother for an afternoon of goodbye sex.

"Mama said something that shocked me." Again, the damn pause. *Please, oh, please, oh, please, God, Allah, Goddess, Great Spirit, Thor, Vishnu, Mother Earth, all the gods ever invented, push him to get this revelation out.*

"Mama told me I was in love. She saw it. She knew it. She said she knew I was gay years ago. She's happy about us." He takes in a long, deep breath to replace the short shallow ones he has been expelling.

"That's a good thing! Mothers know. That's what Mom's always telling me. And the fact that Maria knows and approves is a cause for celebration. So why haven't you told me this good news?"

I feel the warm air he expels. "Truth?"

"Of course, truth. We will always be honest with each other."

"Mama said, with the wedding consuming our lives, I should wait to tell Baba until all this madness is over."

My heart skips. "She doesn't think he'll be happy?"

"No, she says she's certain he'll be fine with it, but if he has a hard time processing, it's best that he's not trying to do so amid all of Aysel's drama."

"Well, I predict he will accept it because your baba's a really nice guy who wants everyone to be happy. And what is it he says?"

We say it together: "That is between you and Allah."

It's good to see a smile break out across Kerem's face for the first time in the last ten minutes. But the darkness returns.

"Okay, babe, spill it. It occurs to me that you still haven't told me why you've kept this from me."

He hesitates. "I—I—I was afraid if you knew about it, you would press me to tell Baba now, instead of later."

I sit up, grab him into a hug, and whisper, "Oh, babe, I'm so sorry you've had this weighing on you. I wouldn't do that. Ever. Coming out is so very personal. Your family will embrace your sexuality like they've always cherished everything about you. I'm absolutely certain of that. But I don't want you to ever think I would try to force you out of the closet or to reveal any secret that is burdening you. That is—" I pause to put a smile on my face and a bit of wickedness in my voice. "—between you and Allah."

He punches me. Then he stands up. "For that bit of wayward humor, you're not getting a goodbye kiss." And he walks away.

I leap from under the covers, totally naked, my dick swinging recklessly in the air, and rush to him, turn him around, and grab him. I smother him in kisses, and then I scream, "Not as long as I walk this earth will you be able to get away from me and my kryptonite kisses. May they protect you until next we meet, inshallah."

"Go on with your bad self," he says, pulling from my grasp. "I gotta go. I still have evening prayers—late, I might add, thanks to you."

"Allah will forgive."

And he leaves, shaking his head.

It takes a while to get to sleep. I'm head over heels with Kerem's mother's declaration. That's half the battle. A battle that I want to believe won't take place. I want to think that his baba will be accepting also. But I know that fathers think differently than mothers, and acceptance of a son's homosexuality, for dads, can be traumatic, bound up in feelings of failure and confusion. I was lucky with *my* dad, but some aren't so blessed. And then, too, Aram Uzun is a devout Muslim. They, as a rule, don't accept this. I pray to God that all goes well for Kerem when he finally does speak to his father.

Exhaustion or a feeling of well-being overcomes me, and I finally sleep.

Next morning, Mom is filled with Aysel this and Aysel that. I am so happy for her that she gets to experience this. When the time comes, if ever, for Kerem and me to marry, I'd be happy to show up at city hall for a quickie ceremony. But that's guys for you—or at least *this* guy. Mom wasn't blessed with a girl she could shower with elaborate nuptials, so doing this for Aysel is the next best thing.

"Aysel has such definite ideas. About everything. Each and every little detail has to be her way. I don't blame her. I get it. Poor Maria gets exasperated with her daughter, but she tries not to show it. I can't imagine the quarrels that might have happened if I had not been there as a buffer."

"She's a stubborn one, that Aysel. At least that's what I've observed. Stubborn, stubborn, stubborn."

"As a mule." Then she laughs. "But not like a Bridezilla, thank God." I remember seeing some of that old show. Those girls were horrible. "Aysel just wants the perfect wedding for her Hasan. And herself. I truly think, though, that she's deeply committed to her man."

"From what I've seen and heard, she's plunged right into the deep end when it comes to taking on his family's ways."

"Yes, she has. Maria tells me that Aysel is far more dedicated to the old ways than Maria and Aram's family ever have been. But that's a good thing. The man she's chosen comes from a very strict family, and her marriage will be stronger if she adopts their ways. But as I told Maria, don't expect Aysel to knuckle under all the time. The girl has her own mind."

"She certainly does. Yessiree, Bob."

"Don't call me Bob," Mom teases. "I'm worried, though, a bit, about Timur."

"What about him?" I didn't think Mom even knew Timur, aside from his brief introduction the day she was there to plan the dress.

"Poor thing, he seems to be getting deeper and deeper into the orthodox version of Islam, and I'm not sure that's a good thing."

"How do you know all this?" I'm intrigued my mother knows so much about this cipher who lives across the street, and I know so little, despite the fact that he's the cousin of the man I love.

"Maria and I talk. She's concerned as well. Timur's life was thrust into turmoil very quickly at a very young age."

"She told you, huh?"

"Everything. You know too, huh? How horrible. Maria says she and Aram have done everything they could to make Timur feel a part of the family, but he remained distant. Lately, though, she says an incident that happened turned him around, and he's opening up a bit more and embracing the family."

"The computer breach?"

"Yes. Timur must be a whiz, solving that problem. Aram and his practice faced a world of hurt. Timur saved them, Maria says. Aram's gratitude seems to have brought him and Timur closer. The boy needs a father."

"He's not a boy, Mom. Tim's a man."

"Not really. He may be a man physically, but after what he experienced, there's no way he has grown up. Not emotionally. He's still that traumatized little boy. And I'm afraid his newfound love for the old ways is just a cover to mask his stunted emotions."

"You think he may be turning to terrorism?" I shudder at the thought, not wanting to believe it. Timur can be unpleasant with that continual smirk on his face, but surely he's not capable of anything that extreme.

"No, no, no. I didn't say that. I doubt seriously that anyone who grew up in that family could turn to anything that vile. It just doesn't happen in most good families—not in our country, anyway. At least I want to believe that. God knows some kids go crazy on their parents. What I'm saying's that Timur is trying to replace his need to process with the outward trappings of Islam."

"So when did you get a degree in psychology, wise mother?" My smile, I hope, is a trophy, a golden prize full of my love for her.

She laughs at me. And it's a chuckle that says I love you back. "You need to skedaddle. You're gonna be late for school."

She's right. So this in-depth discussion of the damaged cousin will just have to continue later. If at all. I'm not sure I care.

SCHOOL RUNS like clockwork, and I love swim practice. With my concentration on my technique, and Coach screaming at me from time to time, I have no room in my thoughts for Timur Uzun. I barely have time to sneak a few memories of last night with Ker—and smile.

After practice I skype with Kerem, figuring he has no time for us to get together.

A warm feeling comes over me when I see his face on the screen. That always happens these days.

"Hey, babe. How's it going? You're all tied up in wedding, wedding, wedding, I suppose."

"Not really," he answers. "Maybe you didn't notice the decorations in your living room?"

I'd walked right past the living room when I came in the house. I called for Mom, but she wasn't home, so I went straight to my computer.

"Decorations?"

"Aysel's wedding shower's tonight. Your Mom's hosting. As soon as I got home from school and afternoon prayers, Mama had me carting all the good silver and china over to your house."

"Why didn't they just have the thing at your house? And why haven't I heard about this?"

"First of all, it seems the bride's mother can't give a shower for her own daughter. It's usually a friend of the bride who gives the shower, but Aysel, Allah love her, has few friends her age, and none who would go to the trouble of a shower. So that left your mom to volunteer. And even if it had been at our house, I'd probably have had to tote all your mom's good silver and china over here, because this is a big shindig. Every woman my mama has ever met's invited, plus all the women at our mosque, and Hasan's mother, grandmother, the grandmother from Lebanon who finally arrived in the States, plus Hasan's sisters, cousins, and whoever else on the street that Aysel invited. It's going to be one hell of a party. Hasan and Aysel will have to rent a U-Haul to return all the toasters to Target."

"I'm astounded. But again, I ask, why haven't I heard about this?" I'm thinking Mom would have said something this morning. But then I remember we got caught up in Timur and his problems.

"Apparently Aysel just mentioned she wanted a shower. Mama figured with Aysel's lack of friends and Hasan's ultraorthodoxy, there wouldn't be a shower."

"Uh-oh. Bad move on Maria's part."

"But super mother Mary—I'm surprised Aysel hasn't started calling your mother 'Mom'—put on her superhero cape and saved the day."

"That's my mom for you."

"So what ya doin'?" he asks.

"Nothin'."

"Wanna visit the MF's?"

I laugh. "I know for a fact that you don't have a whole lot of affection for those two. So I'm hoping what you want is to show a little affection for...." I let my voice trail off.

"Outside. Now." His face vanishes from the screen.

He's waiting when I open the door to my house. I join him as we walk.

"So what're Tim's and your baba's plans for this evening? Looks like my house will be full of hens."

"Tim and Baba are having dinner out—I was invited—and then they're going to Hasan's mosque to pray. I declined their invitation because I went to that mosque with them once last week, and it was kinda creepy."

"Creepy? How?"

"Well, not in a 'terrorist around every corner' creepy. That's a rare thing in our neck of the woods. No, I just found being surrounded by so many Muslims that dedicated was not my thing. The men seemed to pray more fervently than at our mosque, if that's possible. The women were in another room entirely, and when I saw them, I was astounded at so many burqas. This is one old-world brand of mosque. So very unlike the one we go to."

"So with your mama and Aysel at our house, and your cousin and baba away—"

"Don't even think of it." I'm hurt by his curt dismissal. "Until I resolve this with Baba, there's no way I would be comfortable doin' the nasty in his house."

"Doin' the nasty? Is that what you think of what we do?" I'm offended and don't want to be.

"I'm sorry. Don't know where I heard it called that. I'm pretty sure it was some movie, and in that movie, it was a euphemism for hetero-sex. I guess just the thought of doing what we do—which is not nasty and, in actual fact, is beautiful!—in a home where it might not be welcomed, made me want to make light of it. Poor choice of words."

"I forgive ya, babe. You've got to be under a lot of stress over this. The wedding'll soon be over, and then you can have that sit-down with your baba. It'll be okay before you know it."

"Inshallah."

"Allah—God—has already blessed us by bringing us together. There's no way He will let your father be against us."

"Like I've said, I can only hope you're right."

We sit on our bench and watch the swans glide on the water. The weather has started to warm, and they are content to be out and about.

After these moments of God's solitude, I say, "So with your mother's already-given approval and your dad's soon-to-be-given approval, we will be able to be open and honest to the world."

"What about my sister? Tim?"

"Your sister will soon be a member of another household. How she's going to live with Hasan's parents, I can't imagine. I pray for them because they are in for a rude awakening, I fear. But that's their custom, and we both know she has agreed to it. She will be so busy that she won't have time to think about her brother and his lovemaking. And she won't be in your house any longer, so out of sight, out of mind."

"And Tim?"

"Who cares? He'll just have to get over it if he doesn't approve. The only approval you need seek is that of your parents."

"Tim is a part of the family. I want his approval."

"I know he is, and I know you do. I also know he's a conflicted soul. So his approval may be something you shouldn't wish for. For some, they never approve; for others, they accept rather than approve; and for still others, it takes a lot of time to bring 'em around. I'm thinking Timur's in that last category. He loves your family, and he loves you—even though he doesn't show it—and he will eventually understand it's not a choice. It's just the way we are."

"You're so confident." He kisses me. "So supporting." He kisses me again. "So comforting." He kisses me again, and this time, I put my hands on his cheeks, asking him to stay. I've waited all day for this, fearing that he would be so busy we wouldn't even see each other today. Now that we are here, on our bench, away from prying eyes, I want to take advantage of it.

Our time by the pond, on our bench, is always magical. It's a time for us to forget everything else, and a feeling overcomes me—and I'm sure Kerem too—like we are a thousand miles away from distraction.

We're locked in an embrace when it happens.

A rustling noise.

Someone's going past the bushes that conceal us.

CHAPTER 17

Kerem

I YELP.

"It's okay, babe. Probably just a bird. Got too close to the bushes."

I take a deep breath to calm down. I want to think I was simply startled in the midst of Gabe's magical distraction, but my mind goes to other things.

Gabe looks in my eyes. "What? Did you think your baba was closing in, shotgun in hand?" He smiles.

"Believe it or not, I might have been," I say, still breathing deeply, trying desperately to calm my nerves.

"Seriously? I can't picture your father with a firearm, much less being angry enough to use it on his son and his incredibly handsome, pick-of-the-litter lover."

He makes me laugh, and the tension in me breaks.

I stand. "Let's go. I don't want to test fate."

We step from the cover of the bushes that surround our bench, and we see what has whisked past without our being aware. After all, we were busy doing other things.

It's a kid. A boy. Standing near the edge of the pond. Arm raised, ready to chuck a rock at the swans.

"Hey, kid," Gabe shouts.

The boy turns. Lowers his arm. Obviously not pleased he's been caught in the act.

"Leave the swans alone. You make 'em mad, and they'll bite your nose off before you know it. They're mean mother—" He stops abruptly. "They don't like to be bothered."

The kid drops the rock and runs away. I laugh at Gabe as we start walking.

"Kid's lucky. I almost said 'bite your pecker off.' That would have scarred him for life."

That's my Gabe. Funny even when he's rescuing innocent swans. Gotta love him. Thank you, Allah, for this man walking next to me. For now. Forever.

Our walk back is pretty much silent. Gabe's escapade with the kid was only a moment away from my problems. I have so many thoughts rolling around in my head that I'm having a hard time sorting them out. No, I would never expect Baba to show up at the pond with a shotgun. That's absurd. But I do fear the unknown. I want him to be as accepting as Mama about all this, but I simply don't know how he'll react. And that's killing me.

But I do agree it's best to table the whole issue until after the wedding. We arrive at my house.

"Well, you've been uncharacteristically quiet on this jaunt home. What gives?"

"I was just thinking—about everything," I tell him.

"I figured. That's why I left you alone. A walk is a great time to process."

"Yeah." I only wish I had processed it all, but that's for another time, it seems. "Come inside for a drink. Mama keeps all kinds of juice in the house. You don't want to go to your house, or you'll get roped into the madness. I'm sure that Aysel is, at this very moment, making your mom and mine totally frazzled with her demands. It's best to leave them alone."

He follows me into the house, where I'm surprised to see Tim sitting on the couch, calmly eating an apple. He has a large knife, and he's slicing off pieces and eating each off the blade.

"Tim, whatcha doin' home so early?"

He looks at me, sliding a slice of apple from the enormous blade onto his tongue. "Boss gave me the rest of the day off. I finished the big project he gave me, so he rewarded me."

"Good for you," Gabe says. "It's good to be appreciated."

Timur ignores Gabe's remark, looking right through him.

"You wanna go to Hasan's mosque with me for sunset prayers?" Timur asks, still calmly eating his apple from that death blade.

"No—I'll do them in my room, but thanks for asking," I say. "You've sure been spending a lot of time at that place. What gives?"

"I like it. There's a holiness there that we don't have at our mosque. Hasan and his family are truly dedicated to Islam."

I want to counter that remark, but I hold my tongue.

"I only wish Aysel respected that more," he adds.

I can't be quiet at that, not having watched Aysel change so much in the last three months. "Aysel has embraced their ways very deeply. You know that. And it was not to just rope Hasan into marrying her. She really believes in what she has chosen."

"I know that," Tim says, slipping another slice of apple off the knife. "But she disrespected Hasan's family when she refused to let them join in planning the wedding. In the old ways, the groom's family paid for the wedding, and I'm sure that's what they expected to do, not be shut out entirely from paying and planning. Hasan has barely had any input, and his family's had virtually none."

I laugh. "You grew up with Aysel just like I did. That girl has been planning her wedding since she was in middle school. No way she'd bow down to someone else taking over. That's not Aysel."

"True," he says. "But I still think she dishonored Hasan when she insisted on doing it all herself. With Aunt's and *Mary's* help, that is." There is a sinister tone when he says Gabe's mom's name, and I feel Gabe bristle, since he's standing so close to me.

"Hasan and his family don't deserve such treatment," he adds. "If they'd had their way, the *nikah* would take place in their living room, and there'd be Lebanese snacks in their backyard as a reception."

"Aysel wouldn't feel like she'd even had a wedding." I try to keep resentment out of my voice. But my sister needs defending, and that's what I'm doing.

"It would get the job done, and that's all that matters." Tim's voice is cold as he continues eating his apple from that enormous knife.

I'm starting to get hot under the collar, and I don't like feeling that way. Not in front of Gabe. And not toward Timur.

Gabe speaks up. Trying to defuse the situation, no doubt. "What kind of knife is that?"

"Turkish dagger. Bought it on eBay." Tim's curt reply to Gabe just makes me madder.

"Well, don't let the blade slip. You don't want to cut your…." I'm about to say *throat* when my better nature kicks in. Considering what happened to Tim's sister, saying that would be a low blow. And I do care about my cousin, even if I'm angry with him at the moment. I hastily finish my sentence with "finger."

Tim doesn't react. He slices again, and once more eats the slice off the blade.

"Come on, Gabe. Let's go up to my room." I turn, Gabe following.

"You boys have plans?" I have no idea what Tim's implying or if he's implying anything. He's a hard nut to crack.

"I need help with homework," I lie, looking over my shoulder at him. "And after I say sunset prayers, Gabe and I will get some chow."

"Chow? You're getting to be quite the *normal American boy* these days. Who taught you that word?"

I don't like his question. And I don't like his tone.

"Get over it, Tim. I can say—and do—anything I want. It's a free country." He's pushed my buttons, and I unload on him. I'm not even sure why I added the *and do* part. I guess it's because Gabe is standing right beside me, and I just wanted to assert myself a bit, to reassure him and get the upper hand with Tim.

But Tim doesn't take the bait. "Well, you're welcome to join Amca and me for dinner. I'm meeting him after sunset prayers at the mosque. Then we'll return for evening prayers. I hope I can persuade Amca, eventually, to switch to Hasan's mosque permanently."

"Whatever," I say. Disgust drips from my voice, but I've had enough of Tim for now, so I lead Gabe up the stairs.

When we are safely locked away in my room, Gabe speaks: "He's wound up tight. What gives?"

"Who knows? Just when I start liking him more, my cousin goes into inscrutable mode."

"Crazy the way he was waving that giant knife. Why would he want one of those? Especially after what happened?"

I shake my head. "Tim's been trying to get back to his roots. Maybe he thinks possessing a real Turkish dagger will make him an authentic Turk. You never can tell with him."

"My mom thinks he has problems."

"Understatement. But let's quit talking about him."

We go to my bed, and despite the fact that I refuse to do what we do in Gabe's bed, I find myself willing to spend the next half hour kissing and cuddling, chasing away all the dark clouds hanging over me—the fright at the pond, Timur's weirdness, Baba's approval or disapproval.

I am content. With my Gabriel.

And that contentment carries me all the way until Aysel's wedding day.

AFTER MORNING prayers I go back to bed. Then, an hour or so later, I shave and take a long, long shower. This day could be stressful, and I want to look my best, feel my best—for Aysel's sake, although she will likely be the source of any stress.

Refreshed, I head down to the kitchen. I start to prepare myself some breakfast.

Baba sits in his recliner, studying the Quran. As I crack eggs into the frying pan and pop bread into the toaster, I say to him, "You have breakfast yet? I could fry you up some eggs."

"Thank you, love, but I've already eaten. Your mother and Aysel were so worked up after morning prayers, I treated myself to Denny's to escape them."

"They *were* in crisis mode, weren't they? I expected it of Aysel, but Mama is usually a rock."

"It's not every day that her daughter gets married, son. I'm only glad that Gabriel's mother Mary is a part of all this. She came over, took charge, and was carting them off to the salon just as I was pulling out of the drive."

"And Tim? He wasn't with us at morning prayers."

"At Hasan's mosque. The way he's taken to Hasan's family and their mosque, I expect him to announce he's moving in with them any day now." Baba chuckles.

"Oh, somehow I don't think he would want to live with Aysel the rest of his life, now that he's getting rid of her."

"She can be a trial sometimes, my benim küçük kızım, that she can." There is so much love in Baba's eyes. It comforts me. If he can love my exasperating sister like that, then there's hope he will accept and love me for who I am.

"And you?" I ask. "Timur seems to think he's winning you over. That you will be taking us to Hasan's mosque to pray from now on, instead of our own."

"Your cousin's practicing wishful thinking, son. I have no such intentions. I'm only trying to keep Hasan and his family happy for now. After the marriage, our lives will go back to normal, inshallah."

I hope. I shudder, thinking of the message I plan to deliver this very evening.

My eggs perfectly fried and the toast popped up, I make an egg sandwich, then retreat to my bedroom to eat it and get a bit of skyping in.

Gabe's face fills my screen, and my heart flutters.

"Ready for the big day?" he asks.

"As I'll ever be. Closely shaved. Supremely hot shower. Deodorant generously applied. Tux fresh from the rental, pressed and waiting. Brother of the bride, reporting for duty."

"I can't wait to see you all spiffed up in that tux. But I have to say, I'll miss that baby goatee you've been sporting." He leers at me. He's been teasing me unmercifully ever since I sprouted a wayward hair or two on my chin. "Mom was super excited this morning."

"I missed seeing her. After morning prayers, I slipped back under the covers for an extra hour of shuteye. I need my strength."

"Mom couldn't stop babbling. She, I guess you know, was taking Aysel and your mom to the salon to get their makeup done. She said that, and I added, 'and hair too.' She shook her head. Then she went on and on about the hijab your mom was wearing to the wedding. I've never seen your mother in a hijab. What's up with that?"

"Muslim women must cover their heads at mosque. Mama always wears a simple scarf. But she shopped and shopped and shopped for the perfect hijab to go with her mother of the bride's dress. Big deal."

"I'm aware. Mom said she almost wished she were Muslim so she could wear a gorgeous hijab too." He laughs.

"She *could* wear one. And Hasan's people wouldn't blink an eye. At weddings, especially, we Muslims, orthodox or not, are very welcoming to you heathens—er, I mean non-Muslims." He chuckles at the joke he's made at my expense. "No, if Hasan's family shows any resentment, it will be at the fact they're compromising their principles, somewhat, showing up at our mosque for the wedding. If it had been at theirs, Aysel and the women would have been in one room, while Hasan and the men were in another. Aysel was having none of that."

"I'd bet. So are we driving together? I don't have a tux, but I clean up right nice. I don't think you'd be ashamed arriving with me on your arm, babe."

"I can't believe we haven't discussed this before—our riding together."

"This has been the fastest wedding prep in the history of the world, or at least for one this elaborate. I guess we just assumed we'd be going together, or at least I did."

"Yes, we are going together. You're chauffeuring me since both our family cars are being used. You *can* drive me, can't you?"

"You bet."

"Good. I guess I'd have had to Uber over if you'd balked. I have no doubt you'll clean up right nice, as you put it, but there will be no 'on my arm' part. This is a semiorthodox day, you know. We don't want to offend the new in-laws."

"I'll be on my best behavior. Ready to roll in two hours?"

"Yeah."

Time creeps when you have nothing to do, and waiting for this momentous occasion takes its toll on me. I'm apprehensive for Aysel's sake, wanting it to go well for her, and I'm anxious for it to be all over, wondering if I'll find the time and courage to talk to Baba tonight.

Gabe leans over and pecks a kiss on my cheek after I'm settled into the passenger seat. I quiver, from the sweetness of his kiss and from the tiny terror of discovery.

"You look mighty fine in the penguin suit, babe. Is this a preview of our prom night?"

I hadn't even thought about prom. A new terror sweeps over me at the thought of being out and open at school. "You look pretty good yourself."

"You like? Off the sale rack at Nordstrom's. I haven't bought a suit in years, but I figured this event demanded it."

We pull up to the mosque, and Timur is standing outside, acting impatient. He, too, is all tuxed-out. He must have changed at the mosque, because when he left this morning, he was dressed normally.

"You're late." Tim's attitude's showing.

I glance at my wristwatch instinctively. Then I realize there was no specific time given.

"Chill, Tim. Wedding's not for another hour and fifteen. Baba inside?"

"Yeah." We walk past him, and I don't like the look he gives Gabe.

Baba's pacing, so it's obvious his anxiety has increased.

"Mama and Aysel here?"

Baba says, "Got here an hour ago. They're in the prep room." A room had been designated for the bride to get ready in. "Better check in with them, or they'll be sending out smoke signals, asking about you."

I knock on the door of the room, and Gabe's mom opens the door, just a tiny wedge. When she sees it's me and Gabe, she lets us in. This may be a Muslim wedding, but Aysel is an American Muslim, born and bred, and a lot of traditions she's chosen are straight out of the anybody's wedding playbook. She does not want Hasan to see her until she parades to the front of the mosque.

"There are my handsome boys!" Mary kisses each of us on our cheeks.

I gaze past her at my sister. She's radiant. The gown's nothing short of magnificent, a wedding dress fit for a princess. A vision in white, Aysel's skirt is full, with tiers of delicate lace, seeded with tiny pearls. The arms of the dress poof a tiny bit—not too much—at the shoulder, then flow to a point that brushes her hands. The top is a sort of turtleneck-like device that sweeps up over her head into a turban that covers her hair entirely, with a flowing white lace veil coming out the top. Surrounding the veil is a diamond tiara. My sister could not be lovelier.

I rush to give her a hug and a compliment. I'm met with "Careful, careful now. Don't smudge my makeup onto my dress."

That's Aysel. Always giving orders. I hug her gently and whisper into her ear. She laughs.

Mama looks at us and glows. "For a moment I was seeing my two beautiful toddlers, playing."

"Well, one of those toddlers, the beautiful one, is a woman today," I say.

"Ah, my love, you're quite right," Mama says, "and the other, equally as beautiful in his own way, is a man."

"Well, both of us, and I know I can speak for my sister, have the most gorgeous mother in the entire world."

We have a group hug, my mother, my sister, and me.

"Stop it," I hear Gabe's mother say, "you're going to ruin my makeup." I look at her as Gabe gives her a tissue to wipe her tears.

"Shall we?" I offer my arm to Aysel and then escort her to Baba.

He walks her to where the imam's standing with Hasan.

The nikah ceremony begins. Hasan proposes to Aysel in front of the attendees. Then he explains the terms of the mehir. The imam asks if these terms are acceptable and then asks if they wish to be married. Each of them says, "*qabul*, I accept" three times.

Two male witnesses sign the marriage contract, making it legal both religiously and civilly. Hasan and Aysel share a date, eating the sweet fruit, signifying the sweetness of their union.

The imam reads the *Fatihah,* the first of the Holy Quran, and gives them blessing.

Finally Aysel has chosen to say vows, much like the vows in non-Muslim weddings, but these pledges to each other are sworn on the Quran.

After that, my sister and her groom are forever tied. And I truly believe that. Aysel, my sweet crazy Aysel, does not choose lightly—anything. And certainly not the man she will spend the rest of her life with.

If Hasan's family had had their way, the reception would have been done tomorrow, and it would have been a simple meal.

But Aysel's version of a wedding reception is the big blast we are heading to right now—well, after a million pictures are taken—in the giant hall of the mosque where communal meals are eaten.

There's a DJ, about twenty-five feet of decorated tables groaning with food, and an open bar—no liquor, of course, but an open bar nonetheless filled with ten or twelve choices of beverage. I can only hope that those burqa-clad women on Hasan's side can lift their niqabs high enough to enjoy this feast.

There is both traditional Turkish music and pop. Aysel and Hasan actually take the floor to do "YMCA," and it's hysterical watching them, Hasan in his awkwardness.

Baba takes Aysel for a spin around the floor in the traditional father/daughter dance, and I dance with Mama.

Timur, during all this, stands, apart. Once again, my inscrutable cousin is hard to read.

The DJ spins a wild rock song, and drunk with the happiness invading the room, I pull Gabe onto the dance floor, and amid the crowd, we dance together for the first time. Well, not together because this is one of those songs where you just stand with each other and gyrate.

As the music turns traditionally Turkish, even Hasan's family seems to loosen up. They applaud at Baba's attempt at Turkish folk dancing. He pretends to be the whirling dervish, the mystic Sufi. I would need at least two shots of tequila in me—not that I know how that would make me feel—to do what Baba is doing right now.

Bellies full and bouquet thrown, Aysel and Hasan are escorted outside, the crowd tossing rose petals, and a limousine takes them away to the Hilton, where they will spend their wedding night, then leave on a cruise the next morning, the honeymoon orchestrated as carefully as the wedding and reception have been.

It's been a fun, exhausting night. Mama and Mary, with Baba's help, salvage any souvenirs they want. The caterers are packing leftover food for Mama to take and packing up all the dishes and serving pieces to be taken away to be cleaned. A cleaning crew will arrive tomorrow morning to leave the meeting hall spotless.

Gabe and I offer to help, but Mama tells us we're free to go.

As we head out to the parking lot, we pass the ever-lurking Timur.

"Aren't you staying for evening prayers?"

"No, Tim. I'll do them at home. Great night, wasn't it?"

"I suppose," he says noncommittally. "See you tomorrow if I don't see you later tonight. I'm staying."

"Okay."

He turns to go inside, and Gabe and I go to the car.

Inside the car, Gabe touches my hand. "Beautiful wedding, huh?"

I look at him. "Indeed it was. And it was made more wonderful because I shared it with you."

I lean in and kiss his cheek, not caring who might be watching.

CHAPTER 18

Timur

IT'S OVER. This show. This production. This mockery of holy ritual.

I can only hope that Aysel comes back from her honeymoon and settles into being a good Muslim wife for Hasan. He deserves it. He comes from an observant family, and this foolishness of my cousin's must be over.

If Hasan knows what is good for him and his soul, he will demand that she settle down. The Quran doesn't require the wife be obedient, but she certainly mustn't bring grief to the marriage with open defiance. In my heart, I know that Aysel will make a good wife, once she is living in Hasan's father's home, the good Muslim home that it is.

Amca seems to be taking to the ways of the new mosque. I believe that he will continue to come with me to prayer. As for Aunt, she is so American in her ways. Her parents were much too liberal. But if Amca switches his allegiance to Hasan's mosque, Aunt is sure to follow. She does believe in family, and families that pray together are better for it.

Kerem, though, is becoming more and more of a problem. How can he be so disrespectful? Of our family? Of Allah?

What was he thinking, dancing like that, for all to see? Did he not give one thought to the fact that good, devout people were observing him bouncing seductively around that evil boy?

It is an insult that he is named for the angel Gabriel. Gabriel brought the Holy Word to our prophet, PBUH, and this namesake of his has led my cousin into such deep sin that he will be denied his place in paradise.

Because of this unholy Gabriel, Kerem will burn in hell. And he will take his family with him.

They think I don't know what they are doing. Kerem blindly follows, and each time he falters, he thinks he can say his prayers and be absolved. But some sins cannot be forgiven.

Not these sins. I saw them. Kissing in the car. Disgusting. Two men doing that. And one of them a supposedly devout Muslim, led astray by one who lives in sin.

This. This *thing*. This *evil*. Must be stopped.

Kerem will not lead our family into ruin with his degradation.

MAY

CHAPTER 19

Gabriel

SHAUN SPRAWLS on my bed, and I sit in the desk chair. It's a Saturday—two weeks before prom—and Shaun's folks have gone on a much-needed weekend trip. This is the first time they've left him since the accident. Even though he lived at our house throughout his initial recovery, his parents hovered. They were happy that he was in good hands with Mom, but still, they worried about him, checked on him constantly, and then, when he returned home, they were devoted to him.

Shaun still uses the cane, but he's much better. At school, he gets around fine, hardly a glitch in his walk, but his mom—the queen of worrywarts—didn't want him staying at home by himself while they were gone. It took every argument my uncle could think of to get her to go on this minivacation, and when push came to shove, she agreed, but only if Shaun spent the weekend at our house while they took the other kids for a weekend-long treat, just to reassure them that they mattered to them as much as Shaun does. My aunt and uncle are very loving—though frazzled at this moment—parents.

He got here last night, and he, Kerem, and I had pizza together; then we went to a movie. Now the two of us, Shaun and I, sit, shootin' the breeze. I'd rather be spending Saturday morning with Kerem, but I'm playing the good host, plus Kerem is off doing something or other at their mosque. He explained it to me—something to do with some older folks who needed help with repairs on their house, sort of like a Muslim Habitat for Humanity thing. He wanted me to join them—but I had my own project going with babysitting Shaun.

Not that Shaun needs babysitting. If you ask me, he would've done just fine, staying at his house alone. But he's a changed guy after what happened to him, so I'm enjoying our visit.

"You excited about prom?" he asks. "I've been so busy getting caught up at school, I haven't had much time to even think about it, not to mention that you and I haven't talked much since...." He stops. I've noticed he has a hard time bringing up the beating he got.

"Yeah, I have to say, kudos on your determination. Working 24-7 on the stuff you missed at school? That's awesome."

"Well, nothing was going to keep me from graduating with my class." He says that quietly, but with the resolve I know he has.

I feel sorry for Shaun. That's something I never thought I'd say. Yes, he helped me a lot to make the transition from my old school to my new one, but he proved to be such an asshole. But even assholes can change. It took almost losing everything, but he learned from it. And then he fought his way back, back to a reasonable semblance of physical well-being and back to where he was in school when it all happened. Not only that, but we found out our class rankings a few days ago, and Shaun is number twenty-five. Not bad for someone who missed a big chunk of his senior year.

"So—we were talking about prom. What skank agreed to go with your sorry ass?" I joke with him, hoping to lighten his mood.

"Watch your tongue, cousin. My date is none other than Darlene Durham."

"*The* Darlene Durham?" DD, as everyone calls her, is the head cheerleader and was voted Most Beautiful.

"What? Are there a dozen Darlene Durhams at our school? Of course, *the* DD." He has a smile wider than the horizon, and just as sunny, on his face.

"How'd you score that?"

"Poor choice of words, coz. I haven't scored—yet. That's for prom night." He leers at me.

"Okay, okay, letch. Let me rephrase. Why would the most popular, most beautiful girl in school want to go to the prom with you? You're not exactly King of the School, you know. Or did all those painkillers you were on make you delusional?"

He smiles, and it feels good to get to joke and be ourselves with each other. "Maybe gimps appeal to the ladies. Have you thought about that?"

"You're not a gimp. That's a terrible word. You barely have a limp now. If you ask me, I think you still walk with that cane for sympathy." I smile at him.

"Well, it caught me the best fish in the pond, now, didn't it?" Again, that twinkle in his eye. I used to hate that look because he often used it when he said something awful, but these days, he uses his powers only for good. And to snare a perfect prom date.

"Enough about me. Who you takin'?" Shaun asks.

I hesitate. I'm not ashamed, but with Shaun's history, I'm not sure I want to bring it up.

"Hello. I asked a question. Which luscious babe did you snag?"

Still, I hold back my answer, formulating the words.

"Okay, I know you and Kerem will most likely double, but surely you've lined up dates. You two can't go together stag. What'd people think?"

"That we're lovers?"

The look on his face is startling. He knows about Ker and me. Why's he so surprised?

"But no one at school knows about you two. Believe me, if they had a clue, I'd be told. Kerem's liked by everybody—yeah, me too, now—and no one knows that he's gay. You've managed to keep your secret too."

"I don't keep it a secret."

He smirks. "Really now? You haven't told a soul. To my knowledge the only one who knows about you is Kramer, and he isn't telling, for fear someone would find out about him too. Like they all don't already know that little tidbit."

"You got me. At first I didn't make a big deal about it. It bugged me that I kept silent, but I guess because I was in a new school, I had to get the lay of the land. You know, figure out how people would react. Then Ker and I became close, and since he's not out at school, I felt I needed to keep my secret in order to keep his."

"I'm bumfuzzled. You said 'not out at school.' Is Kerem out anywhere else, except to you—and me, by extension?"

"Well, yeah—he's out to his parents. He told his mom before Aysel's wedding. Well, actually, she told him. Like most moms, she already knew. She asked him to wait until after the wedding to tell his dad, so he did. But now his dad knows too. And his sister. And his cousin. Little by little, he told his whole family."

"Okay, but that's a small circle. Coming out to the school's huge."

Is he trying to talk me out of taking Kerem to the prom?

"Look, we've already spoken to the principal. He's fine with the idea. In fact, he thinks that a high-profile student like Kerem coming out of the closet will be a good thing. The district already has a nondiscrimination policy, so our going to the prom together will make it real. And that's a good thing."

"So the head guy needs a test case, huh?" A smirk.

"Lose the negativity, Shaun. Ker and I both know what we're doing's risky. But we want our prom to be memorable, and we don't want to share it with some girls we pick out just to be beards. That's not fair to us, and it's not fair to them."

He shakes his head. "Gabe, Gabe, Gabe. Congrats on your courage." He pauses. "But I fear for you."

"You actually think anybody's gonna care? It's the twenty-first century. This is happening all the time now. Guys're going to proms with guys, girls with girls."

"But not here. Not in a school like ours. I never understood how Kerem got elected class president. That was part my own prejudice." He throws up his hand to keep me from speaking. "That's out of my system now, but I personally know of a lotta kids who, although they were willing to vote a Muslim into office, still harbor bad feelings about gays. When they find out their prez is gay, it could blow up in your faces. I'm just sayin'. And don't shoot the messenger."

I can tell by his expression he's very much trying to help. That he really cares, not only about me, but about Kerem as well.

But what he was saying threw me. Can kids my age—who are usually at the forefront as far as acceptance goes—actually accept a Muslim classmate and still be against a gay one? What's the big deal? It's as if a Muslim's no threat, but a gay's a giant one. Threat to what? Are they so ill-informed and so dense that they can't see that there's no such thing as a *gay agenda*, that we're just like them? That we're not out to ravage them all by force, to take over their cherished institutions— that we're as loving as they are? I never would've thought that of my classmates. I can only hope Shaun's wrong.

WHAT SHAUN said played on me the rest of the weekend. I couldn't stop thinking about it. Doubting our decision, Kerem's and mine. Was our going to the prom together a terrible idea?

Shaun's parents picked him up late Sunday night, and as soon as he left, I was on Skype.

"Gabe, I've been going crazy without you. Fixing the Abbasis' house took a lot longer than we expected. There were ten of us from our mosque, and it took all day yesterday and today to finish. It was in super terrible shape. I didn't have a minute to even text you."

"No prob, babe. I missed you something fierce, but Shaun kept me entertained."

"He's changed, hasn't he?" There is wonder in Kerem's voice, and I understand. It's hard to accept Shaun has made a 360 on his extreme views.

"Yes, he has," I say with confidence. "His mind has healed as quickly as his body. He's doing better in a thousand different ways, and he's actually fun to be around. There was a time when I never thought I'd say that again."

"I'm glad to hear it. May he continue to heal, inshallah."

"Inshallah, for sure." Kerem smiles. He loves it when I parrot his words, especially when they are in Arabic. "Get this: you'll never guess who Shaun's taking to the prom."

"Couldn't be as wonderful as the person I'm taking."

I feel a blush. And a rumbling in my gut, for I know I have to bring that up, and it will not be a good thing.

"Better. He's taking none other than DD herself—Darlene Durham."

Kerem's mouth flies open. His head jerks slightly in disbelief. "*The Darlene Durham?*"

"That's what I said, and he quickly pointed out there's only one in our school."

Kerem laughs, that beautiful tinkle of a laugh of his, like a delicate wind chime. "I guess he's right, isn't he?"

"Righto, babe. The one and only DD will be on the arm of my cousin on our night of nights."

"And I know Shaun's bustin' a gut over that, isn't he?"

"You better believe it."

"Well, good for him. He deserves it, after all he's been through. Yes, he brought it on himself, but he paid for his mistakes. Allah forgives."

"And so do you, I might point out."

"And why shouldn't I? If Allah can forgive, then of course I can and should. I'm glad something good came of all this. Shaun's a changed man, he's almost healed physically, and he scored the best date in school, next to mine."

I love that Kerem can forgive so readily. He's a good, good person. And he's mine.

Then the word he used makes me remember. "As Shaun so wickedly pointed out, he hasn't scored anything with DD. That's for prom night."

Kerem laughs, a hearty one. "I like his way of thinking. For his sake, I hope she's willing." He laughs more. "But God forbid, can you picture a cherub with DD's eyes and Shaun's mug? Use a condom, Shaun!" That last he calls out as if he's shouting across town to my cousin. And he expels an even bigger laugh than before.

He's enjoying himself so much that I hate to bring up what I have to bring up.

"Ker—" I pause, formulating my words carefully.

But he must hear the caution in that one syllable I've spoken, because his laughter ends, and I see apprehension in his face.

"What? I don't like what I'm hearing. Say it. You've got something on your mind. And it doesn't sound like something I'm going to like."

"You heard all that in one little syllable?"

"I know you. I know every little nuance in your voice, every crease in your face, every tell. You've got something to say, and I'm not going to like it."

I take a deep breath.

"Spill it, Gabe."

Another deep breath. "Are you still okay with our going to prom together?" I spit the words like they're venom I have to get rid of or die instantly.

His face darkens. "Of course I am. What brought this on? Was it Shaun? Did he revert to his old ways?"

"No," I say. I pause just long enough to think a second and realize that was a lie. "Well, yes, Shaun did plant the seed. But it wasn't because he's back to his old way of thinking. Far from it. He's concerned that other kids won't be as accepting."

"Maybe. But I think he's wrong. I know them. I'm their president. They know me. It will be okay." He's trying to reassure me, but he's not succeeding.

"But if we casually stroll into the thing with no warning, won't that rile up the ones who might—*might*—be homophobic?"

"Do we care? It's our prom as much as theirs." I can't believe he's so calm, so rational. I'm supposed to be the one who's been out and loud for years here, not him.

"What if something happens?"

"What could they do? The place'll be crawling with chaperones. There'll be metal detectors at the entrance, so it's not like someone can blow us away with a smuggled gun. There won't be any drunken rages because old lady Simpkins will be posted at the refreshment table guarding the punch bowl, and all the other teachers there will have their eagle eyes on the known offenders who might be likely to bring in flasks. I just can't see anything happening. The most I can imagine's a few dirty looks."

"I think you're fooling yourself, babe."

"I thought you'd conquered your irrational fear of prejudice. Four months you've had to process. And it seemed to me, that long-ago January afternoon, that you had processed it instantly. You haven't said a word about being afraid since that moment we sealed our love. And Gabe, even though your fear then was about us being a Methodist/Muslim couple, prejudice is prejudice, and we're gonna encounter it as a gay couple, as well. We just have to ignore it."

"I know, I know."

"Yes, you know. But do you believe? Prejudice can only hurt us if we let it. And I'm here by your side, and I'll be there at that prom."

I think he's finished, and then he winds up again.

"Besides, I can't believe you're trying to back out. You're the one who talked me into doing this." He's supportive and hurt, all at once. "If you don't want to go with me, say so."

"No, no, no—I don't want to back out. It was something we needed to discuss, though." My answer is lame because I know what this is all about: Shaun stirred up those old fears.

"Tell you what." Ker's face lights up. "Why don't we can the surprise and come out at school tomorrow? Big announcement. Very public. Make sure everyone knows well before prom. Any problems, we deal with them ahead of time."

This amazes me. Just a few months before, Kerem was stuck. He couldn't admit to his parents he was gay; he couldn't even admit to himself he was gay. Now he wants to tell the world—or at least his world. I knew he loved me, and this proves it. And instantly my fear is gone, and I'm excited.

"So how will we do this? Do I stand on a cafeteria table waving my hands until calm descends, and then proclaim 'I have an announcement from your president'?" I feel a weight lift from me, and that idea actually sounds like a good one to me, even though I know I'm kidding.

He laughs. I see it. I hear it. I feel it. The love. "A bit drastic, don't you think? Not to mention dangerous. Those are collapsible tables. On rollers. I can see us skating into the wall, felled in a crashing mess of cafeteria goo. Besides, why do I have to be the potential bearer of bad news? We're in this together, bucko. No, let's get to school early, and together, we can start telling people. We'll seek out those who we think are the most accepting, just to bolster our confidence, and then we'll move on to the biggest gossips, so they can spread the word. By the time first period starts, believe me, everyone will know."

"And shit can begin raining down, if shit it be." I smile, hoping to mask the tiny worry that has bloomed. Worry—not fear.

"There won't be any. Trust me. And I'll have my Handi Wipes with me, just in case."

I laugh, picturing us both covered in steaming doo-doo. "Okay, I'll trust you. From your mouth to Allah's ears. There will be no diarrhea shower. But keep those Handi Wipes near," I say. "I love you, babe. Now, I need to sleep to give me courage, and you have evening prayers."

"Salaam Alaykum."

"Wa-Alaykum."

Despite what I said, I am ready for a sleepless night.

Surprisingly I go right to sleep.

I WAKE up refreshed. I shower and dress and head down to the kitchen. A text from Kerem says he'll meet me in front of the house as soon as we both have a nice fortifying breakfast.

Mom says, "You look happy this morning," as I get the milk from the fridge.

"I am," I say. That and nothing more.

A huge bowl of Wheaties, the Breakfast of Champions, and I'm ready to face the task at hand. For courage, I picture me and Kerem, linked together, pictured on the cereal box, like all those triumphant athletes they feature. Onward I go into the fray.

As soon as we get to school, Kerem takes my hand, proudly and conspicuously walking with it clasped in his, even though no one seems to notice. He immediately spots his vice-president, and we stroll toward her.

"Morning," he says. "Excited about prom?"

"Isn't everyone?" she answers. "My dress—incredible, and Tony's cummerbund and tie match perfectly. Dreamy shade of periwinkle." She smiles. "Who are *you* taking, Kerem?"

"You're lookin' at him." He tosses that off with a finger pointed at me.

Her eyes widen, and for a minute I'm thinking, *here it comes*. Then she smiles.

"Good for you. You guys spend so much time together, I was beginning to wonder. Now I know. You wearing matching tuxes? What color are your ties?" And like a lot of girls, fashion seems to be the only thing on her mind. That sounds sexist, but at prom time, girls' thoughts turn to dresses, and tuxes, and corsages, and stuff like that.

As we continue on our rounds, Kerem leans in and says, "Told ya. Piece of cake." We stop to shoot the breeze to a couple of unsuspecting people. One looks in shock but quickly recovers, smiles, wishes us well, and heads off to class. The other, a jock, actually says, "I knew you two were. My gaydar's never wrong." He saunters away, leaving me to wonder. I have always thought only gays have gaydar. Which means.... Now that's a thought to ponder, but it vanishes when I spot Lou Kramer. Something tells me that if we want to tell a gossip, Kramer's our guy.

"Kramer," I call out. He smiles and walks over. "How's it hangin'? Haven't talked to you in ages. Pumped about prom?" I ask.

"As pumped as I can be," he says. "Taking my cousin. She needed a date, and I was *available*." He eyes me like I should know what he means, being two friends of Dorothy, two travelers under the rainbow, two souls in search of Oz.

"I'm sure you'll have a great time. I know I will."

He looks at me like he doesn't understand how I could possibly have a great time under the circumstances, as he perceives them.

"Meet *my* date." I drop the bomb as I gesture at Kerem.

"Wait a minute." Kramer sputters, his voice full of incredulity. "You? Kerem? A couple? Prom? Together?" It's comical how he can't seem to speak in complete sentences he's so knocked for a loop. I love it.

"True, true, true, true, and true."

I can't describe the look on his face. Part totally disbelieving, part admiration, part wishing he'd had our courage. "And you think it's okay?" For someone who wants you to think he's full of confidence, this announcement's done him in.

"We've already cleared it with the higher-ups. We're good to go," I declare.

"And the earth stops spinning," Kramer says.

I've rocked his tiny world.

CHAPTER 20

Kerem

I'M IN shock. There is a Sufi saying that Baba repeats. It goes like this: "Keep a green tree in your heart and perhaps the singing bird will come." Baba tells us this every time we begin to lose hope. Well, I remembered that saying as Gabe and I started our rounds, and I knew everything was going to turn out well. Our coming out was easy as pie. There was absolutely no blowback. Of course, we didn't speak to each and every senior, and I have no illusions. There's bound to be some out there who are, at this very moment, gathering in their covens, preparing their cauldrons of blood. But let's hope not. We didn't pick up on any negative buzz. May there not be, inshallah. As Baba always says, "There are far more good people in this world than bad ones."

This whole thing's been almost a dream since I first met Gabriel. Who woulda thought that in a few short months I would be out and proud, open to the school, my mama, and my baba?

Oh, Baba. That giver of wisdom. I'm blessed to have him. I screwed all my courage up, and after evening prayers the night of Aysel's wedding—Baba did them at home, and not at Hasan's mosque as Tim wanted—I plunged right in.

With Tim at the mosque and Mama in her bedroom, it was just me and Baba in the family room. We were rolling up our prayer rugs when I said, trying to be as nonchalant as I could, "Baba, we need to talk."

"That sounds ominous. Have you at last done that murder I've been waiting all your life for you to commit?" He chuckled as he put his prayer rug away.

I put mine in the same cabinet and answered, "Baba, stop. This is serious."

He sat in his recliner. I continued standing.

"Sit down, love." He pointed to Mama's chair. "Nothing is so serious that you must stand over me to tell it."

I sat as commanded. I didn't say anything. There was a long, long silence.

"So, son, spill. You know you can tell me anything."

The love that's always been in his eyes was there, shining on me. Would it be there after I said what I needed to say?

I opened my lips to speak. But still, nothing came out.

Baba's eyes narrowed. He leaned over and took my hand in his. "Nothing is so bad that it can't be spoken, love."

I tried again, and this time words formed and spilled from my mouth. "I'm gay."

A huge smile broke out on his face. "Is that all?"

I looked at him like he was crazy. Is that all? Isn't that enough?

"I was afraid you were going to say, 'I'm not going to medical school after all; I'm running away to join an ashram,' or 'I've joined a terrorist cell, and I'll be leaving for Syria tomorrow,' or 'I've decided to get a pet alligator.'"

"But aren't you upset about what I told you?"

"Who you love is between you and Allah. It is not for me to judge. I only know I love you, and that will never end." He squeezed my hand. I'd forgotten he was still holding it. It suddenly occurred to me that Gabe had called it: Baba did indeed say it was between me and Allah.

"But most fathers would not be happy." I can't let it go.

"Your baba is not most fathers. Who you love is not important. What's important is that you love. But I have a sneaking suspicion I know the 'who.' It's Gabriel, isn't it?"

"Yeah." Months of holding a secret, a secret that apparently was an open one. Mama knew; Baba knew. Who else knows just by looking at us?

"Yeah? Is that all you can say? I saw you on the dance floor with him tonight. Those people didn't have a clue—none of them—but your baba sees things. I saw how you smiled at him. How happy he made you, as you made your tiny little public statement. My heart swelled, knowing my son had someone in his life, someone besides his old baba who has spent his life totally devoted to him."

I was in complete shock. I believed him when he said no one knew a thing. It was ridiculous to think you could always tell by looking at someone. My classmates didn't know I was Muslim until I told them. Gabe is as much a jock as the quarterback on the football team. No one would know he was gay. He was very open at his old school. He'd only kept it a secret here because of me. And I was pretty sure my friends would never suspect that I, a Muslim, could even *be* gay. It's a weird world we live in. But Baba and Mama knew. Parents always *know*. They may need to be told specifics sometimes, but they can always sense when something's up.

But this… this total acceptance… I never expected this. Why I doubted, I didn't know. My baba is not your typical Muslim, but he's Muslim nonetheless. How many Muslim fathers would accept this news so well? How many would embrace the idea with as much love and gusto?

"Love, I'll be beside you all the way, in everything you do. Whether I'm physically beside you or not, I'll be there. Now—do we need to call your mama downstairs? She should know as well."

And guilt set in. A tiny twinge.

"She already knows," I said, quietly. "She asked me not to tell you until after Aysel's wedding." I waited for the hurt to set in, that I had told one parent and had chosen Mama instead of him. "Actually *she* told *me* I was gay."

"Surely you already knew." He laughed. *Laughed?*

"Yeah, I did." I grinned, grateful the tension had broken. "But I had no intention of making the big reveal at that point."

"Oh, love, how can you get to your age and not know that mothers know everything? I'll let you in on another secret: they frequently choose what and when to tell things to their husbands. They know us men can't always handle things like they can." So he was not upset that she knew before he did.

I have the two best parents in the entire universe. Gabe says that about his, but I won't tell him he's wrong.

Baba lifted a weight from me that night. And telling people at school was another step. I feel as if I'm no longer shackled. Oh, I know that there will be situations when being in the closet is preferable for survival. In those times I'll step back in for the brief moment it takes to figure out how to burst out again. For life is nothing if you don't live it honestly. And I will live honestly, from now on, inshallah.

And now, this morning is a wonder. I awakened with newfound happiness, the happiness that comes from knowing that I need hide nothing, from my family, from my friends.

Aysel sits in the kitchen when I go down for breakfast. Baba is frying eggs, and Mama is squeezing orange juice.

Timur sits, sullen. He's been more and more out of sorts since Aysel's wedding. You'd think three months would be plenty of time for him to come to grips with reality: Aysel is different but the same. A new husband, a new family, a newfound orthodoxy has not changed her into the burqa-clad good little wife Tim was hoping for. Mama and Baba have not suddenly switched their allegiance to Hasan's mosque. And I, well, I am living more openly, and since so many Muslims frown on homosexuality—and I'm sure that includes Timur—then enough said about that. I couldn't live as unhappy as Tim seems to be.

"So, love," Mama says, setting glasses of fresh juice in front of us all. "What brings you over this morning?" She directs her question to Aysel.

"Yes, my benim küçük kızım, we've missed you at breakfast," Baba asks. "One egg or two?"

"Actually," Aysel says, "I don't care for any. My stomach's been bothering me a bit lately."

"What, love? Have you been sick? Why haven't you told me before this?" Mama is totally concerned, focused on her little girl.

"What are your symptoms?" Baba asks, ever the doctor.

"We-e-e-ell," Aysel says, drawing out the word. "Let's see. I wake up in the mornings and immediately I have a queasy feeling in my gut. It's like the worst hangover I could ever imagine. And since I've never touched a drop of alcohol, imagining is all I can do. But this has to be worse than that. The sight of a fried egg makes me want to puke. And I frequently do."

Baba's face is full of concern, like the physician he is, wanting to delve deeper. Mama, however, knows. I can see it in her eyes. I don't know what she knows, but she knows. Like I said, mothers always do, don't they?

"Oh, love, when are you due?"

Baba smacks his forehead like he should have figured that out as fast as Mama.

"January. I'm barely five weeks, now," Aysel says, proud that her little secret has come out. I know my sister well. She came over this morning to break the news. But she does love her little games.

"How does Hasan feel about this?" Tim asks. How *would* he feel? Surely Hasan is over the moon about this. "You will raise this child strictly Muslim? All the old ways?" Tim continues.

"Of course, Timur. I didn't pledge my love to Hasan, join his family, to suddenly break with his traditions as soon as I brought his child into the world." Aysel sounds offended.

"Then, good." That's all the reply Timur gives.

"Oh, darling, there is so much we must do. We'll ask Mary to plan a baby shower for you, and we'll go shopping to outfit a nursery. Who's your doctor? Do I know her?"

"Dr. Saddiqi."

"Theda Saddiqi. She's the best. I'm glad you chose her," Mama says. "She'll take good care of you."

"Hasan's mother wanted me to use the midwife at their mosque, but I knew you wouldn't rest unless I went to a doctor, so I chose the best. Hasan is backing me on this."

Timur glares at her, like she's committed treason.

"I'm glad," Baba says. "There is nothing wrong with a good midwife. A midwife brought me into this world, but we live in a different world, and proper medical care can work wonders if complications arise." He smiles at Aysel. "Not that there will be any, my benim küçük kızım."

"Don't you worry, love," Mama adds quickly. "Fathers are worriers by nature. You'll do fine."

"You haven't said anything, Kerem." Aysel looks at me. "Are you happy for me?"

"Will you name him after me?" I ask with a grin.

"How do you know it will be a him? It might be a girl, you know," Aysel says.

"Either one, I'll teach them everything I know about school politics."

"Ugh. That's all I need. A class president for a daughter or son. No, I want to raise a painter, a musician, an actor. Someone creative."

"And what," I say, "if he or she turns out to be a mathematician, a scientist?"

"Then she will love the child as much as your baba and I love you three," Mama declares.

I look at Tim to see his reaction to Mama including him in our family.

He beams.

I gobble down my eggs and gulp my juice. "Well, sister, congratulations. Your politician brother has to go to school now."

GABE AND I meet up outside. We've gotten to where we're in tune with each other. It's strange, but most mornings, we are coming out our front doors at the exact same time.

"Salaam Alaykum," he greets.

"Wa-Alaykum," I respond. Then I kiss his cheek, not caring if the neighbors notice or not.

"What's up? Your smile is wider than the Grand Canyon."

"I'm going to be an uncle."

"An uncle? You mean Aysel's knocked up?"

I know he means nothing mean or nasty, but I sock him on the arm anyway, not hard.

He rubs his arm like I've just given him the worst bruise of his life. "Ow! Play nice."

"No, you play nice. Stop talkin' 'bout my sister." I say that all gangster.

"So Aysel's really having a kid? When?"

"Next January."

I can see his lips move as he counts the months. "So she's only a month or so gone, then."

"Yeah. I guess she waited to make sure it took before she told the family."

"Well, when you see her again, tell her I'm happy for her. Also tell her Gabriel's a nice name for a baby boy. For a girl, Gabriela."

"In your dreams, guy. I've already put my bid in for Kerem. It's a good name—means noble and kind."

"And they gave it to *you*?" he mocks.

"Yes, they did, and I would be proud to pass it on to my new nephew, wiseass."

His smirk turns to a loving smile. "And your new nephew would be proud to have it."

We get to school and get settled into our respective first-period classes. I'm about to open my notebook to copy the day's objective from the board when a student aide knocks on the door.

My teacher goes to the door and retrieves a call slip from the aide's hand. She walks over to me and hands me the slip. "They want you in the principal's office, Kerem."

I don't get called down often, but I think nothing of it. Probably some class business.

When I near the office, I see Gabe coming from the other direction, a call slip in his hand as well.

I immediately feel a pit in my stomach. This has to be about the prom thing. They've reversed their decision. Some parent must have called. The school board has rescinded its nondiscrimination policy. The ax is going to fall. We aren't going to be allowed to go to the prom, at least not as each other's dates. I want to rant, rave. How could this happen?

"You here too?" There's not a trace of worry in Gabe's face when he sees me. How can he not know what's about to happen?

He opens the door and motions for me to go through first.

Mr. Zynco's secretary looks at us and says, without emotion, "He's in there." She points to the closed door of the principal's office. "Don't knock. He's waiting for you."

Again, Gabe opens the door and lets me go first. I step into the tiny office. We're greeted, and there's no disdain or worry in his voice. "Have a seat, guys."

We both sit, side by side, in chairs placed in front of his desk. There's a third chair in which a young, frizzy-haired woman sits, a spiral-bound tablet and pen in her hand. "This is Ms. Christopher. She's with the *Neighborhood Tribune*. She's asked to interview you for the paper. What say, guys? You game?"

I look at this strange woman. Interview us? Why?

She must see and understand my expression. "Gabe didn't tell you? He came into our offices last evening and pitched the story. This is big. We're just a tiny paper. You probably get a copy thrown into your yard for free, but for this area, two gay guys going to the prom together is big, big news."

Gabe? My eyes, I hope, ask my question: *what have you done?*

"Ba—" He stops himself. I know he was about to call me *babe*. But he was wise to stifle, here in the principal's office, in front of a reporter, no less. "I would have run it by you," he says to me, "but when I got the idea, you were at prayers."

"Like those take two or three hours," I say with disdain. How could he make this decision and not tell me when it involves both of us?

This Christopher woman pipes up. "Kerem, if you're not on board with this, I'll understand. Gabe said I'd need your principal's approval and yours as well. So if you're not cool with it, I'll kill the story. But I really do wanna do it."

Gabe looks at me, pleadingly. "Ker, this is a good thing. We've come this far. This is just another step in our coming out. Do it. For me?"

How can I resist? He's right. Yes, everyone at school knows now. But if the whole community knows, there can't be any backlash. Living openly. That's what we agreed on.

"Fine. What do you want to know?"

"Is there somewhere private?" she asks.

"I'm afraid," Mr. Zynco answers her, "right here is as private as you're going to get. I'm all for first amendment rights, but you have to understand that schools are little dictatorships. I need to know what you ask and what they answer. If there's anything that will reflect negatively on the school, I must try to dissuade you from publishing—at least that part of your story. Agreed?"

"Agreed."

And we spend the next forty-five minutes answering her questions. Nothing even borders on negativity, so I know this will be a really nice profile we can all be happy with.

She thanks us for our time when we've exhausted all her questions; then we leave. The bell has rung for second period, so the secretary drones, "I sent aides to pick up your stuff for you." That woman is, and always has been, a sour personality. She's either very efficient or the principal is sleeping with her because she wins no one over with her nonexistent smiles.

"Thank you for doing this," Gabe says when we're in the hallway.

"I didn't have much of a choice, now did I?" I can't believe I've said that because I thought I was over my initial pissiness at his volunteering our lives to the community.

"You could have said no." His voice is quiet, full of hurt. I melt.

"No, I couldn't. I know this was important to you. And I know it will be good for us. I just hope that my parents are on board with it. If not, you can explain it to them."

He pecks me on the cheek. "I know your folks. They'll be happy as clams you did this."

"What does that mean? Happy as clams? How do you know mollusks can be happy? Huh? Huh?" I keep saying *huh?* over and over as we head to our classes. I would guess he's glad to be rid of me when we split at the first hallway intersection. I say one more *huh?,* loud, when he's about ten feet down the hall to my right.

He looks back at me and grins.

I forgot to ask when the story would appear, but the next afternoon, the *Neighborhood Tribune*'s in my yard, and I remember it comes on

Thursdays, regular as clockwork. I snatch it up because I haven't told Mama and Baba the fact that our lives have been immortalized in print. They were both out last night, and this morning, wouldn't you know it? I got up late and skipped breakfast.

Gabe scoops up the copy off his lawn, and together we head to the pond. Neither of us is expecting anything earth-shattering in this article, but we'd agreed yesterday that when it came out, we'd read it together and in private.

Nothing's said as we walk to the land of the MFs. We sit on our bench, and still we don't talk. Like a solemn ritual, we each remove the plastic sleeve from our copies. We unroll the papers. We snap them to unfold them to make them readable. Like synchronized swimmers, we turn the pages until we find the article, tucked away on page six.

I scan; he scans. There's a picture Ms. Christopher took of us both, standing with the principal, all smiles. The article's flattering. It tells of Gabe on the first day at a new school and how he sees me and wants to get to know me. Christopher weaves our tale, not in gruesome detail, but enough to paint a love story like anybody else's. Even the "two boys going to the prom together" thing is treated as nothing very unusual. She states it simply, like something that happens every day in the modern world. The only thing the least controversial is the Muslim angle. In answer to one of her questions, I did tell her that many Muslim families would not be okay with a gay son. But I was quick to tell her of mine, and how loving they are. All in all, it's an article to be proud of.

"What do you think?" I ask.

"What do I think? I think I will cherish this forever. I think Mom will be pasting it into my senior scrapbook tonight. I think your folks'll be honored by what you said about them. I think we'll be showing this to our kids and our grandkids. That's what I think. And you know what else I think? I think this article'll do more to convince a skeptical community than anything ever written before. Certainly it'll do more good than all the stories about conflicted gay children who've been bullied and who commit suicide, feeling unloved. And it'll do more good than any stories about crazed Muslims who radicalize and kill people because they're convinced their god wants them to. This article is about love. And the world needs more of that."

"Wow. You really speak your mind," I say, so proud of him right now I can burst. "I'm glad we did this."

"So am I, babe, so am I." And he grabs me and plants a lingering kiss that has all the love in the world in it.

We sit in silence, basking in the warmth of the kiss, the warmth of this article.

And then that kid is back. I notice him first. He's chucking rocks at the MFs once again. I pray to Allah that He send the male swan swooping in to bite the kid's little pecker off.

"Hey, kid," Gabe yells. "What did we tell you? I'm calling the cops if you don't lay off. And if one of those birds bites your eyes out, don't come stumbling blind across the park, crying your nonexistent eyes out to us."

The startled kid, who had no idea we were there watching him, I guess, turns, rock in air. There's a "deer in the headlights" look in his eyes which we can see from fifteen feet away.

Gabe stands, and the kid takes off running. Then Gabe turns, laughing. "I think we made a believer out of him."

Joining in the laugh, I stand. "I need to get home. Mama and Baba will be home soon, and I want to show them this." I wave the paper in the air.

When I enter the house, I call out, "Mama? Baba? You home?"

There is no answer. I decide to get some juice, so I go to the kitchen. As I'm pouring myself a glass of apple juice, I notice Tim sitting on the sofa, his back to me. He hasn't said a word.

I start to speak. Then I notice what he is reading. The *Neighborhood Tribune*, page six.

CHAPTER 21

Timur

OUTRAGEOUS! THE whole world is going to read this and think it's normal. There's nothing normal about these two. Why can't Aunt and Uncle see that?

Now it's in print for all to see. Hasan's family will read this. We are disgraced.

The one thing that can save us is that surely Uncle will be shamed by this article and put a stop to this. Kerem and this pervert cannot go to the prom together. What makes them think this is okay?

Are there no authorities in this school? No one with morals? With good sense? Why have they not forbidden this? The principal's an idiot. I knew that from my time there. A Godless fool. But surely someone higher up will see this sort of behavior leads to disgrace.

If the school board has no morals and condones this, then someone— the mayor, a politician, a preacher, an imam can do something. This is a community newspaper, it's nothing, barely any circulation at all, but I will post this article online. Someone of importance and authority will see it and call a halt to this.

This is the only way I can save our family. It is bad enough that Aysel defies Hasan's family, refusing the midwife. And now Kerem's abomination. I can't let them destroy us. I can do very little about Aysel. She's proven that, over and over. But I can't allow Kerem to attend prom with a queer. I should beat Gabriel within an inch of his life, put the fear of Allah into him.

But that would not stop Kerem. He'd run to his side, cry over him, make a fool of himself even worse. They made it into the newspaper already; whatever I could do to Kerem's abominable *love* would make the news again. That would compound the disgrace.

Stopping it is the only way. Then Hasan's family will see that we are good Muslims, that we are not sinners.

And that, coupled with this baby, will go a long way. Despite her refusal of the midwife, Aysel must redeem herself by raising this baby to be a good Muslim, an Allah-fearing Muslim. She must make her parents see that the one path to heaven is through a clean, true way of life.

Our family can be redeemed. We can sit at Allah's feet someday.

If Aysel doesn't utterly disgrace us.

If Kerem doesn't throw us all into dishonor.

Neither can happen.

CHAPTER 22

Gabriel

"WE'VE GONE viral, babe," I shout to Kerem, who's waiting for me across the street.

As I cross, he says, "What're you talking about?"

"The article. Somebody tweeted the link."

"Who would do that?"

"I don't know, but I do know it's been retweeted so many times that we may never know who posted it the first time. And you know what?"

"No, but I'd bet you're going to tell me," Kerem quips.

"Most of the comments I've seen are positive—very few negatives. Yeah, I did see a few nasty remarks, but those got shot down quickly. People love us!" I grab him and hug him.

"I'm in shock. Yeah, I've seen Facebookers fawn over all the 'two guys going to the prom together' stories, but this is a different angle. One that could be explosive. We have the all-American swim teamer crossing over to the dark side and dating a terrorist."

I hate he has phrased it this way, but he does have a point.

"Don't talk like that. We both know you're not a terrorist, and I didn't cross over to any dark side. We fell in love, and that's exactly how Christopher wrote us—brilliantly, I might add. She was able to take potential controversy and make it normal, as American as apple pie and baseball. Score one for her."

"It *is* a good article, isn't it?" he says. "I guess I'm still stuck in the old world, the one where I was convinced that no one would accept us."

"It's a new world, babe, and this thing on Twitter just proved it."

Everyone at school is talking about the article. They are all basking in our glory, happy that we, and they, have all that Twitter attention. More than one of the other seniors come up to us to tell us how happy they are or how proud or how we should ignore the naysayers.

And we may never graduate, having failed to attend our first-period classes, because once again we are both called into the principal's office.

This time it's the local NBC TV station. They want to do an interview. Who knew we could start something like this?

Again, first period and today, even second, is obliterated by our newfound fame. Not only that, but the station didn't just assign one of their reporters, the morning anchor has shown up to do the interview himself. Rumor has it he's gay, so I have to wonder if he didn't volunteer.

They've set up in the school library, where a Do Not Enter sign has been posted on the door. Principal Zynco takes us in to meet Jesse Milian, the news anchor. He seems to be a really nice guy. He leads us over to four chairs and shows us each where to sit. Apparently, like the day before, we will not be interviewed just the two of us. Milian briefly explains the process; then he thanks us for doing this. He also tells us to call him Jesse, even on camera.

An assistant director/cameraman counts us off, and the filming begins. Jesse begins with an explanation of the situation, telling of how our article has gone viral overnight. Then he begins his questions.

"So how long have you guys known you were gay?"

I look at Kerem, and he signals for me to answer first. "I've known for a long, long time. I was totally out at the school I went to before I transferred here this year. I've always believed that being open is the best path to acceptance."

"I see. And Kerem?" Jose asks.

"Well, I guess I knew I was different all my life, but it was a long time before I pinpointed why. I've spent most of my school years running for office—as you know, I'm our class president—and politics, even elementary school politics—haven't left me much time for relationships. I know that sounds crazy, that little kids could get that caught up in running for office, but that's me. So when I met Gabe, I felt something, and I was scared of it. But our friendship first, then our relationship second, grew."

"And has being Muslim been a problem in your relationship?"

Kerem smiles, and I know that smile is lighting up the TV screen.

"Actually Gabe's interest in Islam was the first thing that attracted me to him. That, and the fact that he's a beautiful man. Gabe stalked me—" He pauses, and I laugh; he follows with his own laugh, then continues. "—and saw me praying. After I realized he wasn't an ax murderer—" He laughs once again. "—he was full of questions. Gabe's Christian, but questioning's always a good thing, about anything. My classmates have always accepted my religion, but none were interested enough to ask me about it. Or maybe they were afraid. Islam's so misunderstood in this country. I've been blessed because they, my friends, have simply accepted me for who I am. Anyway, the more Gabe and I talked about Islam, other topics came into the mix, and before we knew it, we were ready to take our friendship to something bigger."

"And how do you feel about going to the prom together? Are you excited?"

We both begin to speak at the same time.

"One at a time, guys. You first, Gabe," Jesse directs.

"I couldn't imagine going to prom without Kerem by my side."

"And Kerem?"

"Likewise. And I want to thank the powers that be for not objecting, and in fact for welcoming us."

At that, Jesse looks at our principal. "Principal Zynco, you have anything to add?"

"I'm pleased as punch that these two'll be breaking barriers that've needed breaking for a long, long time. Our school board and superintendent believe in equality, and this year's senior prom is proof."

"Thank you, Principal Zynco. And thank you, Kerem and Gabriel. What you're doing, who you are, is an inspiration to us all.

"And that's what it's all about, folks," Jesse says directly to the camera. "It's not about some controversial relationship or some over-the-top act of civil disobedience. It's about two guys in love and a world who accepts them.

"And on a personal note, let me say this story has touched me in a way that no story I've ever covered has done. I'm not making a big deal of this, and I'm not looking for praise or headlines. Let me just make a simple statement: I, too, am gay."

I'm glad the camera isn't on my face right now. I'm in shock and awe.

"This is Jesse Milian, reporting for *Channel 12 News*."

"And we're out," the assistant says.

"That was unexpected," I say, not to Jesse in particular. I just can't seem to not say something.

"As I said, you two're inspiring, and I've needed to do that for quite a while," he answers.

"Well, we're with you," Kerem says to him.

The assistant walks over, his fingers on the earbud in his ear. "Station manager wants to see you pronto, Jesse."

Milian looks at him questioningly.

"We were on a live feed," the assistant says.

"But I thought we were filming for the five o'clock," Milian says. His voice is filled with apprehension. Maybe he thought he could get back to the station, and if he had second thoughts, he could cut out that revelation of his before it hit the air.

"We were, but somehow the live feed button got pushed too."

Milian turns white as a sheet. I don't blame him. Although what he's done is a courageous act, it could also be a career ender.

Then his color returns. "Well, guys, looks like either there will be rainbows or the shit will hit the fan. Wish me luck. Either way, I don't care. I feel liberated."

He fist-bumps both of us and leaves.

Kerem and I are in disbelief.

"For his sake, I hope his boss likes what he just did," Kerem says.

The interview airs as recorded, complete with Milian's revelation, on both the five o'clock and ten o'clock news. I guess only his boss saw the live feed. Which was enough.

Like most news stories, ours fades as his takes over.

Google News is filled with links to newspapers across the nation. It seems that Jesse Milian's station manager fired him when he returned to the station. Then the station owner got wind of it—thanks to a friendly whistle-blower. The owner arrived at the station in a rage. He told the station manager he was out of line and a bigot. The guy who got canned was not Jesse Milian, but rather the homophobic station manager.

Next morning, Jesse Milian was flown to New York City for a *Today Show* appearance. Unsubstantiated reports are that he is being considered to replace a national newsperson who quit to "pursue other interests," as they say.

Who would have believed that our little story, in the local neighborhood throwaway paper, would lead to this? That's the power of openness and honesty.

And that's the power of love.

Kerem and I have become even bigger celebrities at school.

I'm glad Jesse Milian came out. For his sake. But selfishly I'm glad he came out so publicly because it took the pressure off Kerem and me. When we did that TV interview, I was really afraid our prom night would be ruined by TV cameras, following our every move. But now they're all chasing Milian and leaving us alone.

Our prom will be as magical as it's supposed to be. Nothing can go wrong.

BUT FIRST, we need to get outfitted. It's Saturday morning, and Kerem and I plan to hit the tuxedo rental place. It's really no big deal. Kerem is wearing his dad's tux, and I'm wearing my dad's tux jacket. I need to rent pants, plus we want to get ties and cummerbunds. Neither of us actually cares what we wear. We're just glad we're going to the prom—and going together.

I pull the car into a spot right in front of the rental store nearest our neighborhood. We get out, and go in.

"Can I help you guys?" the clerk asks.

"Yeah," I say, "our prom is next Saturday. I need to rent pants, plus we want ties and cummerbunds."

"You're the two in the *Tribune* story, right?"

I smile and say, "Yep." This notoriety could be addictive.

"We can't help you," the guy says. No smile. No emotion. Just *we can't help you.*

"What? We know it's pretty close to our prom, but surely you can rent me some pants," I say, totally not reading anything into what he's just said.

"Look," he says, "I don't do business with guys like you. Go somewhere else."

"What do you mean—guys like you?" I'm beginning to understand. And I may pounce on this guy.

Kerem tugs on my sleeve. "Come on, Gabe. We'll go someplace else."

I'm ready to stand my ground and demand service, but I know he has the right to refuse it to me. The asshole. What I really want to do is pound him into the ground. Which is what I almost start to do, but Ker stops me.

"Come on, Gabe. He doesn't deserve our business. Let's go," Kerem says, trying to pull me away.

"Be my guest," the guy says, and he motions toward the door.

In the car, I say, "It's a good thing you stopped me."

"We cannot steal the fire. We must enter it."

"Come again?" He's making no sense.

"It's a Sufi saying. I think it means this: if you had attacked that guy, only bad things would come of it. You would have tried to 'steal the fire.' But if we enter the fire—that is, accept that there are people like that

and that we can do nothing about it, not right here, right now, anyway—
then we enter the fire, feel its wrath, know that we can use it to fuel us
and extinguish the haters, and we have then conquered the prejudice."

"You're a wise man, Kerem Uzun. Sort of like what the AA people
say, 'Accept the things you cannot change; change the things you can.'"

"Exactly. We both know we'll encounter fools like that guy our
whole lives—gay haters, Muslim haters. But we just enter the fire. Let
it ignite us to do what we can to combat it all. In a sense, giving that
interview to the *Tribune* was entering the fire."

"And that—you," I say, "are why I no longer fear. But the fact
remains. What do we do now?"

"We try every rental place in town until we get what we want,"
Kerem says. "They can't all be like that piece of shit."

I look at him. I know he can pop a good phrase every now and then,
but this one surprises me, and I laugh at him.

He joins in, and at last, we're back in the good mood we'd started in.

"Okay," I say. "Guide me, o great wizard."

He says there is another place two streets over, one block down,
and I head there.

A bit warily, we go in the door and an older man, short, bald, a bit
humpbacked, greets us. "Welcome, welcome. What can I do for you today?"

I repeat my request.

He looks at us, and it's like a light bulb has gone on over his head.
"You're the two boys in the newspaper, right?"

Uh-oh. Strike two.

I nod, but Kerem enters the fire. "Yes, sir, we are indeed."

"Well, I'm not giving you a pair of pants."

"But…," I say, ready to do battle. After all, he's a little old man. I
won't hurt him. I'll just change his mind.

"No, sir," he continues, ignoring my defiant stance. "I don't know
what you plan to wear with those pants, but it's not good enough. I'm
outfitting both you guys in our finest, free of charge."

Both our mouths drop.

"My grandson—the sweetest boy you could ever meet—didn't get
to go to his prom. Broke my heart. But times have changed a bit, thank
Yahweh, and you two are going, and I intend to see you go in style."

He motions for us to come with him to a nearby rack. "Let's see,
you're both slender and tall. I say the Joseph Abboud silver heather slim

fit. It's perfect." He pulls two amazing suits off the rack. "Try 'em on." He loads us up with accessories, as well.

We head to adjoining dressing rooms, and when we step back into the main room, we are mirror images. Two fashion models decked out in suit, vest, ties, and even shoes to match.

"I knew it! Absolutely perfect. You two are magnificent. Girls are going to be wishing they were your dates. Boys are going to be green with envy."

I don't need a mirror, because if I look half as good as Kerem, then we are very much fashion magazine cover models.

"How's the fit?" the man asks. "*Nu*, the pants on you, young man"—he points to me—"are a tad bit long. I can fix that." He reaches down and pins up my pant legs. "And you," he says, turning to Kerem, "you need to eat more, boychik. Even the slim fit is a bit baggy on you." He grabs the sides of Kerem's jacket and pins them.

"When's your prom?"

Sheepishly I say, "Next Saturday. I know that's soon, so if you can't do all this...." I didn't know how long alterations took. I had thought I was only getting a pair of pants off a rack.

"*Nisht gefloygen.* It doesn't matter," he says with a gesture. "I'll have these finished and pressed for pickup Wednesday afternoon. Okay?"

"Fine with us. And we really appreciate it. But you can't do all this for free."

"Yes, we insist on paying," Kerem adds. "Please let us."

"Nonsense. *Es iz meyn fargenign.* It's my pleasure. Tell you what, all I want is a picture of you two in the suits. Best advertising I could ever get."

Of course, we've been in the newspaper and on TV.

"Anybody," he adds, "who comes in here and sees you two looking so good, will think this is *the* place to get formal wear. I couldn't ask for better models for my product."

"If you're sure," I say.

"*Ikh bin zeyer zikher.* I'm very sure, indeed. And if anybody asks where you got these suits, tell 'em Bennie's Formal Wear. I'm Bennie, by the way."

We both shake his hand. "Good to meet you, Bennie," I say.

Kerem adds, "It's not every day we meet one of Allah's angels."

"Your grandson is very lucky to have a granddad like you."

A slight sadness tears away his genial smile. "My Daniel is no longer with us, I'm afraid. *Alav ha-shalom.*"

Neither of us ask, knowing that far too many gay teens take their own lives, and that might be the case here and what has motivated Bennie to be so nice to us, total strangers.

"Sorry to hear that," I tell him, almost at a loss for words. "I know you miss him."

I see a tear in his right eye, but he manages a smile. "My Danny was very special. Now, boys, in case my assistant is here Wednesday afternoon and not me—I'm an old man and sometimes have to take an afternoon off—" *I bet that happens almost never*, I think. "—will you both be picking these up, or will one or the other of you, or will someone else be doing your errands for you?"

Kerem answers. "I'll get here. Gabe has swim practice, but I'm free Wednesday. What time do you close?"

"Five, sharp."

"Then I'll be here at four. Count on it."

"Wonderful, wonderful. And don't forget that picture."

"We won't," I say.

"Mazel Tov!" he calls as we leave the shop.

"What a nice, nice man," I say when we're back in the car.

"He surely was. Allah blessed us. What do you think happened to his grandson?"

"I don't even want to think about it because my imagination can take some very dark turns."

"That's what I'm thinking too," Kerem says. "We're lucky, you know."

"Yes, we are." Despite what I said about not wanting to think about it, that's all I can think about until I decide forcefully to banish the thoughts. Danny, Bennie's grandson, might not have even been gay. He could have been killed in a car crash or hit by a bus, for all we know. We only know he was blessed with a wonderful grandpa, and Danny's death was a great loss to Bennie, and to the world. If Bennie thought that much of him, Danny had been destined to do good things. If fate hadn't stepped in.

AND THE big day arrives. I've known for a long time that our final swim meet of the year was on prom Saturday. But Coach told us it would be over by 2:00 p.m., so we would have plenty of time to prepare for the big night. The meet is a short drive across town, so no sweat. Which is not to say that the girls on the team aren't crazed over the idea. I'm surprised they didn't quit the team, knowing they had such a short time to get their hair and makeup done, and then get all dolled up in their dresses. Most girls are spending the entire day getting ready. But swim team girls are a different breed, and they didn't want to disappoint Coach. He lives and breathes swimming, and he sees nothing wrong with this meet being on the biggest day of the year.

Things run over, and before we know it, it's three, heading for four o'clock. The girls're frantically phoning their moms, having hair appointments switched. Calling friends to beg them to take their earlier appointments and giving them their later ones. Hoping that this thing is over in time for it all to happen.

And, victors, we drive away straight up four o'clock. I rush home to shower and get into the monkey suit.

As the shower pounds its rejuvenating heat on me, I wander back to that first day, the day I saw the vision that is Kerem. So much has happened. Who knew that my life would change so drastically? I've found love, and no one can take that from me. Kerem is perfect in every way. And the most perfect thing is that he loves me, with all my faults. He'd say he's the one with the faults, but that's not true.

I want to think this'll last forever. If we somehow take another path, I'll be content to have this year. It's been amazing.

I dry off, gel my hair, and suit myself up. Bennie was right: silver heather's perfect for both of us. I can only imagine how sexy Kerem'll be. Especially since I got just a taste of it in Bennie's store.

As I gaze into the full-length mirror in my room, I say out loud, "You're a fox, Gabriel. And you're the luckiest guy on earth tonight. Stylin' in Joseph Abboud, Kerem Uzun and Gabriel Dillon proudly strut the red carpet. Into the prom. Together.

"Thank you, Joseph. Thank you, Bennie. Thank you, God. Thank you, Allah.

"And Danny," I say, looking heavenward, "thank you for paving the way for Kerem and me, just a bit, in your own way. If you did take your own life, I hope you've found peace."

With that, I head downstairs.

There, in our living room, I find Mom, Dad, and Kerem's mama and baba. Mom asked them to dinner so they all four could give us a big send-off. Dad and Aram both have high-end cameras near them. No cell phone photos for their sons. Uh-uh. Dad even bought a new camera to capture the moment.

"Where's Kerem?" I ask. "Surely he's dressed."

"My son worked all day, once again at the Abbasis'. He was in the shower when we left," Maria says. "I'm sure he'll get here soon."

"I'll go give him a nudge," I say. "He told me he didn't want me to see him until he was fully decked out, but he didn't say I couldn't skype."

I run back upstairs and go to the computer.

Kerem's head fills the screen.

"Where you at?" I ask.

"Getting ready. I'll be over soon. Give me five more minutes."

I hear a knock on his door.

"Someone's at the door. Must be Tim. He's the only one in the house, as far as I know."

CHAPTER 23

Kerem

"JUST A sec. I'll get the door. It's gotta be Tim because Mama and Baba are at your house, right?"

"Waiting for you. My dad even bought a brand-new camera to capture your mug in style. When are you getting over here?"

There's another knock. Louder.

"I've got to get the door. I'll be there as soon as I can get my tie tied and my shoes on. Bye."

"Halt." Gabe stops me from signing off. "I'll wait. You get rid of Tim or the rapist who has broken into your house, and you can finish in front of the computer. The tie is tricky. You may need my expert advice."

"Okay—hang on."

I go to the door and open it.

"Hey, Tim. Where you been?" I say.

He doesn't come into the room. Just stands there.

"Praying. At the mosque. The good one." His voice is monotone, but that's the Timur voice I've come to expect these days.

"The good one? What's that supposed to mean?"

"Hasan's. Where the people know how to pray."

Strange bird, my cousin. I don't know if he's trying to provoke me, or if he's just speaking his mind. He certainly has gotten totally bound up in the old ways of Hasan's mosque, so knowing Timur, he probably does think we don't know how to pray at our mosque. At any rate, I want him to leave so I can finish getting ready, but he just stands there. I guess I'm doomed to yet a little more small talk before I have to be blunt and tell him to leave.

"It's pretty late for sunset prayers. Those were over at least an hour and a half ago."

"I took extra time. On the private part. I had a lot to talk to Allah about. A problem I needed solved. A question I wanted an answer to."

"And did you get what you wanted?" I ask.

"I did." Nothing more. I still can't fathom why he came to my door. And he's not sharing. But then again, what he prayed is between him and Allah.

"Well," I say, "I'm late as it is." I'm hoping he'll take the hint. I glance at the computer screen, wondering if Gabe is still there. I see his face, and I get all warm inside. This is going to be one magical night.

"You're still doing this?"

What's that supposed to mean? Timur is all riddles tonight.

"Doing what?"

"Going to the prom with *him*." There is extra emphasis on the *him*, like it's a curse word or something.

"Yes, Gabe and I are going to the prom. And I'm late. I need to finish getting ready." I turn to go back to the closet. I figure if he won't leave of his own accord, I'll just finish what I have to do. Surely he'll leave when I leave.

"I'm surprised." His voice doesn't come from across the room. It's right behind me. He's followed me. I turn to face him.

"Surprised at what?" And then I turn back to get the tie that is clipped to the hanger the suit came on.

"Doing this to the family."

That sounds weird. I turn around, and he's right in my face. "Doing what to the family? Going to prom has nothing to do with them."

"It does if you are going with *him*." Again the emphasis. Why doesn't he just say Gabe's name?

"Look, Timur, I love the family and would never do anything to hurt them. But my going to the prom with Gabe is okay with Mama and Baba. So if it's not okay with you, so what?"

I can't believe what I've just said—that last part. I love my cousin. I think. But he can be a royal pain, and right now, I don't want to deal with him. He's got me wound up as it is.

I lash out. "Timur, if you can't accept that I'm gay, that I'm in love with Gabriel, that Mama and Baba, and Aysel too, are all supporting me and accepting me, then I can't make you see otherwise. That's your problem, not mine."

I see it. Something growing in his eyes, something that looks like an ember flaring up.

"It's wrong, Kerem. And you know it."

"Timur, I know in my heart that there is nothing more right than the love I feel for Gabe. And I'm not going to stand here and argue the point with you when I've got to finish getting ready. So leave, would you?" I point to the door. "You can continue your rant tomorrow, okay?"

Dismissing him, I turn away to get the shoes, hanging in a Bennie's bag on the hanger. That's when I feel it. A cold metal across my throat.

"Come on, Tim. Cut it out. I don't have time for this." I try to remain calm. My mind flashes to what Tim's father did. That long-ago night when my cousin Delal was killed. But Tim, as crazy as he can be, is not murderous. He may want to scare me, but he wouldn't hurt me. "Tim, I've got to finish getting ready." The assurance in my voice will surely make him leave. "Funny joke. I'm laughing." I force a laugh, hoping to defuse the situation if it indeed needs defusing.

His arm forces me around. Still behind me. The blade still at my throat. He pushes me toward the mirror above my computer. "Does this look like a joke to you?" His voice is harder, colder, more menacing.

"Timur, please," I say as calmly as I can muster. "Why would you want to do this? I've done nothing to you." Skype's still connected. Gabe's listening. He'll do something.

I feel sweat trickle down my forehead. I try to reason with myself. Tim's not a crazed killer. He grew up right beside me. In the same loving household—same adoring parents.

"You've brought dishonor." That statement is so quiet that it sends chills up my spine.

My mind is thrust back.

Is this what it's all come to? Is he repeating that ritual he witnessed so long ago?

"Timur, listen to me. Your father was executed for what he did to your sister. What did he gain from doing what he did? What did you gain? Did it really save your family?" I know I can get through to him. We're almost *brothers*, for Allah's sake.

He doesn't answer, but I feel the blade dig into my skin.

Is this the payment I deserve for forgetting, all too often, he was raised as my brother?

I've got to keep talking to him. To get through to him. "Timur, your family and its honor are gone. I know hearing that hurts. But you have a new family now. Mama and Baba love you. Aysel loves you. What would they think if you did this? Please, Timur, you're my brother. Don't do this."

"Your brother? That's the first time those words have ever left your lips."

I put every bit of conviction I have in my voice. "It's true. You're one of us. Our family's your family." I have to stay calm, gain his trust, reason with him.

"But don't you see? That's exactly why I have to do this. Our family is disintegrating. Aysel took the right step by marrying Hasan, but she is still not the obedient wife he deserves. Aunt and Uncle are far too liberal. I tried to steer them to the righteous path, to make them see they must attend Hasan's mosque to save themselves. Aysel. Aunt. Uncle. Those are transgressions that can be forgiven. They can still choose to walk the path.

"But you. Kerem. The golden child. You have chosen to stray so far that Allah will not forgive. What you have chosen to be—it's an abomination, a sin so terrible that you are destroying our family. And you can't even do it quietly. No, you must tell the world. The newspaper. The television. You will burn in hell, and you will take the family with you. But I—I can save Aysel, save Mama, save Baba."

I'm surprised that he has switched from calling Mama and Baba *aunt* and *uncle* to calling them what Aysel and I call them. He truly does feel a part of our family, and my heart hurts for him, because if he does this, it is not I who will burn in hell, but he.

"Mama and Baba love you, Timur. And they love me. Don't take me from them. You will be taken away, and they will lose both their sons if you do this."

"Don't you see? I'm saving them. It matters not what happens to me. I am insuring their place in the Garden of Paradise by ridding our family of this sin that is destroying its honor."

I hear a noise outside in the hall. It is faint, like whoever is out there is trying to be as silent as possible.

A millisecond. Baba appears in the doorway. He looks calm. I know it's an act.

"Timur, son, what are you doing?" he asks, his tone measured. "Put the knife down, love."

At the sound of Baba's voice, Timur's body jerks, almost imperceptibly. Still pressed up against me, I feel the quiver run through him. Baba will reach him. But will he drop the knife?

The blade cuts deeper. I feel no blood, so he hasn't broken the skin yet. But it's only a matter of time. And one quick slice is all it will take to sever my carotid. *Please, Baba, speak reason. Stop this.*

Baba steps into the room. He's followed by Mama, Mary, and Gabe's dad. They are like a human shield, advancing toward the enemy. But their steps are tiny. Nothing that will upset Timur. I hope.

"Timur, love." That's Mama speaking. There's anguish in her face, but there's love in her voice. "Can I come to you? Will you give the knife to me?" She makes a slight move, a ministep.

"Don't come near us! He deserves this. He has dishonored us all."

Baba pulls Mama back. "Timur," he says, "there is no dishonor here. You have to understand that what Kerem does is between him and Allah. Who he is, the choices he makes, are not yours to dictate. Only Allah can accept or forgive him. You can't make that decision. It is for Allah. Only Allah."

"Listen to Baba, Timur," Mama says. "He speaks truth. If you take Kerem from us, you will not be honoring the family. You'll be destroying the family."

Suddenly I feel a tug. Timur's hand, the one holding the dagger, is pushed away from my throat. The force is such that I stumble and fall. From the floor I look up. Gabriel has his arms locked around Timur, and they are struggling. He has one hand on Timur's wrist, trying to wrest the dagger from his grip.

Timur is strong. But Gabriel's stronger. It's happening so fast I cannot think of where my savior came from. But I do know Allah sent this angel to rescue me.

Gabe has Timur on the bed now. They are so tightly wound together that if Gabe weren't wearing the tuxedo, it would be difficult to sort out whose arms and legs belong to whom. At last, Gabriel is on top of Timur, and he manages to get him to release the knife. It goes flying across the room.

At that, Baba and Ken Dillon rush the bed. Ken pulls his son off Timur, and Baba tugs at Timur. On his feet now, Baba holds Timur in a tight armlock.

But the fight has gone from Timur. He's lifeless. Drained.

As soon as his father lets go of him, Gabe pulls me off the floor and smothers me in a hug that feels like safety. He kisses me, over and over, my eyes, my cheeks, my forehead, my lips. His kisses are frantic, but they speak love.

I look over his shoulder, and his mother stands there, longing to grab him away from me, no doubt, because she needs to feel her son's warmth. Know he is okay. I don't want to let go of him, but his mother needs him right now. So I push him into her arms.

At that moment, the tears start flowing. She floods him with tears of joy and relief.

By now, Mama is cradling Timur, trying to comfort him. I can almost see her message, though she speaks no words. She's trying desperately to tell him that it'll all be okay.

But it won't. My cousin may very well spend the rest of his life locked away. In prison. In a hospital. I will pray to Allah fervently that Timur is healed, that he comes to understand. But I fear his life is over.

I walk to him, put my hand on his chin, lift his head so I can look him in the eyes. "I forgive you, brother."

Forgiveness. Allah commands it. And I obey. It will be quite some time, I think, before I truly understand, feel the depths of Timur's anguish. After all, I didn't see my father kill my sister when I was ten years old.

But I can forgive my cousin. The rest is up to Allah.

With everyone at some semblance of normality—well, at least the immediate crisis is over—my brain works well enough to remember I do have french doors that lead from my room onto a balcony. In a Joseph Abboud silver heather slim fit, my lover climbed the tree outside my room to save me. I'm truly in love with a knight in shining armor.

"Thank you," I say to him.

"Thank you? Is that all you can say? I almost ripped a thousand-dollar pair of pants climbing up that tree." Leave it to Gabe to bring us all back to normalcy with one sentence.

I smile at him. No one laughs at his joke, but I know they're all grateful that he's made it. The tension's broken somewhat.

I top him. "The pants are only five hundred. The coat is the other part of that thousand." I can't believe I'm joking after all that's just taken place.

Mama takes Timur from my room, to where, I don't know. He goes with her willingly. Or, at least, he doesn't put up a fight. He's a broken robot now.

"What's going to happen to him, Baba?"

"I don't know. Right now, I must take him to the police. What happens after that is up to them. And the court system. If I have my way, he will be committed. Your cousin is a good boy. He just went astray. I blame that on me. I should have seen the signs."

"You couldn't have known, Baba," I say, hoping to comfort him.

"He was following in my brother's footsteps. Surely I could have taken measures to see that would never happen. We brought him, your mama and I, into our family, a broken little boy who'd lost his entire family, his mother taken from him, his older brother too, his sister murdered right in front of him by his own father, and we simply acted like nothing had happened. Some doctors we are."

"Don't be so hard on yourself, Aram," Gabe's dad says. "Those were unusual circumstances. No one could have dreamed all that would happen in such a short time, and you and Maria are only human. You thought love would take care of it all. You made him your son and hoped for the best."

"And now I must turn him in to the police." Baba sighs. "It will be the hardest thing I've ever done. Harder, even, than going with my brother that night."

Ken puts his hand on Baba's arm. "I'll go with you." His words are few and simple. But Baba's body changes. He becomes taller, filled, it seems, with resolve. Allah has sent him his angel to guide him through this horrible task. And I love Gabe's dad for that.

Still with his hand on Baba's arm, Ken leads him out of the room.

So here we stand, I half-dressed for a prom that is never to be—at least not for us. Gabe, remarkably put together, for a man who has just climbed a tree, sneaked into a room, caught a potential killer off guard, and saved his lover. And Mary, beautiful Saint Mary, standing quietly, her gaze showering love on us both.

"Well, this has been quite the ordeal," Mary says. "So what now, boys?"

"I suppose we get changed out of these monkey suits and get on with our lives. It's not every night you face death and live to tell it," I say.

"Yeah," Gabe agrees, and then he grabs me and kisses me. After all I've been through tonight, Gabe's kiss instantly makes me feel safe.

"You have no idea what was running through my mind as I shinnied up that tree." He gazes into my eyes, filling me. "I'm fast, but it put the fear of God in me. In those thirty seconds, I kept praying over and over, 'Please, God, please Allah, please God, please Allah.'"

"They're the same, you know." He's made me feel so secure that I can joke again. I laugh at him.

"Allahu Akbar, huh? God is great?"

"Yes, he is," I affirm and hug him like I'll never let him go.

"Uh, guys," his mom says hesitantly, sounding embarrassed for intruding into our moment, "it's only nine."

Why do we care about the time? Then I get Mary's drift. We could still make it to the prom. And I want some distraction. It's not every night you almost get your head cut off and live to tell it. No. That's a fleeting thought. Forgive me, Allah. I could never have fun after what's taken place, knowing Timur's in hell right now.

"So—it's only nine," Gabe says, wonder in his voice.

"I think your mom's suggesting we could still get to the prom before the last dance." My words are quiet and even. I don't want to betray myself. I can't have anyone thinking I could even consider going to the prom now. Am I considering it? After I just dismissed the idea?

"Mom, I think going to a prom's a bit trivial compared to all of tonight's events," Gabe says. And I love him for that.

"And why?" It's my mama's voice. She has come into the room. "You boys have been looking forward to this for weeks. My Kerem's almost dressed, and Mary here can work her magic and get you put back together." Her eyes lock on to Gabe's. "Why shouldn't you go?"

"Because Timur's going to jail, for one thing," Gabe says.

"And so? My heart is breaking for him. In many ways, I failed him. I wanted to be a mother to him, and I could have done better. But I have another son, here. A son who has been put through hell tonight. My heart swells knowing he's okay, that he's alive, that he can live to see this prom."

I look at her with all the love I can put in my eyes, my smile. But I can't face going to this thing. Not tonight. I shouldn't.

"Kerem, love, I'm in the mood to celebrate. Celebrate that Allah spared you tonight. I will mourn the loss of Timur—and I will grieve, as I already have started—later, but now, won't you humor me, and give me the joy of seeing my handsome son and his equally handsome suitor go off to make some happiness for themselves? And for me?"

I can't do it. I can't play while my cousin—my brother—sits in jail for what he has done to me. If I'd treated him differently. If I'd shown him the love he deserved. If, if, if….

I know Gabe will back me up.

There is *why-not?* in his face.

I can't disappoint him. If he wants to go. If he thinks I should go. If, if, if…. What can I say? "Okay. But don't expect me to be the life of the party."

"Just be *the life*," he says. "I was so terrified that you couldn't be that for me anymore."

Mary holds out her arms to Gabe. "Strip, kid." Then she turns to Mama. "You do have a steam iron, right?"

"Certainly," Mama answers.

"You hop in Kerem's shower, and I'll press your glad rags," Mary says. "Kerem, get crackin'. You got a prom to go to."

She rushes off with Gabe's suit, and he takes a five-minute shower while I finish dressing.

Mama insists on taking picture after picture before she'll let us leave. I guess Bennie will have that shot for his wall after all.

With hugs all around, Gabe and I are off to prom, the dance we anticipated forever, the dance that we made history for, the dance that I hope will erase, or at least temporarily make me forget, what has happened tonight. Allah, if it be Your will, make this the night we hoped for, finally.

And actually, though we are both a bit low-key, we do enjoy ourselves. We start our abbreviated evening with me full of guilt, and if I know Gabe, he is too, if only to support me. But everyone seems so happy to see us when we arrive. They are so alive. They are so accepting. We fought for this. We started this venture not knowing if we'd even be allowed to be here, then we had to screw up our courage to come out to everyone, then bare our souls to the entire community, and then, yes, fight our way here. Allah took care of us. We entered the fire. We needed to be here tonight. Allah will continue to take care of us, just as I know He will take care of my cousin.

After all the crap that went down, I realize I am starving, so the first thing we do is hit the refreshments, old lady Simpkins flashing us the evil eye when we fill our cups of punch. Who has punch at parties anymore?

Our bellies full, we make it to the dance floor. And unlike the wedding dance we shared, this time we do a slow dance, arms firmly wrapped around each other.

It's cool. Exactly like the movies. Everyone fades off the dance floor and makes a circle around me and Gabe. There in Gabe's arms, I feel safer than I have ever felt. When the dance finishes, everyone applauds us.

I realize something. During that dance, I didn't think of Timur once. I know that he will be on my mind for the rest of my life, but for now, not thinking of him is blessed relief. Praise Allah.

And then—the best thing of the night, the thing that makes the night and that I would have missed if I hadn't reluctantly been pushed into coming here: Gabe and I are crowned King and King of the Prom. It's the first office I've ever held I didn't have to campaign for. An honor just handed to me simply because I love the right person.

The night ends, and we head home. Gabe pulls up in front of my house. He walks me to the door, like a proper gentleman. At the end of the walk, he kisses me, a sweet and gentle good-night.

I turn to open the door, and I feel him right up against me.

"Hey," I say, "what's going on? Prom over. You go your house. I go mine." I use the caveman voice to make him laugh, and it works.

Then he says, "Let me walk you inside. I want a follow-up on Tim. If I know my dad, he's still here with your dad. And besides, you know our moms are on pins and needles to get a prom report."

And yes, the two moms are sitting at the kitchen table, having coffee. As soon as they see us, we have to sit and tell them everything. Mama, who is not the squealing type, yelps when we reveal we are King and King.

Baba and Ken acknowledged our presence when we came in, but then turned back to their conversation, sitting in the recliners in the family room.

With the prom saga exhausted, Gabe and I go to the family room.

"So how's Tim?" I ask Baba.

"He's holding up. By the time Ken and I got him to the police station, he was babbling. The desk sergeant took one look at him, and I could tell he had compassion. I explained all that happened—by the way, you'll need to give a statement at the station tomorrow, both of you—and the sergeant called the hospital. They came to take him away for observation. We don't know yet what charges, if any, will be filed. You guys can go with your moms tomorrow morning. They want to talk to each of you."

"I'm glad they didn't put him in a cell," Gabe says. "He will get the help he needs, inshallah."

Baba looks at him with love.

"So," Ken says, standing, "you ready for this night to end? It's been a long one." Gabe nods at him. "Aram, if there's anything—anything— day or night, you can count on Mary and me." Then he calls out, "Mary, you ready to get outta here?"

And Gabe's mom comes to join us all, followed by Mama.

Mama hugs Mary. "Thank you, love. Allah has blessed us with saints for neighbors. Or in-laws, maybe?"

Both of our mothers look at Gabe and me.

"Stop it," Gabe commands. "Let us graduate high school first, at least."

And everyone laughs. Perhaps the first truly carefree laugh of the evening.

I follow them to the door, holding Gabe back as his parents walk the sidewalk toward the street.

Our eyes lock and I kiss him good night. It is sweet. Gentle. Joyful.

"Salaam Alaykum," I whisper in his ear.

"Wa-Alaykum," he says. Then he adds, "Do you think Allah would approve? Repeating these words as your warm breath is making my…." His voice trails off.

"Oh, Allah approves, yes He does," I tell him as I kiss his earlobe.

When I return to the family room, Baba looks at me. "Evening prayers? Or is your mind fixed on carnal pleasures?"

I feel the heat well up inside me as I turn beet red. He really does know.

We spread our prayer rugs, and Mama joins us.

The three of us say prayers, more fervently than I've ever heard them said. The last part, where we talk to Allah with our personal thanks, hopes, and wishes, takes longer than usual. I can't look into Mama's and Baba's minds, but if their prayers are anything like mine, they are full of thoughts of Timur.

LIFE CONTINUES. Before prom night, I would have taken that as a given. Now I'm very glad it does, thank Allah.

Gabe and I graduate. The ceremony is long and boring and wonderful, for it marks a passage that I might not have been able to make. About the only lighter moment is Shaun's little dance he does as he goes across the stage to get his diploma. The dance itself is funny, but what makes it even better is that he does it without his cane.

Aysel is big as a house. The baby blew up in her very, very fast. And she milks it for everything it's worth. I wouldn't want to be Hasan. But it's clear he loves her dearly. He caters to her every whim.

And Timur. He is in a state institution. Allah willing, he will come out of this. Right now he's lost in his madness. But who knows? Maybe someday, sometime, some doctor will lead him to a breakthrough. I pray for that—five times a day, seven days a week.

At any rate, there was no honor in this attempted honor killing. There never is.

CHAPTER 24

Timur

HE BROUGHT dishonor on our family.
He brought dishonor on our family.
He brought dishonor on our family.
He brought dishonor on our family.
He brought dishonor on our family.
He brought dishonor on our family.
He brought dishonor on our family.
He brought dishonor on our family.
He brought dishonor on our family.
He brought dishonor on our family.
He brought dishonor on our family.
He brought dishonor on our family.
He brought dishonor on our family.
He brought dishonor on our family.
He brought dishonor on our family.
He brought dishonor on our family.
He brought dishonor on our family.
He brought dishonor on our family.
He brought dishonor on our family.
He brought dishonor on our family.
He brought dishonor on our family.
He brought dishonor on our family.
He brought dishonor on our family.
He brought dishonor on our family.
He brought dishonor on our family.

RUSSELL J. SANDERS is a man on a quest. In his travels all over the world, he searches out Mexican restaurants. A lifelong Texan, raised on Tex-Mex, he wants to try the enchiladas and other delicacies that pass for Mexican food in the far reaches of the world. He has been pleasantly surprised in Tokyo and Indonesia and left wondering in Rome and a few other places. Sometimes what the menu says and what you are served is not what is expected. But the joy is in the quest.

Russell's also on a quest to spread a very important message: love is found in many forms in this world, and being gay or lesbian or bisexual or any other variation is normal, healthy, and wonderful. He wants his novels to bolster the confidence of gay teens and change the minds of or educate further all the others who may stumble upon his prose.

Russell's writing joins his long career of acting, singing, and teaching, adding to his passions for cooking and reading. He has won awards for his acting and directing and has taught theater to hundreds of teens. He has also taught additional thousands of teenagers the art of writing and the love for literature. He is always in the middle of a good story, whether reading it or writing it. And he can whip up a delicious meal in minutes. He does all this with the support of his husband, a man he has loved for over twenty years and married a few years ago. They live happily in Houston, Texas.

Website: russelljsanders.weebly.com
Facebook: www.facebook.com/russelljsandersauthor

RUSSELL J. SANDERS

ALL YOU
NEED IS
LOVE

It is 1969 when Dewey Snodgress, high school theater star, meets irrepressible hippie Jeep Brickthorn, who quickly inserts himself into Dewey's life—and eventually into his heart. Meanwhile, Dewey prepares to appear in a production across town, a play about protestors of the Vietnam War, where he befriends the wild and wonderful Lucretia "LuLu" Belton, who is also determined to follow her dreams and become an actress—whether her parents approve or not.

The show has a profound effect, especially on Dewey's father, who reconsiders his approval of the war after his son's performance. But Dewey knows his dad won't be so accepting if he reveals the love he's developing for Jeep, so he fights to push his feelings away and keep the peace in his family.

Still, Dewey can't ignore the ripples moving through society—from the impending Woodstock Festival to the Stonewall Riots—and he begins to see that the road to happiness and acceptance for him and Jeep might lead them away from conservative Fort Worth, Texas—and Dewey's dad.

www.harmonyinkpress.com

RUSSELL J. SANDERS

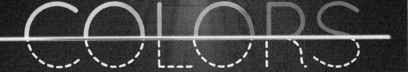

COLORS

With a beautiful girlfriend, a scholarship to a prestigious musical theater school, and talent to spare, life is good for high school senior Neil Darrien. He's on his way to stardom, but then newcomer Zane Jeffrey secures a place in the school show choir, rousing Neil's envy. Neil soon sees there's more to Zane than a talented performer, though—he's funny and charming, and the two boys become friends.

Neil's girlfriend Melissa doesn't like Neil spending so much time with Zane, and she draws Neil into her church. There, Neil is faced with a choice between righting a wrong and risking revealing a secret that could cost him everything he's worked so hard to achieve.

As Neil's relationship with Melissa deteriorates, Neil starts to see Zane in a different light—one that has him thinking of Zane as more than just a friend.

www.harmonyinkpress.com

TITANIC

RUSSELL J. SANDERS

SUMMER

It's a summer of revelations for Houston high schooler Jake Hardy. Along with his estranged father, Jake embarks on a trip to Nova Scotia to visit the Titanic museum and the cemetery where the victims are interred. There, Jake's father's biggest secrets are revealed. Hurt and confused, Jake flees—not only from his father's confession, but from his own feelings.

Jake is gay.

Back home, the proposed Equal Rights Ordinance is polarizing people. As Jake faces a difficult choice about where he stands—and how far he's willing to go for his beliefs—he soon discovers that he's not the only one in hiding. When confronted with how his actions have hurt those he cares about, purposefully or not, Jake must learn to accept his friends, his father… and himself.

www.harmonyinkpress.com